THE FIFTH ERA OF MAN

Joshua Banker

First Publication, 2018

ISBN: 1983515027

ISBN-13: 978-1983515026

Logo font is Qhytsdakx by Brandon Schoepf.

http://www.tepidmonkey.net/

Also from Joshua Banker

The Realm of Tah'afajen Series

Not Gods But Monsters

A Prison of Flesh

For Heather,
without whom none of this would be possible

01

As the last moments of the gloaming waned in a slowly-graying atmosphere, a rainbow-hued haze slowly pulsed to life, flowing along the streets like radioactive lifeblood in the city's circulatory system. Light pollution hovered over the metropolis, a brilliant halo that outlined the skyline's dark industrial columns.

Though technically not behind schedule, Cal pushed through the growing crowd like a man on a serious timeline. After barging past the herd at the northern entrance to Urigo Sector, he forced his way through a group of sailors who were seeking a night of entertainment. One seaman complained at being shoved aside, only to quickly lose sight of the shabbily-dressed man as Cal disappeared in the burgeoning throng.

A thick mist, illuminated by the prismatic hues of the surrounding street signs, gave the densely-populated avenues a hallucinatory quality; much like inebriation induced one's senses to dance between dreams and reality. However, Cal knew better. He hadn't touched an intoxicant in weeks, though not for lack of trying. His sober mind was a sharp as could be, which left him all the more suspicious of his surroundings.

Urigo Sector was a haven for all manner of debaucheries found within the boundaries of Greater Decedistadt and offered anything for a price. In light of his current predicament, what was for sale did not concern him. On a good day, he might have indulged, but he had been summoned.

Cal slipped two wary fingers beneath the hem of the patchwork leather jacket. They settled on the ivory-inlaid revolver barely concealed behind the heavy coat that kept the night's moisture off his shoulders.

He was mindful of the robbers, pickpockets and the usual hooligans who hid in the crowds, preying on visitors. With what little he had to his name, the last thing he wanted was to be picked over. While they would find nothing of value in his pockets, the matching pair of revolvers that hung off his waist would be a prize more worthy than his own life.

If it came to it, he'd fight his way clear of any trouble, even if it ultimately proved counterproductive. At best, it would cause him to be late. At worst, it would draw the attention of the city's security forces. Urigo Sector was by and large self-regulating, with the business owners left to police themselves. If a spot of unexpected violence broke out, a legion of Magistrates, Greater Decedistadt's main source of security, would fall upon the streets like an axe on a dead tree. The result of which would clear the area; most businesses would be forced to close up until the city's constabulary were gone.

He'd walked the streets many times before and could pick out the people working the crowd by dress and mannerisms alone. Ladies of the night, barely dressed in silk, lined the curbs on his right, occasionally flashing extra skin to seduce patrons from the crowd. The dampness in the air only served to make their outfits all the more stimulating.

At each street corner, garishly-dress barkers filled the air with their enticements, beckoning with the promise of a valuable night's amusement. An overlapping drone of advertisement floated atop chatter roiling through the watershed courtyard that fed to all corners of the sector.

As he crossed through the horde, his head popped up as he looked for specific signage on the south end of the court. With his free hand, Cal brushed the sogginess from his ash blond hair. It had been some time since it had been cut and the humid air quickly pasted it down over his forehead. The kaleidoscope of colors that glittered throughout the district reflected in the pale gray of his eyes. During the day, hints of blue could be seen in his irises, but now those were muddied in the irradiated haze.

Eventually, he found his exit, an unmarked lane between the exterior walls of rival gambling halls, and peeled away. Between the pair of multistory brick edifices, the crowd's clamor faded to a dull murmur behind him. A nearby streetlight threw a long shadow that was swallowed a few yards down.

A few paces along the way, he spied the gaudily-neon, rectangle-shaped light at the far end of the alley. The vermillion-hued sign was a hard-light construct that hovered midair only a few inches from the nearby wall. Two lines of text flickered luridly in the murky lane. The glowing sign cast a pale outline on the surrounding brick walls and the thin stream that had collected in the uneven stone path.

As he picked up his pace and jogged along the narrow back alleys, Cal brushed against a man heading in the opposite direction. He was overdressed for the weather and the brim of his hat was pulled down over his face to hide what was not obscured in the darkness. With a grunt, the man continued on, without a look at Cal. Cal ignored the incident; it wasn't the first time he had encountered someone who desired anonymity.

After a few sharp turns, Cal came upon the innocuous-looking building, hidden between two taller ones. Each was topped with a large sloping roof that almost concealed the discreet business entrance. Pink lights that hovered above the lintel stated plainly "D'RIAN OBIX" without further clarification. Cal knew the strange name meant many things to many different people. Some said it was a phrase from a long-dead language. Others claimed it was a lewd expression that originated from Thosa Prathvi to the south, on the other side of the Byrathium Sea.

He trotted down the steps to the front door and gave it a firm rap with his knuckles. As the rattle echoed back into the lonely passage, the dense steel barrier swung wide to reveal an incredibly broad-shouldered man in a suit that stretched tightly across his chest. Lit from behind, the thick shelf of his brow cast shade down his craggy features.

Recognizing the recently-arrived patron through a rose corona, the doorman groaned as if disappointed and stepped aside. With a cockeyed grin, Cal slid inside and bypassed the man.

The rank odor of wet garbage was replaced with the sultry musk of booze, tobacco and unfettered lust. The interior was lushly decorated in dark wood and deep green wallpaper, with a series of brass and colored glass sconces lining the walls. A thick burgundy carpet swished under Cal's booted feet. Two rows of dense rosewood benches were set facing each other in the entrance hall, one of which was occupied by an older gentleman negotiating over the price of a young lady's services. From beyond the curtains separating the hall from the main chamber, rumbling promised pleasures that Cal was sad to miss.

As he stepped through the velvet drapes, familiar sights came in view. Dozens of felt-lined tables were spread out across the room. A few dozen men of varying ages and classes were fixated on various card or dice games. Smoke hung like a dense cloud over the proceedings.

A bevy of half-naked women wandered, many carrying trays lined with drinks. They moved luridly, the sway of their hips and unconstrained breasts as lusty advertisements. From time to time, patrons who had no financial stake in the competitions would pull one of the women aside. If the terms of their proposition proved agreeable, the newly-formed pair would disappear to other rooms, including a row above the bar at the back of the main hall.

Cal let the curtain swing closed behind him and

carefully stepped around the maze of tables to avoid disturbing the clientele. His view wandered from one barely-dressed woman to another. The acres of flesh were hard to ignore. A few eyed the new arrival, only to turn away once they recognized him. A dealer from a nearby table gave him a sideways glance, warding him off.

To the right of the bar was a set of stairs to the second floor. At the foot of the steps waited two mountains parading as men outfitted in suits who glared at Cal as he arrived. One of the well-dressed bouncers that served as checkpoint for the brass-and-redwood stairs leaned in as he held up a hand.

Cal cleared his throat and raised his voice to be heard. "I'm Cal—"

"We know who ya are, Reeger." The man on the right stated as his brow furrowed.

"Well, then, you know why I'm here, right?"

"Ya gots Jaefor's credits?"

"Uh…" Cal sputtered, which caused both men to grin.

"Well, den, ya should heads on up. Boss has sometin' for ya ta do."

The bouncer with the crew cut and block-shaped jaw stepped aside as if to let him pass. The second stopped him with a hand on his collar. Cal's heart jumped as he skidded to a halt, turning to the dark-skinned muscle whose long black hair was tied back behind his head. Icy blue eyes scanned Cal before they paused on the leather jacket draped over his shoulders.

"Dat is not yers," he announced, punctuating each syllable with a poke at Cal's chest.

"What isn't?" Cal's head turned to the side to avoid the man's gaze.

"De jacket. I seens it on ole Jecobis nots a week ago. Orange patches on the shoulders an' elbows. Brass clasp closures." He pointed to each section of the coat as he spoke. "Ya can't waltz aroun' in sometin' like dat an' people not notice it."

"I won it fair and square."

Both men shared a laugh. After a minute, Crew Cut spoke up. "We all know you're too chicken shit to kill a man for it, so I assume you stole it from him when he was sleeping in the next alley over. 'm I right?"

This time, Cal was more insistent. "I tell you I won it justly on a bet. On rodent races in Golland Park."

"Get this," Crew Cut nudged his coworker in the arm. "Ain't got two coins to rub together, nowhere to sleep even, so he bets for a leather jacket. What a riot. On rats, no less. Big spender, he is."

"Indeed," Black Hair said with a smile before eventually waving him up the stairs. "Get yer ass movin' along. Ya hang out 'round here too long, we might catch a bit of yer luck."

They separated and let him climb the steps. Usually, they would have vigilantly patted down anyone who was to head upstairs; no one was to carry a weapon anywhere near Jaefor. Even though the two revolvers that hung from matching holsters were plain to see, they let him through unmolested.

7

With a hand on the brass bannister, Cal took the steps two at a time. Once he reached the second floor, he hung a hard left, dashed around a pair of women who turned up their noses at him as if he were spoiled meat, and headed for the last door on the right.

A quick knock elicited a call to enter. After taking deep inhalations to calm himself, he slipped into the room.

Cal came to an immediate halt as the door shut with a click. His breath caught in his throat as his eyes widened.

Framed foremost in Cal's view was the older man, Jaefor, entirely naked and standing beside his bed, his creaky hips moving back and forth in a constant loop of hungry thrusts. Kneeling on the bed on her hands and knees was a young, busty redhead softly moaning in response. A sickening beat of wet flesh on flesh caused Cal to gulp as a blush colored his cheeks.

The juxtaposition of the aging and wrinkled Jaefor, who had an extra thirty pounds hanging from all the wrong places, and the young woman left Cal a bit confused, puritanical shame warring with voyeuristic arousal. His eyes jumped back and forth between her swaying breasts and Jaefor's own bloated torso. Eventually, he turned away.

"Uh, s-sorry about the interruption. I-I didn't know," Cal sputtered. "I'll come back once your—"

"No need," Jaefor raised a hand without turning away from his conquest. The other remained on her hip, fingers digging into the soft flesh. "I'll be able to pause in a min…" He stopped as his entire body clenched. After a series of grunts and a long breath through his nose, he slapped the girl on the ass and extricated himself with a gooey sound. Any desire that might have remained for Cal was surely gone now.

Still naked, with all of the signs of a life of excess shown on his mottled skin, Jaefor turned and dropped to the edge of the bed. As he reached over and gathered up a green silk bathrobe, the girl slumped forward and fell face-first into the mattress. Her breathing was deep and regular and she made no effort to cover herself. There was a hint of blush on her pale skin, but she remained face down on the top of the mattress.

Jaefor rose unceremoniously as he wrapped himself up and met Cal halfway across the room.

"Is she… okay?" The words left Cal's mouth before he could remind himself to keep out of Jaefor's personal business.

"Does it really matter?" Jaefor rubbed at the graying stubble beneath his chin. The pupils of Jaefor's brown eyes were dilated; Cal scanned the room for the man's main vice of choice. A mirror covered in tan powder sat atop a nearby bedside table.

Cal's lips opened and the words began to spill out. "But—"

Fortunately, Jaefor interrupted him. "She knows better than to bother rising from the bed. She'll only have to return to her original position when our business has concluded. I find that I truly enjoy taking a woman from behind. They can't see my face and I don't have to see theirs. It ruins the mood to see what a woman is feeling.

They're awful at keeping the little ticks that show the truth in their expressions. When it comes to the more detestable of their roles in society, they're horrible liars. In fact, once you and I are done with our transaction, I will return to complete receiving payment for her father's lost earnings."

Cal struggled to hide the grimace on his face. He had heard the smallest pained whimper through the pillows. *Thank the gods he's not interested in men. I can't imagine the kind of payment he would put to me if he did.*

"Would you care to go a round?" Jaefor offered politely. An evil grin creased his weathered face as watched Cal. "You seem stressed. Maybe a little exercise culminating in an enjoyable release of fluids would loosen you up a bit. Might make you more receptive to your future assignment."

"Uh, I think I'll take a rain check."

"Are you positive? Because getting my man-bits worked over, getting the blood flow moving from one place to another, makes me a far more agreeable businessman to bargain with. In fact, if my dear girl hadn't been in such a receiving mood, we might be having this discussion with *you* on your knees and two very large men breaking an assortment of bones."

Cal gulped. Despite the cheeriness of his mood, Jaefor's words rang of a ghoulish truth. "No, I'm sure I'm all good."

"Ah, it's all for the best, anyway." Jaefor cast a glance over his shoulder. "If you had defiled her with your miscreant's seed, I certainly would not have seen it in me to stick my meat back in. And then, how else would she finish paying off dear old father's obligation? Perhaps with a lengthy stay at the local brothel. Not here, mind you. This is far too upscale for the likes of her family. Down the street, at the Red Wench, perhaps. Fortunately, your gentlemanly declination has kept her single night of indignation from turning into a month of slogging through a hundred cocks, I guess."

At that comment, the girl placed her hands over her ears. Jaefor frowned.

"Damn it all, don't soil the sheets with your whoring tears!" Jaefor snapped before turning back to Cal. "Well, Mr. Reeger, let us be formal now and get to the matter of our business before her cunt dries up. I'd hate to have to go through all the effort to warm the child back up again. I only have so many hours in the day to waste. As it is the bedspread will need to be cleaned if not outright thrown in the fire."

"Yes, sir." Cal replied sharply, hands behind his back.

"Since you still owe a debt to me, I have a very specific task that I need you to take care of. One of a dubious nature, as you might imagine. Considering the amount in which you are indebted, I'm quite sure you understand the potential for lethality and illegality. I expect you to act accordingly. Keep it hush-hush and all." At this, Jaefor walked across the room to a liquor cabinet and poured from a decanter of whiskey. His rings clinked against the glass as he gripped it in one hand.

"Of course. And what would be this job?"

"I hear tales that the Archaeology Bureau in Rian Sands has unearthed a rare find in Natx Hollow. How rare is yet to be determined I hear. Something about a Third Era site buried deep, almost a half-mile below the surface. I want whatever of value can be seized from there, no matter what it is. To sell for a profit or to keep for my own. Makes little difference. I want it. I have an empty place in my sitting room that needs something ancient and/or expensive as a conversation starter."

"Do you even know what it is?"

"Unimportant," Jaefor flicked a hand in the air as he sipped. "As you would imagine, the excavation site is likely under guard. So, normally, getting you in would cost more coin than it's worth to me. Having said that, though, it's been brought to my attention another means of entry. The Athenaeum of the An-Sebban already has a relationship with the Bureau and can gain access to Natx Hollow without too much difficulty. A recently-submitted petition has been approved to allow one of their own to catalog the site and bring the information back for their collection. As you may know, the An-Sebban are not the most… sturdy or world-wise of people, so they have sent out a contract to the Merced League for the services of a bodyguard."

"And you need me to—"

"Shut the fuck up… is what I need you to do." Jaefor clenched his teeth. "My resource in the League already has the contract set aside, to be filled at my discretion. As such, I want you to pick up the An-Sebban, escort them to the site and when the time is right, appropriate all of that ancient shit that your filthy hands can hold. Smuggle as much as you think would balance your debt to me. I have little choice but to leave the decision-making to you as to what you would appropriate, but in light of your history, I would consider that you aren't good with that sort of critical thinking. Assume that anything you acquire is likely worth half of what you think it is."

Cal nodded quietly. He didn't care for Jaefor's tone, but he kept his tongue in check.

Jaefor downed his drink and dropped the glass on the bedside table, scattering tan dust from the mirrored surface. He crossed the room to a birch hutch desk, opened a drawer and removed a sheaf of papers. "Make no mistake, Reeger: I am sending you on this task because you owe me a grand amount. This is the most important thing you will ever do with the rest of your life. The rabble that scurries to and fro from my establishments may see you as a pathetic roach, doing your best to avoid the boot that will crush the life from you. I, on the other hand, see the raw talent, the once-capable gunman, who squandered a life of promise in the pursuit of wine, women and wealth, only to end up with none of them."

Jaefor turned back to him. "Understand me when I say this: fail in this endeavor and I will find value from you. I will strip the skin from your body while you still live, have it tanned, and then use it to upholster a new piece of furniture. I will task men to find everyone in your bloodline and do the same to them. And in the end, I *will* sell this fine collection of furnishings to the highest bidder to at least recoup a portion of my lost capital."

He reached out his hand, offering the papers to Cal, who quickly snapped them up.

"In the morrow, you're to arrive at the Athenaeum's

property in Nipir'x Sector and report to the headmistress, Grande Dame Hru-Gatta, to retrieve your ward. These documents will be enough to appease any curiosity she may have. Also, there are the required papers of transit to get through Ilgyngate and on the continental rail to Quartewuste."

"There, uh, there is a slight matter." Cal was hesitant to bring up his concern.

"As expected, I assume that you have no spending money to make any arrangements of your own. Speak with Illgosses at the cashier's window downstairs to get a stipend that will be added to your debt. Pick up a little extra and possibly buy an outfit that doesn't leave you with all the appearances of vagrancy. You *are* working for the League. Also, do the An-Sebban a favor and spend a little time to wash the stench from your body."

Cal clutched the documents tightly against his chest.

"Now get out of here, lest you wish to pay a viewing fee."

Cal was out the door as quickly as his feet would take him.

Cal's steps had a dancing quality as he approached the cashier window at the back corner of the main hall. Though the bouncers by the stairs heckled him, he offered no retort. He was too relieved to be out of Jaefor's presence with all of his limbs intact to care what anyone in the building thought of him.

A dour countenance greeted him from behind the metal bars. On the other side of the window reclined the pale-skinned banker, coated in flop-sweat and sporting green-tinted glasses. His thinning hair was brushed out of his face, and a long scar that ran diagonally along the crest of his scalp created an odd part in the oily coif.

Another man entered the cashier's cage from an adjacent room and closed the steel door. A rattle of metal jingled with every footstep. Draped in a suit of slate-colored armor plating, the sentry was an athletic man, leaner than the bouncers, who waited in the shadows at the back of the room. The outfit under the armor was black fabric that had the appearance of snakeskin. The fingers of his banded gauntlets rested on a belt that hung from his hips. On one end swung a baton and the other a pistol.

In the faint light from a nearby lamp, the features of his face were dark behind his bronze helm. If Cal was not already familiar with Raxus, whom he had seen on prior occasion, he might have been caught off-guard by the glistening faceplate. Even still, he found himself pausing at the window for a breath too long, which caused the cashier to bark at him.

"What brass-plated balls you must have to show your face here. I told you last time you don't have any more credit with us. Why Jaefor—"

"He's why I'm here," Cal interrupted before Illgosses could continue on what would certainly be a spit-spewing tirade.

At this, Illgosses looked to the sentry, who only shrugged.

"Educate me as to how you've acquired additional credit." Illgosses narrowed his eyes and leaned in.

Cal pulled the recently-acquired papers from within his jacket and flashed them at the cashier. Illgosses eyed the top sheet as he ran a jagged finger along the more pertinent parts of the legal documentation. By the time he reached the third page, he appeared convinced and pushed the notes back to Cal.

After counting and recounting the stack of currency, Illgosses slid the funds to Cal and leaned away. "Don't spend it all in one place," he said as Cal slipped back with a sarcastic salute.

02

At the heart of the western territories, before travelers reached Treyets Coast, was an expanse of desert known as the Quartewuste. While the northern acreage was dotted with small villages, most of the southern terrain was an unhospitable wasteland. Wind-blasted dunes of blanched sand shifted back and forth as they baked in the arid climate. Only in night's darkness did those who remained in the barren region find solace from the relentless heat.

To the west, almost a hundred miles from the nearest township, was Natx Hollow, a five thousand year old complex long lost beneath the sea of sand. The site rested within a naturally-formed depression, framed on three sides by a ridge of earth that rose hundreds of feet above the largest structure. Its original purpose was still up for debate within the Archaeology Bureau; while the central building appeared much like a place of worship, surrounding structures resembled remnants of a marketplace. There were only a few hovels that were believed to have served as housing, though not in a quantity to support the theory that the site had been a proper community.

To the north was a collection of matching olive tents,

temporary housing for the Archaeology Bureau's current expedition in residence. At or before sunrise, the inhabitants were up and about as they made preparations for the day's tasks. During the daylight hours, the heat made it unbearable for the crew of ten to remain outdoors for any length of time. While the above-ground temple itself provided sufficient shade in the dry air, it was when the staff escaped to the underground passages that they found extended relief.

Peter Mathester, Junior Associate of the Archaeology Bureau tasked with recording Segment D103 of the Quartewuste, waited in the entrance of the main temple as his gaze scanned the familiar courtyard below. His face, burned days ago, now peeled along the thin bridge of his nose and plump cheeks.

Seated on a crate that was once filled with supplies, he fanned himself with a free hand and finished a handful of dates before he rose. His luncheon—a lamb-filled pita, fruits and nuts—was taken out of necessity; he had been wholly-absorbed in his work since sun-up.

He often found himself needing to get away, to stare at the sand as the winds blew it inch by inch across the landscape before him. Only once his senses were focused on unimportant stimuli could he start to piece together the information absorbed during his time below. Usually, he would return to his work refreshed and able to compose his records accordingly.

This time was different, though. He felt stuck, as if in a quagmire.

As he walked along, he produced a rag from his back

pocket and wiped his brow and the back of his neck. His hair, dirty brown and parted to one side, was coated in a fine layer of dust. Until he returned to civilization, he felt there was no need to brush his locks clean, as they would only collect more of the tan grit. It was a losing battle; the sand found a way into everything, no matter what precautions were taken.

He was dressed in a short-sleeved button-down shirt and khaki pants. A chocolate gingham vest hung loosely from his thin shoulders. Peter was a small-framed man, almost swallowed by the folds of his clothes. His black cap-toed boots had once been neatly polished, but over the past months, his attention had been more on his work than on his appearance. It wasn't as if there was anyone within a hundred mile radius that he felt the desire to impress. The expedition was entirely male and the nearest village was to the east through the dunes.

As Peter traveled, his mind wandered and his body went on autopilot. At times he added items to his mental checklist of supplies to purchase. Other times, he mulled over notes for the eventual documentation he would submit once his time at Natx Hollow came to an end.

There were no major routes that passed in the vicinity and it was only in recent decades that anyone from the Bureau had taken an interest in the site. After the second expedition unearthed underground catacombs, which dated back at least a hundred thousand years, administrators in the Bureau became far more interested.

When Peter received notification of his assignment to Natx Hollow, he assumed that his career was on the upswing. While the Bureau kept its associates busy cataloging recent archaeological finds, the rarer, ancient locales were considered special, for more than just their historic value. To be dispatched to one of these sites was an honor; a person's success in the Bureau could be gauged by their résumé of assignments and the discoveries attached to their names.

This was Peter's opportunity and he knew that to be successful, he had to uncover something truly extraordinary. He was certain there was some as-yet unseen object or piece of data to be exhumed. Evidence seemed to hint at something unique within the site, though he was unable to make the connection just yet.

In the back corner of the courtyard, near the eastern colonnade, was an opening in the floor. Time and the tectonic shifting of the earth had caused the thin soil to give way, revealing a subterranean network of chambers below. A thirty-foot long rope ladder was anchored to the ground. From the echoes rolling up, Peter could tell that his fellow associates were back to work in a nearby compartment.

Natx Hollow mystified members of the scientific community, since the underground structures were so unlike any in mankind's history. At their age, they should have been total ruins. If Peter were prone to whimsy, he might have considered that the edifices were touched by magic. The interiors stayed in excellent condition despite millennia of disuse.

The above-ground structure showed all expected signs of extended age, with the wear and tear of the arid environs leaving few exterior details. Below, however, even in the topmost floor, the site was in far greater condition than was to be expected. The structural integrity was especially astounding and left more than one man dubious at the validity of the earlier carbon-dating.

Peter descended and touched down on a small mound of sand. He looked around for a moment and caught a glimpse of activity a few dozen feet to his right. A number of his fellows remained intrigued by a triptych of murals in the nearby chamber, so much so that they were recreating the artwork for submission to the Bureau.

As Peter kicked the dust from his shoes and began to walk away, a voice hailed him.

"Hey, Mathester," Quillin called out as he stood in the doorway. This caused Peter to halt midstride. Quillin was of similar age and had entered the Bureau at the same time, but Peter in no way considered him a friend. At best, he was tolerated. "Headed back to the Blue Room?"

"Of course," Peter said curtly.

"You're *wasting* your time," Quillin heckled. "Why don't you just join my group? I'll be sure to add your name to the fine print of my dissertation. At least you'll get credit for something. Maybe even considered for the next round of promotions."

"Thanks for the offer," Peter replied without looking back.

"You're going to keep at it until you excavate something of worth, eh? Better bring something bigger than a pick axe! I hear we have demo charges! Maybe you could use one or two to blow out a wall and find an even emptier chamber. Or, maybe you can author a thesis on the pigmentation of ancient metal." Quillin hollered with a cupped hand to the side of his mouth. When Peter failed to respond, he shrugged his shoulders and retreated.

Peter knew better than bite. While they all were under the employ of the Bureau, there was a bit of competition amongst the group, as if recognition was a finite resource to be squabbled over. Though Quillin wagered on the mural, Peter was far more interested in a room considerably deeper in the site. He left his co-workers behind as the sounds of their chatter echoed down the long hall.

The passage itself was a peculiar structure, and from the style and its age, constructed by different hands than the above ruins. While much older, by at least a hundred thousand years if science was to be believed, it was in surprisingly stable condition, with only a few areas deemed unsafe to explore.

Set at intervals along the long corridor were sconces, each lit with glowing sapphire jewels. The tiled floor was covered in powder that had seeped inside over the millennia. Dyes that once decorated the pavers were largely scrubbed away, with only faint markings left to show the original artwork. The walls, composed of maroon-dyed bricks, featured a number of ornamental arches and square columns. Only a few murals existed and no evidence of statuary had been unearthed.

At the end of the hundred-yard-long walkway was a curling staircase, broken into segments of twelve stairs each, which led downwards to the lower floor. Peter followed this to a similar hall, that also ended in steps, which drew him deeper into the complex.

By the time he reached the bottom-most floor, the heat trapped within his clothes had dissipated. He now felt a cool dryness in the air. On his lonesome in the stretch of interconnected chambers and alcoves, Peter picked up his pace and came to a stop outside a room in the back corner of the level. It had gone undiscovered until a recent shift dislodged a limestone block that had masked the entrance. With the obstacle cleared, Peter had thrown himself into determining the cube-shaped area's purpose.

Peter went to the opposite side of the strange room and stopped within arm's reach of the far wall. He was intrigued by the unusual markings along the floor and vertical surfaces. Unlike the rest of the rooms that were lined with dense earthen blocks, the room seemed to be constructed of a cobalt-tinted metal. No evidence of furniture or personal belongings was originally found within.

In fact, everything that now occupied the space had been arranged by Peter himself. A single table, covered in handwritten notes and a few books from his own collection was set to the side of the entrance, lit by a lantern of amber glass and brass. In the corner, hanging from a wooden chair, was Peter's khaki jacket and leather satchel.

Along the exterior were row upon row of etched lines, none more than three inches in length, arranged vertically from floor to ceiling. They were carved in an irregular pattern. At first, Peter speculated that it was a form of written language, but as time passed, he struggled to make sense of it. A second theory was that it was some record, a coded number system, but he did not have the experience in this area so his efforts on this idea went no further.

On the back wall was a small square panel, in the middle of which was a tiny hole. Peter ran a pair of fingers over it and for a moment, an aquamarine light shape formed midair, inches above the panel. The light was projected from within the pinprick opening. The quadrangular shape was filled with similarly-colored squares, each with a foreign symbol of intersecting lines in the middle. Though its purpose remained undetermined, it had the appearance of a keyboard.

He ran his open hand above the construct, which allowed the aura to shine on his palm. After a few seconds of inactivity, the complex fabrication faded, leaving no sign of its existence. Even the faint hint of warmth that accompanied it quickly dissipated.

Peter had been aware of the electric manifestation for some time now, but had not yet pressed any of the buttons. To tap at a few of the icons might be like punching in a keycode. Perhaps he didn't feel ready to find out what it would do. As it was, the walls around him left plenty to decipher.

As he stood in place, considering the mysterious, radiant formation, a gravelly baritone addressed him. Peter jumped at the sound.

"Mr. Mathester? Is all well?"

Peter turned to find Apello framed by the doorway. As the lamplight barely revealed his flat nose and wide cheeks, the dark-skinned man seemed to meld into the shadows. A thick tangle of brown hair obscured his brow.

Apello was a sizeable man, one who towered over his Bureau wards. Even Peter, who was taller than most, could not look directly into his goldenrod eyes without tipping his head back. Hired as security officer for the group, Apello was garbed in a leather cuirass formed of crisscrossing strips and closed with a quartet of brass clasps. A kermes-red cashmere kaftan with gold embroidery hung from the pauldrons atop his shoulders.

Peter felt various embarrassments, a fresh one from the surprise, another longstanding. He was riddled with guilt about imposing on Apello despite the fact that the man was hired to help. He was the only person operating so far below ground and, because of that, Apello was regularly forced to go out of his way to check Peter's status.

"Ah, Apello, good morrow to you. Or rather, good... afternoon?" Peter frowned as he cocked his head to the side. He hadn't paid much attention to the sun earlier and had no clear idea of what time it was.

"I'll take your word for it," Apello replied politely, even though his voice was taciturn enough to imply disinterest. His eyes scanned the metallic surfaces and lingered for a moment to the patch behind Peter. When he seemed to show interest, Peter took this as a sign to initiate conversation.

"Curious as to what I've discovered as of late?"

"Not to be impolite, but my only concern is for the site's safety. Merely making my rounds."

"So you have no desire to investigate our recent find?"

"It's not within my purview to care. I have been tasked with keeping you alive and relatively safe, considering the situation." After a moment's pause, he continued. "What was the nature of the illumination I just saw?"

"Oh, merely an ancient light formation," Peter responded with a cheerful smile as he motioned to the panel over his shoulder. "Would you—"

Apello held up a single hand to cut short the inquiry. "Are you certain of its safety? What is its purpose?" He took a single step forward, looked around the cobalt-colored walls and curled his lips in distaste.

"Perhaps, would you be a… superstitious fellow?" Peter inquired as Apello refused to progress further. The inquiry drew a glare. "I assure you there's nothing to be concerned with here. Just because it does not share similar features as the rest of the site does not make it a danger."

"I am a pragmatist, sir." He emphasized the last word, as if to maintain professionalism. "As it is, we have no idea of what anything in this room does. That is something you are currently attempting to determine. The fewer in here, the better, I say. I have been paid to guard and not interfere. This entire chamber is a find, is it not? It would be best that I not stomp about, like a clumsy oaf. I leave *that* to you."

How rude, Peter thought to himself. He took a long breath, counted to five and eventually responded. "Well, I assure you that nothing is of issue, as of yet. Any interaction I've had with the room has yet to produce any tangible effects. Much to the detriment of my career…" Peter trailed off.

At this Apello bowed and began to depart. As he withdrew, the sound of weapons banging against the back of his armor rang out. Peter had seen the pair of khukuri in use before; the inwardly-curved blades were prized possessions that were ornately-decorated along the upper spine.

"Before I continue my patrol," Apello paused in the doorway. "Master Contrell advised that we should expect visitors in the near future."

"Oh? Do tell?" Peter was earnestly surprised. Natx Hollow was not a place one casually visited. If someone was to make it their destination, there was a reason.

"An-Sebban. Under escort. The Athenaeum is sending a delegation."

Peter nodded. He had heard of the An-Sebban before but had never been in their presence. Others within the Bureau had and such tales were passed around in the Bureau's halls like campfire stories. He found himself excited by the prospect. "How soon should we expect them?"

"A week, barring travel complications."

"Well, that will certainly give me time to clean the place up."

Apello left Peter without further comment.

03

The Athenaeum of the An–Sebban's campus was centrally located on a 130-acre plot of land in Nipir'x Sector. Bordered on all sides by middle-income housing districts, the estate rested firmly between the heart of Greater Decedistadt and the northern harbor. The property was bounded by forty-foot tall, ivory-colored stone walls, which kept the inhabitants secluded from the rest of the populace. The only public access to the grounds was through a portcullis at the southernmost tip of the main yard.

Cal had set out well before sun-up. Still, his trek from Urigo Sector to the estate took hours; it was mid-morning before he arrived at the blackened-iron gates. Even with liberal usage of the city's taxi system, he had to weave his way through the industrial districts before cutting through the central business and legislative zones. North of that was a series of higher-income neighborhoods which fed white-collar employees into the adjacent sectors. Among tightly-packed homes and apartment buildings, the white fortification and monumental structures within were distinct.

As he travelled, sometimes on foot and at other times by cab, Cal thought back to his meeting with Jaefor. He felt both anxiety and revulsion at the means by which he was pressed into service. Every time the loose change jingled in his pockets, he felt awkward that not a single piece of it was his. On top of that, if he completed his task, he'd be none the richer; success would merely clean the slate with Jaefor.

With a portion of the stipend, he had done as suggested. While he still retained his orange-and-brown jacket, recently dry-cleaned to eliminate the worst of the trapped odors, the rest of his attire was new. Beneath the lined coat, he wore a white linen shirt, left open at the top. A pair of black suspenders held up tan slacks that were still stiff with starch. Occasionally, he would tug at the legs in hopes of softening the rigid fabric. Two holsters hung from belts strapped across his waist, beneath his jacket.

Once within the wall, Cal paused as he took in the unexpected panorama. To one accustomed to the overcrowded city, the open spaces of the piazza came as a refreshing change. Leading away from the gate was a brick-laid walking path through the concourse that ended in a terrace that bordered the main hall. On either side of the central aisle were rows of well-tended topiaries and, beyond those, were lush thickets of flowering trees.

In a circular planter a dozen yards from the portcullis stood a tree fashioned into the shape of a woman. The branches and trunk appeared to naturally take a feminine form with her chest protruding and her arms stretched out behind her. There was no sign of recent pruning which left Cal doubly impressed at the creation. From its back spread laden boughs formed into the shape of wings. At the center of its chest was a ruby that glistened in the morning light.

Through the canopy of saplings, Cal located the central administration building, a colossal slab of gray limestone that towered multiple stories over the courtyard. A number of small spires, ornamented with iron-formed trefoils and rosettes, were set at each corner of the complex roofline. The steeply-pitched roof itself was topped with slate tiles. The asymmetrical façade was flanked on each side by a pair of wings connected to the entrance tower. Above bronzed doors that shone warmly in the mid-morning light was an open loggia that overlooked wide stairs.

Flanking the main building were what appeared to be residence halls. These red-brick dormitories were newer additions, with more contemporary architecture evident in the archways and eaves.

With his mind focused on the vista's details, Cal ignored the foot traffic around him. He was seasoned at tuning out the ebb and flow, concentrating on the things he wanted to see. It wasn't until his scan of the grounds was complete that he took notice of those enjoying the greenspace. While there were a few people dressed in business attire speaking casually amongst themselves, he found himself drawn to a couple on a bench by to the unique planter.

Though neither of the pair looked older than twelve, the manner in which they wore their vestments suggested a maturity that the illusion of youth could not obscure. The layered robes, an ankle-length gray sticharion with a brown epitrachilion across the shoulders, were pulled tightly about them, as if to conceal as much of their bodies as possible. Both sat upright with their hands crossed on their laps. On closer examination, Cal noticed a wariness in their eyes.

One of the duo, whose gender he could not determine, met Cal's gaze, causing him to look away. Feeling self-conscious at being caught curious, Cal hurried along.

There was no doorman to greet Cal as he slipped into the foyer. The front doors closed behind him with a resonant thump that rolled deep into the bowels of the hall.

Cal felt like he was casing the lobby as he eyed the decor. The floor was a glossy black marble and the bannisters on the curling staircases were polished brass. At the peak of the vaulted ceiling, in the faceted dome coated with a metallic silver paint, was hung a crystal chandelier. In each of the lamp sockets rested a teardrop-shaped gem that glowed with a cold, yellow light. Constructed of black leather and lusterless metal, the furniture felt utilitarian by design, odd in a lobby intended to be hospitable.

A young man, dressed in a charcoal suit that accentuated his thin frame, approached. His flaxen hair was brushed back and his lean features were soft and welcoming. He bowed with his hands clasped and addressed Cal kindly. For a moment, he had to remind himself that he was no longer in Urigo Sector, where almost everyone was rude to him.

"I am Golette, how might I be of assistance?" His voice was like velvet; consonants rolled from his tongue like water off of a duck's back.

"Cal Reeger. I was sent by the Merced League on a contract. Protection detail as I understand it." He made a move to reach for the papers tucked inside his jacket.

"Ah, say no more," Golette replied with warm smile, even though surprise appeared in his raised brow. His eyes widened for a second.

The mixed signals made him all the more wary of what awaited him. He began to wonder if Jaefor knew anything at all about the An-Sebban before he dispatched Cal.

"If you'll remain here, I will retrieve Grande Dame Hru-Gatta for you. Please, have a seat." Golette motioned before he slipped away. Cal watched him for a moment before he disappeared beneath one of the stairwells.

Now alone, Cal shrugged and dropped into the nearest seat: a blocky settee that was curiously stiff, as if the upholstery was not yet broken in. As he stretched out, with the leather creaking beneath him, Cal could hear the movement of others elsewhere in the building. As he honed in on the sound of footsteps, he noticed a lack of heavy tread usually associated with more upscale settings. *No big men? Or no security personnel making the rounds. That's odd. One would think a place like this would employ a force of some kind.*

Cal fidgeted, shifting his weight from side to side as struggled to find a comfortable spot on the couch. When Golette eventually returned, he readily jumped to his feet, relieved to be on his way.

From behind Golette stepped a petite woman, who, at

Cal's best guess, could be no more than five feet tall and 90 pounds soaking wet. She was dressed in a tailored, three-piece pantsuit of charcoal silk with an ivory ascot. Pulled away from her face and pinned back with a carved-bone hairpin, her long straight hair had once been a solid sheet of black that was now streaked with lines of white. Her soft cheeks and rounded jawline were offset by wrinkles etched around her mouth and across her forehead. Her pale blue eyes narrowed as she moved in to greet Cal.

"Mister Reeger, is it?" she began with a slight curtsy. The fabric swayed faintly at the movements of her body.

He wondered if he should bow or offer her a handshake. He gave her a quick nod, replying. "Yes, Calvin Reeger. Sent by—"

"The Merced League? Yes, I am versed with your organization. You are not the first, nor shall you be the last. I am Grande Dame Hru-Gatta, Head Administrator." Her words were sharp, on the verge of being impolite. There was no congeniality, though Cal did not get the impression that she was being intentionally stern. It was as if she had no capacity for polite niceties. "I have no recollection of prior encounters with you. Is this your first sojourn to the estate? Have you any previous experience with the An-Sebban?"

Cal's knee-jerk reaction was to fabricate a backstory, to make himself seem more experienced than he was. After a moment, he spoke up.

"No, ma'am, I–I have not. First time for both, I must admit." *Sometimes the truth is the best backstory,* he reminded himself. *Just don't give her more of it than she needs.*

"Then I shall escort you through the facilities and to the Central Archive. That is where we will encounter your ward." With a flick of two fingers, she beckoned him. Golette waited, hands behind his back, as the pair departed through oaken double doors at the back of the foyer.

As they progressed through the building's winding halls, including a corridor lined with dorm rooms and a dining hall, Cal tried to keep his eyes on Hru-Gatta. She moved swiftly, cutting corners sharply. With his attention on his guide, he had little time to notice the interior, much less observe the decorations. Out of the corner of his eye, he would occasionally catch a painting or bas-relief that stood in stark contrast to the near-colorless decor. The carpet was a dull ashen tone bordered by slate baseboards.

As he caught up with Hru-Gatta, when she whirled down a curved staircase, he spied something at the back of her neck as her hair whipped to one side. Cal wondered if it was a trick of the light or maybe a tattoo. He knew of inked skin—there was a rose on his left shoulder blade, a sign of affection for a girl whose name he had forgotten long ago.

When Hru-Gatta's locks swung the other way, he saw it again. Located centrally on the back of her neck was a quartet of small holes, each framed by foil, which reminded him of electronic sockets. Before he could open his mouth, Hru-Gatta spoke up.

"What do you know of the An-Sebban, Mr. Reeger? Or, rather, what are your prior experiences with the Athenaeum? You've stated that you have no prior working relationship, though you must have some knowledge of our place in society."

"No more than the average person, I would guess. From what I've heard, they're… well, you're considered gatherers of data, collecting information for the purposes of a single research library. Izzat right?"

"I would consider 'gatherers of data' to be a rather appropriate turn-of-phrase." Though he couldn't see her face, Cal was almost certain he heard a single note of laughter. "I have heard the Athenaeum referred to as many things in my time: a business guild, a religious sect and even an intellectual collective. We retain a retinue of staff, like Mr. Golette, who perform in various official capacities within the institute. Most are groundskeepers, personal assistants, or even concierges. At times, they may even be tasked with acting as liaisons with the outside world. Their sole capacity is in support of the actual members of the An-Sebban. Those of who are the true 'gatherers of data,' as you so eloquently termed it. I am certain you have witnessed them lounging in the campus yard, have you not?"

Cal was reminded of the seated pair outside. "A few, yes."

"Noticed, did you, how different they appear to the average human living outside these ivory walls?"

"Well, I didn't want to say anything that might be considered rude, but… yes."

At this, she turned her head slightly. Cal saw a smile that quickly faded as she continued.

"The An-Sebban are distinctive, a separate strain of humanity forged by the circumstances of their duties.

They possess all the physical attributes of underdeveloped adolescents, even though most are decades old. Their purpose is to act as witness, to collect evidence with all of their senses and periodically return to transfer this data to the Central Archive. It is within this structure that their records become one with the already-existing directory."

"And the purpose for collecting all this info?"

"To know."

Cal frowned briefly. Before he could press, his guide ushered him through a doorway into a vaulted hall that was once a cathedral. Alcoves on either side were now used for storage or administrative offices. At the far end, where an altar would stand in the apse was a landing, where a long, circular desk manned by two assistants sat. Behind the counter was a wide staircase that led to a balcony which overlooked the oratory.

For a moment, Cal wondered which of the two structures had been built first: the sanctuary or the connected mansion.

"It will only be a few minutes, Mr. Reeger," Hru-Gatta stated as she escorted him along the nave. He only nodded quietly as his mind struggled to keep up. "As a part of the process, your charge is finishing the final stages of her transferral before departure."

"Certainly." He had no idea what she meant. As they continued down the aisle, Cal cast sideways glances at the rows of pews.

A few of the robed An-Sebban were seated throughout, most by themselves, though none appeared to be praying.

Many were intently perusing literature of one form or another, while others were staring off into the distance. A concierge paused to collect one of the An-Sebban, who was lost in a trance, and quietly escorted her to a side room out of Cal's view.

As they crossed the transept, Hru-Gatta bypassed the manned desk without a word to the employees. Neither offered a welcome, and only one bothered to react to Cal's nod as he passed. He once again had to hasten to catch up with Hru-Gatta, who was halfway up the flight of steps.

On the second story landing, Cal noticed an entrance to his right that was barred with a placard that stated "No Entry: Administration Only." He almost lost sight of Hru-Gatta as she disappeared behind a gold-trimmed mahogany door marked "Central Archives" in block letters. Cal caught it just as it was about to close and propped it open long enough to slip inside.

Cal was taken aback at the sight before him. The Central Archive was an expansive column, at least 100 feet in height, most of which appeared to be below ground. As the lowest levels were hidden in darkness, he could not determine how deep it descended. The curved walls were lined with stone tablets, each ten feet in height and sunken into row upon row of niches. Even from a distance, Cal could make out alphanumeric symbols along the face of each slab, as if some manner of filing system was in place.

From the entrance descended steps that sloped to a platform at the center of the room. On one end was a mass of instruments, twinkling lights and glowing gauges. Extending from this central hub were five rectangular podiums which fanned out like playing cards. A single tablet was seated on the central pedestal. Incandescence flickered behind the carved icons along its exterior.

At the base of the machinery was a trio of oval-shaped divans, attached to the controls by a series of wires and hoses. In the middle bed was a small female form, dressed in the familiar gray-and-brown robes, her head inside an elliptical device that cradled her skull. A few wisps of straight colorless hair could be seen beneath the webwork of wires which led to the main device behind her.

As he stood quietly at the side of Hru-Gatta, she looked to him and narrowed her eyes. Eventually, she spoke up. "Apologies for the delay. Ms. Nsu-Ogette should have completed the process earlier, but felt she had additional information to collect before her scheduled transferral session to the archive."

"Not a problem."

"To be honest, the earliness of your scheduled arrival was unexpected." The casual tone caught him off-guard. Since his introduction, she had been excessively formal, but now Hru-Gatta seemed nonchalant. "Usually, the Merced League takes longer to respond to a contract request. Their punctuality, or lack thereof, can be problematic. Days, if not weeks, pass before a member is eventually dispatched. It is not my place to presume why that is the case. Perhaps they lack the requisite amount of manpower to meet demand, or perhaps, the Athenaeum is not deemed a prominent account."

"I wouldn't know anything about that, ma'am. I only just found out about it yesterday," was all he could offer.

Perhaps she was probing him to ensure he was legitimately with the Merced League.

"Indeed." She fell silent and stood with her arms crossed behind her back. He chose to do the same, relieved that she had not asked anything that he could not comfortably answer.

After a few minutes, sounds of air escaping hoses issued from the machinery, which signaled the end of Nsu-Ogette's session. Her hazel eyes flickered open and she slowly sat up. Braided cables disconnected from the sockets at the back of her neck and dropped to the pillow behind her. Once free of the gear around her head, her thin hair became more noticeable. In the room's sallow light, Cal was uncertain whether her tresses were gray or a stark platinum blonde. Perhaps they were both.

A metal armature descended from the shadows of the ceiling. It latched onto the tablet on the pedestal and lifted it into the air with a single vertical movement. Except for the sounds of the hydraulics, the entire process was quick and quiet. With a swift 180 degree rotation, the stainless steel arm flipped over at one of two joints, swung about and replaced the tablet into its once-empty socket along the wall.

As Hru-Gatta joined the woman and helped her to her feet, Cal waited and watched. Side-by-side, Hru-Gatta appeared both taller and more casual. Where her previous mannerisms seemed stiff, in comparison to Nsu-Ogette, she appeared relatively laid-back.

Initially, Nsu-Ogette's features were a bit baffling to Cal. The oval shape of her face, along with the soft slope of her cheeks and her button nose, gave her the appearance of a pre-pubescent girl. In contrast, though, the dullness of her eyes, the creases that lined her sockets and her cracked lips hinted that someone far older was trapped within the frame of the young woman. Even after seeing others of her kind on his path to the archives, his ward's puppet-like appearance was unnerving.

Hru-Gatta led the woman by the hand. "Mr. Reeger, this is your ward, Oebe Nsu-Ogette. Oebe, this is Cal Reeger."

Oebe only blinked in response.

Reflexively, Cal offered her an open hand, only to slowly pull it back moments later as she looked dimly at it. At this, Hru-Gatta spoke up. "I guess I was remiss in fully explaining the situation. Since this is obviously your first time on such a duty for the Athenaeum, I would warn you that she will not react in a manner to which you are accustomed."

"How do you mean?" He grasped what Hru-Gatta might mean from the near-catatonic manner in which Oebe stood.

"An An-Sebban, once completed with the archival process, is much like an empty vessel. Except for the basest understandings of human functions and interactions, they retain little to call their own. It is for this reason that we hire escorts such as yourself. Even though your role is contracted as bodyguard, protection during their transit abroad, much of your time will be spent as chaperone, not unlike a guardian for a young child. On her own, she would be unable to reach Natx Hollow."

"So, not much for small talk?"

Hru-Gatta ignored the quip. "You must understand that, for them, memory lies in layers within the mind. The process of transferral removes the top layers, the recent recollections, where everything she has observed and learned since her previous session is stored. What remains is the formative memories. The base human functions. A side-effect of this is that she will lack the subtleties of social interaction that I am certain you are accustomed to."

"Will she… improve in time?"

"As she spends more time abroad, collecting information? Certainly."

He nodded as he watched Oebe stand silently, her eyes still except for the occasional flicker of her eyelashes. He felt a twinge of guilt about speaking in so cavalier a manner.

"I take it, then, that she doesn't give a whit about us talking about her right in front of her face like we've been doing."

"I do not mind," Oebe spoke, her soft voice surprisingly raspy.

04

Within the hour, Cal escorted Oebe from the estate. Only out from under the watchful gaze of Hru-Gatta did he feel that he could relax. He remained unsure if the headmistress doubted his legitimacy; her stoic nature made her unreadable.

On foot, he led Oebe across to their point of departure: the Langspur Rail Station at the north end of the city. As they paraded through the crowded avenues, he took her hand, as if guiding a child. He had never considered himself paternal. Perhaps the gesture was borne from the need to keep his way to freedom safely within his grasp.

She remained silently compliant over the entire length of the crossing. To Cal, her eyes seemed always trained forward, as if unfazed by the surrounding distractions. Even with the occasional outbreak of raucous chatter, she appeared unmoved by any stimuli.

Cal noticed that her slender fingers felt cool against his skin. When it became clear that he didn't need to tug on her arm for direction, he realized that she didn't require constant vigilance. She seemed to have some idea of their destination, though she struggled with navigating dense crowds as the lunch hour unleashed assembly-line and dock workers into the streets.

It was after noon by the time he purchased passage vouchers from the ticket booth near the station's entrance. With the tickets in one hand, he took her by the sleeve and headed directly to the staircase that led to the rail platform. Cal drew Oebe in close as they pushed their way through the horde offloading from the recently-arrived train.

Oebe offered no protest though they were constantly jostled in the midst of the throng. More than once, Cal swore fruitlessly at someone who quickly disappeared beyond them. Such congested traffic was rife with pickpocketing opportunities. With his free hand, he frantically patted himself down. He sighed with relief: both revolvers and the wad of currency in his jacket pocket were still on his person.

As they reached the top of the steps, a sight caused Cal's heart to skip a beat. At the other end of the enclosed corridor stood a pair of Magistrates who maintained watchful vigil on either side of the entrance. His breath caught in his throat as he came to a stop. Her hand in his, Oebe continued to look forward.

The Magistrates served as the uppermost tier of the city's law enforcement hierarchy. Except for those members of the Central Judicia that held seat in the metropolis' interior wards, the justices-at-large enforced order within the boundaries of the legal system. While Cal had never had the ill fortune of running afoul of them, the horror stories of their punishments coupled with their domineering presence was enough to cause him distress.

Each wore a suit of black armor, featuring angular plates layered over a Kevlar bodysuit. Along the back of their vambraces was a trio of diagonal blades that appeared like raptor's claws. Hanging about their waists was sheathed a steel baton that, once brandished, became electrified. Cal had witnessed a street-level reprimand in which one was used with alarmingly-violent results. A lever-action repeating rifle was slung over one shoulder.

The most intimidating feature proved to be their obsidian helmets, fashioned to completely obscure their faces. At the center was a pentagonal opaque glass panel that glittered crimson in the light. Welded on the crown at either side was a curled piece of steel, like a bull's horns.

Cal began to mull over viable excuses as to why he was there, just in case he was pulled aside. Perhaps he might tell them he was Oebe's uncle, escorting her to visit family in Westhaven. He would have to concoct the details of their relationship. Would she be able to corroborate under interrogation? *No, she wouldn't because she's... Wait a minute, you dumbass. You don't need to make up an excuse. You already have a reason to be here. You have all the necessary paperwork and a legitimate explanation for being here. Stop trying to make it more complicated than need be.*

He patted his breast pocket again. Once he felt the lump of paperwork beneath the fabric, his heart rate returned to normal and he picked up his gait. Hidden within the traffic that dumped out onto Platform One, they passed by the watchmen without issue.

Still preparing for the approaching departure was the northbound train of the Langspur Line. At the fore was an older-model diesel-fueled engine, fashioned from matte black steel and lined in orange trim. The hearty slab of metal and horsepower was the first of a string of twelve cars that ran between Greater Decedistadt and the mainland. There was an ornate luxury to the train that became less opulent the further back one embarked. The first-class car shone golden, making the sienna-dyed wooden panels of coach seem downright pedestrian in comparison. To Cal, it mattered little; the green-tinted glass windows and brass ornamentation were more upscale than anything he'd enjoyed in years.

Posted at the end of each carriage was a porter busy managing arriving customers. With a two-in-one tally counter/ticket punch, they welcomed commuters onto the passenger cars. Without the burden of luggage, it took only a few minutes for Cal and Oebe to board. Once up the side steps, Cal escorted her into the coach.

Paneled in stained timber, the interior featured aged-leather furniture in rows over a beige carpet, with linoleum at either entrance.

The pair reclined in the first open bench on their left. Oebe was quick to settle as she gathered up her robes. Her vision remained forwardly focused and unresponsive to the turmoil of others as they boarded. On the other hand, Cal took a few moments to peruse the other passengers, wary of seeing a familiar face within the crowd. He cast a glance out the window to confirm that the Magistrates were still at their posts. Once finished with his scan, he let out a sigh and slumped back into his seat.

After a series of multi-toned whistles, the train lurched

forward and slowly began to build up speed as it left the station. They trudged briefly through a warehouse district that bordered the northern edge of the metropolis. Once free of the city limits, Cal's gaze fell on the surf crashing against the peninsula, a sight that he had not beheld in years. In the distance, he saw a pair of fishing boats bobbing on the undulating waves.

The northward rail line ran along the Langspur, a thirty mile stretch of land that connected the Decedistadt Peninsula to the main continent. As Cal had learned through his limited schooling, the city was founded almost a thousand years ago on what was then believed to be a manmade earthen formation. The fourteen-mile wide circular patch of earth, which rose dozens of feet above sea level at its highest point, was attached to a long corridor that jutted out of the mainland's southern coast in a seemingly-straight line. Along this length of land, a series of curved formations spread out on either side, and ran dozens of miles, parallel to the northern perimeter of the city. On these rib-like peninsulas, a number of small fishing villages were established.

With the city shrinking behind them, Cal relaxed. His shoulders drooped as he turned to his ward. She sat quietly, with both hands crossed in her lap. Once he turned away, she spoke up, her soft voice barely catching his attention.

It took him a second to process her comment.

"You're new."

There was no judgment in her words. No accusation or suspicion in her intonation.

"New to the Merced League? Yes." He shifted to meet her hazel eyes. The pupils dilated with the subtle changes in light from the nearby window.

"You've done this manner of work previously." The statement sounded less like a query and more like a declaration of fact.

"Well, in the vein of paid protection work? Yes. Once or twice before. Or maybe more. I've kinda lost count." He mulled over a litany of previous jobs he had taken to make ends meet. "Wait a minute… How do you know that? For all you know, I could be a fresh new face in the League looking to make a name for myself."

Without missing a beat, she responded. "You already have a name. It is Calvin Reeger."

"That's… not what I meant."

"Your clothes are clean and new, either recently purchased or well-tended, yet your equipment is broken in to the point of being threadbare in places. You wear it comfortably, more so than your pants, if the discomfort at the chafing around your crotch is any indication. The leather of your belts and holsters do not exhibit the stiffness of being recently purchased. The guns show age but have been maintained, as if prized possessions."

Cal wasn't sure he whether to be impressed or unnerved by her assessment. "Have you already started *observing*? It didn't seem like you were too interested in much of anything on our way over."

"Recording the minutiae of the environs surrounding the Athenaeum property would only serve to provide duplicate information to the Central Archive."

"So you do have some capacity for choosing what and when you want to observe. I was under the impression from the Grande Dame that you wouldn't able to function like a, uh, normal human." He cringed at his questionable use of the word 'normal.'

"Autonomic nervous system functions work like any other. I am capable of self-motivated transportation. Wherein the complication lies is that processes of recording and recalling are difficult to manage simultaneously. Witnessing the factual details of humans walking through my field of view takes precedence over the decision-making required to propel my limbs in one direction or another."

The phrasing was above his education level. Cal's brow furled.

"You must understand that memory for An-Sebban is not like your own. Whereas you have short- and long-term memory where both facts and experiences can be stored throughout your mind, we retain information in layers, where each piece is sorted by its nature. The data that is accessed and moved during the transfer process is composed of facts generated through sensory stimuli, including but not limited to: the names of locations and people, the dimensions of a building's exterior and interior, the tactile sensation of a surface defining a material's composition. Emotional attachments to a memory or theoretical postulations generated as a side-effect of the data are moved to deeper layers, though without the requisite factual information associated, many of these experiences are without context. Such items are often archived in the deepest layer if no such need for reference is required within a certain timeframe."

"And that affects your ability to travel on your own, how?"

"The An-Sebban brain prioritizes documentation. The recollection and instantaneous decision-making required for self-driven transit is secondary and often interrupted by the arrival of new data."

Now that he had her speaking, Cal was surprised by Oebe's eloquence. At the opportunity, he pressed her for additional details. "So, then, I take it that you're capable of recognizing faces from prior trips? Even making the connection that you know people?"

"I retain a level of statistical familiarity concerning facial arrangements. This form of information is not deemed necessary to be archived. Only in rare occasions is the Athenaeum concerned with chronicling the facial arrangement of specific members of the population. There is a subsection focused on portraiture in which that data would be stored. The features of your face were initially unfamiliar to me, which registers that I have not interacted with you prior to this date. Considering your current means of employment, I do not expect the Central Archives will have occasion to retain your facial arrangement. When next we meet, I will be aware that I have interacted with you previously."

"Do you recall the names of those you've travelled with?"

"Their names are stored in the same locus as other facts treated as necessary data and therefor transferred to the Central Archive. I will not maintain ownership of those. Faces I have the ability to recognize based on a series of points which allows me to comprehend when I meet people I have interacted with."

"So, in fact, you don't actually lose everything when you undergo a session?"

"My role is in recording observational data. The transferral system is uninterested in appropriating theoretical interpretations and assumptions. Whether a face is recognized or not is unimportant. A name, though, is a fact and therefor transmitted. Because of how moniker data is treated within our brains, there is no current means to separate that from the rest of the information recorded. As example, I am aware that this is a means of conveyance, but until our arrival at the station, I did not have ownership of a recollection that it is called The Langspur Line. This designation is expected to be removed as part of the data set upon my return."

"Do you have memories of your own? You know… like not data. Like celebrating a birthday or flirting with a boy."

"I have recollections in which emotions are attached. Many of these exist before a time in which I was An-Sebban. Since that moment, I have other memories that are stored deeper within the layers of my mind. Without an immediate need for these during my daily assignments, they are a part of the deepest layer. Accessing them is irrelevant to my duties, so there is no need for them to be considered."

"So, no treasured tales to share with your fellows?"

"No such discussion comes up."

"That's a shame. Think of all the happy memories you'll lose out on."

"Think of all the unhappy memories you are burdened with."

This caused Cal to look away. "I think I preferred it when you were quiet," he said under his breath.

05

Despite the air-tightness of the dwelling, there remained a whiff of clay rich with the offal of a millennium of human existence. No matter how many times the air was recycled through the filtration system, it seemed to linger. Over the years, he had grown accustomed to it. It seemed less pungent during the times he remained active, as if mental acuity reduced the sharpness of his senses.

Laid out on a flat slab of steel, covered in a woolen cloth, Erudatta's thin form rose from his rest. Whether it had been an hour or six was unknown to him as he sat upright and placed his feet on the cold stone.

Erudatta's private quarters was a series of circular limestone cells consisting of multiple stacked levels connected by a staircase against the exterior wall. The interior chambers, which served as his home and personal laboratory, were steel and concrete, lit with radiant gemstones in simple steel sconces. Without any exterior-facing apertures, there wasn't a bit of natural light.

On the far side of the living space was a slab of metal, the color of rust, that was set into the wall and glistened in the light. Along the surface, row upon row of irregularly-spaced lines were etched, each between one and three inches in length, covering the entire face.

Once he was up, the bunk receded into the wall as the drawer retracted. A subtle hum of gears from within ceased as the end rolled flush with the surrounding panel.

After a few unsteady steps, he disrobed and dropped the ochre cloth to the floor. If he was in the presence of others, they would have seen a series of alloy plates in various locations: a pair on opposite sides of his thighs, a trio along his spine, and another pair below where the deltoids connected with the triceps. On each of the metal surfaces were square ports and within those were arranged rows of copper-coated pins.

He had long ago replaced his right hand with an apparatus of his own design. From the rim of the oblong metal bulb, shaped eerily like a fingerless hand, could be produced various tools. While he had briefly mourned the loss of the limb, its replacement became indispensable. Time had taken a hefty toll on his dexterity. He was no longer as adept with his fingers as he once was. As it was, he only retained his left hand for the tactile sensory information it could provide.

While his mind was fresh, filled with ideas generated during his dormancy, the long period between his lengthy rests had impaired his physical deftness, making him more like an older man.

As the grogginess of sleep faded, Erudatta located the empty carapace of his exoskeleton in the nearby chair, left open like the discarded skin of a snake. The support structure was built of multiple alloys fashioned into polygonal plates, linked together with of flexible rods lined with wires and cables.

Gingerly, he reclined into the sheath. The curled metal clamps folded inward and clasped him firmly over the panels imbedded in his skin. On each, a single green LED flashed brightly. From beneath the base of his skull, a thin strip extended and cradled the occipital bone, flattening the small patch of brittle hair that remained there

Once the process was complete, he rose and stretched, as if testing the fit. Moving his limbs in odd angles, he let out a groan and collected a robe that he draped over his shoulders. As he departed, he cinched the garment tightly around his waist.

Taking the steps one at a time, he began the climb to his laboratory, pausing for a moment to tap on a door set halfway up. The metal barrier responded with a dull clang that faded almost instantly, confirming to Erudatta the airtightness of its seals.

It was decades since he closed himself inside the chamber. Any interest he had in the outside world had vanished. Since then, he had not spent much time mulling over the reasons for his choice. The isolation allowed him to focus on his work, but the reality was that he grew disillusioned with the general populace. Erudatta had walked amongst them for a time, only to be overwhelmed by ennui in the course of his interactions.

This melancholy precipitated his retreat into the shelter, to shut himself away. Beyond the door were multiple layers of earth and numerous barriers and constructs between the vermin that existed beyond him and his sanctuary.

The dense fortification allowed him to think freely, unencumbered by the monotony of social obligations. The rabble seemed singularly occupied with their own chatter, as if conversation provided purpose, or barring that, sufficient distraction from their short and futile existences.

As Erudatta pondered, it occurred to him that he hadn't spoken a word to another living being in years, though the term "years" struck him as a gross understatement. To keep his vocal chords from atrophying, he would speak aloud to himself from time to time. Of course, he was careful that his monologues did not take the form of a madman's ranting.

He continued upward and eventually reached his workroom, where his latest effort was spread out across the central table. The laboratory resembled an operating room; the main table was encircled by machines and instruments. A pair of white LED lamps, which flickered to life upon his entry, towered over the central dais.

Along the back wall was a console that had gone unused for years. Erudatta only used the attached desktop as a dumping ground for notebooks and spare parts. Above the string of control panels was a display, on which a list of twelve entries in a peculiarly-written iconography was scribed. Each record was composed of a series of vertical lines in groupings. Beside ten of the indexed items was a rectangular LED that radiated white. The fifth entry was curiously dark, the LED having long ago gone out. Beside the tenth item, the light was a lime green.

Erudatta approached the central table and leaned in. He took a long gaze to refresh his memory where he had last left off. Laid out on the cold steel slab was an incomplete skeletal frame, with unattached parts organized in a logical fashion. They were arranged in neat little rows, like an exploded-view drawing, on the space beside the metal structure to which they would eventually be attached.

Though the mechanized golem was his latest project, it wasn't his first time working on such a creation. Ages ago, he had assembled similar objects, larger and slower than the model before him. If one of them was still functional, it was in such a distant locale that it was best for him to consider it lost. Rather than revisit old designs, he chose to create anew and threw himself into this lengthy project to occupy his time.

Previously, he would not have been able to invest so much energy into the creation of mechanical life. The small windows of time he had been afforded before his retreat did not allow for long-term projects. At best, he had been able to focus on smaller, quality-of-life experiments that could build on one another.

During one such stretch, he had developed a mechanism that, once attached to the brain, would dictate his thoughts via transmitted brainwaves. During the early tests, it became readily apparent that it would never work as intended. Instead of recording specific thoughts that he wanted, it chronicled all of his thoughts concurrently, which made the transcripts a mass of incomprehensible fragments overlapping in a massive wall of words. He had not considered the possibility that the device would register the many simultaneous sensory and subconscious workings of the mind as data to record indiscriminately.

After choosing to extend what was known among

his kind as the Waking State, he had all time to invest in the more-complex projects he had been contemplating. Foremost on his mind was a new robotic manservant to act as bodyguard or willing minion to be dispatched abroad. Information and objects still warranted his interest, even if he no longer had the constitution to fetch them himself.

With all the technical details that such a project entailed, he'd spent months, if not years, on the build. Fortunately, he had completed the largest undertaking: the silicon hardware that acted as its brain. He had already fashioned the body parts, so finishing would only take days.

He moved to the golem's cranial unit, which was already partially-attached to the upper torso. Fashioned in the shape of a galea, it featured a curved faceplate of polished bronze, unbroken except for rectangular slots that represented optical sockets. The remaining parts of the android's exterior were within Erudatta's reach, but until he was finished with the interior work, there was no reason to attach them.

For a moment, he considered his next steps. From a circular opening in his prosthetic, a small tool extended. As he rubbed at his chin, the pentagonal screwdriver spun about. After a shake of his head, the implement receded, and he placed his right arm behind his back.

Erudatta raised his hand and placed it above the faceplate. He extended his little finger and thumb. He made a quick twisting motion with his wrist, which caused a circle of green light to form over the polished metal. He extended two fingers in a V-formation and moved them about quickly, the stiffness of his joints relieved by the supportive bands of metal that covered his fingers. A series of green lines filled the halo. He completed his movements and the glowing formation pulsed once before it descended. As it settled across the metal, the light dissipated, as if absorbed by the uneven surface.

He reached beneath the bottom edge of the faceplate and touched a small circular pad. After a second, the rectangular slits lit up a bright vermillion.

"Good. Now to get the rest of you together," Erudatta spoke, his rusty voice cracking.

06

Cal dearly wished the suspicion that it grew hotter by the mile the further west they traveled was solely a product of his imagination. The beads of sweat that streamed down his forehead and between his shoulder blades told another story.

Unable to shake the sogginess, Cal disembarked from the caravan as it came to rest a few hundred feet from Natx Hollow's eastern edge. His leather jacket was over one arm and sweat spots darkened the armpits of his shirt. Oebe, on the other hand, seemed unfazed by the weather, without even so much as a dotting of perspiration on her pale features. A warm breeze caused her robes to flap in the wind.

For an instant, he thought to ask how she was faring, but he feared the potential response she would give. She might not answer so much as recite a convoluted sequence of information from the depths of her mind.

It took Cal and Oebe six days to make the trek from Greater Decedistadt to Natx Hollow. The first leg along the Langspur Line brought them to Ilgyngate, the industrial city that separated the Langspur from the mainland. The smaller metropolis, a quarter of Greater Decedistadt in acreage, was a regional hub for trade, where most goods passed through on their way to other locales.

In Ilgyngate, they transferred to a railcar headed west along the D'Riwia Line, with several stops before it reached Geinnburg on the southern edge of Treyets Coast. This segment was a multi-day trip through a rolling panorama of the Itiri Uplands, as they slowly transitioned into the arid plains south of the desert. During their time together on the train, though, neither spoke much. Oebe was focused on her observations while Cal kept to himself, lest a careless word reveal too much of his situation.

Early on, Cal became frustrated with her inability to carry on a casual discussion. Having to explain everything was almost like speaking with a toddler. He was not a patient man, and before too long ceased any attempts at idle pleasantries. A brief conversation about prior travels made Cal wary. Her questioning, however innocent it may have been, ignited his paranoia and he opted to stay silent.

Once they finally reached Nibin Ray, a village on the southern edge of the Quartewuste, they left the comfort of the railcar. Since there were many traders headed to other points of call, Cal was able to secure transit. With a bit of negotiation, he convinced a caravan bound for Rian Sands to take them on as passengers. While he did not get the best deal, in fact the caravan master fleeced him, Cal was relieved that they agreed to the detour for their sake.

With the howling gusts blowing sand up over the tops of his boots, Cal looked around. He had never been to the Quartewuste before, so he had to trust that they were at the correct location. The merchant, having taken the payment, could easily have dumped them off in the middle of nowhere and left before they caught on.

Better make this quick. They could bail at any time. Leave us high and dry. If I don't see—

Something caught his attention through the heat haze. There was a slight depression a few hundred feet in the distance, but because of the ever-shifting sands, he had difficulty discerning what was within.

As he placed a hand above his eyes to block out the scorching sunlight, a male form rose from between the dunes. The man, dressed in a cream shirt and tan vest, waved as he began to trot in their direction.

"It appears the Bureau is expecting you," the caravan master announced. "Good travels to you both."

Cal was briefly ashamed at thinking ill of the merchant. He watched the procession of carriages slowly depart, carving a pattern of curved trails in their wake.

Oebe tugged at his arm.

"Yes?" he inquired as he followed her gaze. Across the ridge of a distant sandbank was a row of ten men on horseback, their forms almost obscured by sun's glare as it reflected off of the bleached soil.

"By what designation would you refer to those?" Oebe inquired as she motioned to the dark forms. They continued eastward, oblivious to new visitors at Natx Hollow.

"Don't... don't point at them." Cal reached out and

lowered her arm. "It's best you don't draw their attention to us."

"You did not answer my initial question."

"They're the Harenas, Desertfolk of the Quartewuste. One of a number of small tribes that live in the heart of the desert. Not in any of the border towns, mind you, but actually *in* the desert. Not to be messed with and people you want to stay clear of."

Oebe nodded before turning to focus on the approaching man, who slowed to catch his breath as he drew near. The peeling skin along his forehead and cheeks was flushed. Squinting in the daylight made his eyes narrow tightly.

"Greetings," he began between gasping breaths. "I am Peter Mathester, Junior Associate with the Archaeology Bureau. Master Aellis Contrell regrets being unable to greet you at this moment. He was detained on a personal matter."

Cal chuckled to himself. He'd used the phrase "personal matters" to describe a bowel movement on more than one occasion. In that moment, he wasn't exactly proud that his mind went there first. "Cal Reeger, Merced League. This is my ward, Oebe Nsu-Ogette of the Athenaeum. Glad to see we were expected as I don't think we'd want to stand around too long in this heat."

"Yes, yes," Peter nodded, waving to them that they should follow. "I'll escort you to the main site and, once inside, we can discuss what requirements Ms. Nsu-Ogette has. It's a bit too *hot* out here to discuss anything at length."

As Peter led them back the way he had arrived, Cal was

able to view more of the depression formed by the earthen ridge. By the time they reached the wooden stairs that led down into the valley, the entire site was on full display. If his motivation had been different, Cal might have been impressed by the ruins; as it was, he began to ponder what, if anything, of value might be found within.

"So, Mr. Mathester," Cal spoke up as he followed behind Oebe, who on occasion would pause to take in the scenery like a tourist photographing the landscape. "What is your role here? Besides fetching the occasional visitor during the hottest part of the day."

"Like my fellows, I am part of the main archaeology team, responsible for delving into the site. Each man is tending to various assignments, be it the examination of ancient murals, detailing the relevance of the architectural elements along historical timelines or merely mapping the location to determine the usage of certain chambers. Initially, I was interested in an array of carved idols found in an upper floor vestibule, but that was largely resolved a few weeks in. There lacked little new information in the unearthed sculptures that I had not previously documented, so they were relegated to storage."

"Uh, congratulations…" Cal then trailed off, muttering under his breath. "…on being the foremost expert-slash-collector of other people's junk, I guess."

Peter frowned, hearing the droll comment as he reached the bottom of the steps. He waited for his guests before he headed along the winding path to the central building. As they progressed, Peter pointed out structures of note to Oebe. After brief stops, she responded with a polite nod.

As they drew near the steps that led to the temple's entrance, Cal cleared his throat and posed the question that preoccupied him.

"So, does that mean there's not a lot of *stuff* to find here? Not a lot of pretty baubles and bric-a-brac to put on display?"

"No, not really." Peter replied huffily. "Though I believe Ms. Nsu-Ogette will have *plenty* to examine before she is done here."

"You don't say," Cal responded, casting a sideways glance at Oebe, who matched the pace of the two taller men. While Peter was shorter than Cal, he was almost a head's height taller than the An-Sebban.

"Yes, I do say. Plenty of historically-relevant locations within the main temple and the attached substructure. The main building and surrounding structures are estimated to be five thousand years old. The sublevels, though, predate that by a significant span." Peter paused at the top of the steps and waited for the pair to enter.

Once in the shadow of the temple's entryway, Cal let out a sigh and wiped his brow with the back of his hand. Even in the shade, the temperature was sweltering, but a dry breeze that rolled in behind them brought relief. They passed into the covered courtyard, where Peter indicated sights of interest to Oebe. He made a few observations about the decorative friezes and cornices before directing her to the interior column-work. He made no effort to include Cal, who reclined against a nearby wall.

Oebe maintained her silence as Peter continued his guided tour, speaking at length about the features of the above-ground building while they paraded around the enclosure. Eventually, they came to the opening in the floor by the eastern colonnade. Cal trotted across the dusty tiles to join them.

"Should we move further in?" Oebe inquired when Peter had run out of commentary.

"Of course. I assume that the more *pertinent* details that would be of interest to the Athenaeum are located deeper within. There are a few stops along the way, if you don't mind following me. I'm sure my fellow associates would be put right out if I didn't have you make observations on their current efforts."

A few minutes later, Cal was left by the foot of the ladder as Peter escorted Oebe into a nearby room, where he made quick introductions.

He overheard another member of the team ramble on like a sideshow barker about the historical value of the room's murals. Oebe remained silent. By now, Cal wondered if she had a personal opinion of any kind.

Cal kept an ear open in case he might catch something worthwhile. Maybe if one of the Bureau members let slip a hint of something particularly juicy elsewhere, he could sneak away.

He looked down and noticed the white grains in the creases of his boots. He had been on site less than an hour and he was already fed up with the omnipresent sediment.

By the time Cal had kicked the sand from the top of

his footwear, Oebe was patiently standing by his side. They shared a silent look that might have been meaningful if Oebe was anything other than an An-Sebban. Her lashes flickered for a moment as they batted airborne particulate from her eyes.

"Got all you need from there?" He looked over the top of her head and past the unfamiliar face in the doorway. Beyond was an aged painting, composed of thick red and blue lines dyed into the plaster. He had no knowledge of the iconography, but the art itself certainly had the attention of a roomful of men.

"Only necessary to inspect the mural once," Oebe replied earnestly. "The superfluous postulation provided in addition will be filtered out as noise during transferral."

"If you'll follow me, we'll move onto the next site," Peter stated as he joined them. There was a slim grin on his lips as if he had overheard their exchange. "Next floor down."

After a few stops for discoveries made by other members of the Bureau, they started down a curving set of stairs at the far end of the corridor.

"We just passed through what was once named the 'Passage of Consumed Light.' This, here, is the 'Steps of Dead Men,' so titled as it leads to the burial chambers located below," Peter announced as he descended, occasionally taking a look over his shoulder.

"You don't say," Cal spoke up as he followed a few paces behind. "Bit odd, ya think? Were they always so obsessed with naming things? And strange-like phrasings on top of that."

"No different than your every-day city-planner's habit of naming city streets, like Black Alley in Geinnburg or Harters Square in Nibin Ray. Perhaps they didn't feel the urge to name them after deceased famous people."

"Fair point."

Upon reaching the next floor, Peter ushered them to a burial vault. As before, they were greeted by men more gregarious than Oebe required. Cal noticed that the Bureau members regarded her like a celebrity or head of state. At one point, he wondered if they would break out champagne.

As Cal watched Oebe quietly acknowledge, in her own reserved manner, the crowd of archaeologists, he felt a presence come out of the nearby doorway.

Cal straightened as he caught sight of the armored man. He was draped in a red kaftan with his hands on his hips, standing across from the crypt. The umber complexion made his golden eyes glitter in the low light. From the way he carried himself, it was obvious he was an experienced fighter. Perhaps he had even killed a man or two. Certain he was armed, Cal reminded himself to give the man a wide berth.

"Oh, introductions are in order," Peter spoke up. "This is Apello Satonay, head of security here at Natx Hollow. Cal Reeger, Merced League, and Oebe Nsu-Ogette of the Athenaeum."

Neither Cal nor Apello offered to shake hands. Oebe observed his features before she returned to the Bureau members that begged her to join them.

"You Thosan?" Cal inquired, to which Apello cracked a thin smile. When he didn't respond verbally, Cal turned his attention back to Oebe, who had headed into the nearby chamber.

As Peter followed, Cal remained beside Apello as the crowd of researchers enveloped the An-Sebban.

After a long pause of awkward silence, Cal spoke up as if needing to fill the air with conversation. "So, why they need you? Can't imagine too many bandits looking to swipe something from a dirt pile like this place. The Harenas? Maybe they'd be interested in your supplies, but I haven't seen anything worth lifting in this stack of sand bricks."

"You would be surprised," Apello finally responded. "There are some regional vermin who prefer the dark corners of an underground dwelling as such. Sand rats, blood beetles, burrowing scarabs, serpents and the like. A mechanized golem was unearthed at the ruins of Archenon some time back. Didn't function and was missing mechanics within its torso, but it was believed to be left as a tomb guardian. Since then, the Bureau has regularly employed muscle as a part of their retinue. Wouldn't want to chance running across a working one without someone who is good in a fight."

"You a part of the League?" Cal asked.

"Freelance."

Cal let out an internal sigh of relief. After some time in which silence between them grew uncomfortable, Apello excused himself and headed to the steps which led upwards. Cal watched out of the corner of his eye until he was out of sight.

While Peter and Oebe were distracted, Cal took the opportunity to slip away. As he slowly moved out of the halo cast by the lanterns in the vault, he looked up and down the hall.

He snuck glances into each of the darkened alcoves as he passed, eager to discover something valuable. Once it became clear there was nothing that the archaeology team hadn't picked over, he headed for the next set of stairs.

At the bottom, Cal was greeted by stillness in the air. Except for the sounds that echoed against the stone walls from above, there were no signs of life. The atmosphere was stale, and, except for a sliver of light that fell a few hundred feet in the distance, most of the hall was smothered in darkness.

This thin beam of illumination gave Cal a faint glimmer of hope. The only thing he had seen so far that was even remotely precious was the mural two floors up. He had no way to take it off the wall, much less leave Natx Hollow with it. It certainly wasn't something he could slip into a pocket. Not without damaging any value it had.

In that moment, a strange passing thought slipped into Cal's mind. *Jaefor's the kind of man who would want the mural framed and hung in his bathroom rather than sell it for profit to a museum.*

Cal followed the light to a lantern set outside a back room. Within was a sizable slab of limestone that had fallen and was now in pieces. The shattered rock revealed an open doorway in the far corner. A faint blue-tinted radiance, which originated from the adjoining room, highlighted the nearby brick surfaces.

Cal stepped over the shattered chunks and passed through.

"Well, this is... unexpected," Cal muttered. He took in the stunning view of cobalt-tinted metal walls.

07

After ten minutes, even Peter was overwhelmed by the incessant chatter of his fellow Bureau members. While Oebe showed no visible evidence of discomfort, he thought that she might be on the verge of over-stimulation. The younger associates had pawed at her and often competed for her attention as they went on and on about the minutest details of their assignment at Natx Hollow. When one even went so far as to pull out his personal journal, Peter intervened on the An-Sebban's behalf.

On some level, Peter could understand the excitement. Despite having heard the Athenaeum discussed at length in the Bureau's halls by his elders, he had never met an An-Sebban in person. They were a highly-regarded business partner to many, including the Trade and Cartography Guild, the Uplands Lodge and a number of religious institutions in various corners of the world. Their presence meant an opportunity for those in the Bureau to have their work immortalized as a part of the Central Archive, something that would always be available for future research. Nothing validated one's career like having their labors on permanent record.

"Okay, gentleman," Peter raised his voice to cut through the din. "I think it's time that Ms. Nsu-Ogette moved on. I'm sure she will be around for a while longer. Perhaps you can continue your discussions then." Peter usually lacked a commanding presence, but with his junior associates, it worked enough that he could draw Oebe out of the room.

Each of the fresh-faced boys thanked Oebe for her time and wished her well, as if buttering her up would sway her opinion of them. It did no good since Oebe had no say in what data was ultimately retained post-transferral at the Central Archive. The information would be removed from Oebe's mind and any nonfactual content would vanish. Peter's own understanding of the process was purely from second-hand accounts, spoken in casual conversations with Master Contrell and his contemporaries.

Once free of the chaos, Peter took a deep breath. "Where's your keeper?" Peter asked, realizing they were alone.

"Not present," Oebe commented with her dry affect.

"Does he *usually* wander off on his own?" Peter frowned. Maybe he could ask Apello to locate the bodyguard.

"I have no prior experience with Mr. Reeger's tendencies. Outside of his proclivity to avoid certain topics of conversation."

Peter let out an exasperated breath.

Just as one of the junior members stepped out of the burial chamber to join them in the corridor, Peter turned and pointed at him. The associate came to a skidding halt before the finger jabbed him in the chest.

"I need *you* to locate Apello for me. Tell him that the gentleman from the League has gone missing."

Cal spent a fair amount of time standing in the middle of the Blue Room. At first, he could only blink furiously, rubbing at his eyes with the balled knuckles of his index fingers. The rows of silver lines etched into the cobalt steel proved retina-searing to him. It appeared that they were undulating, as if the walls themselves had a heartbeat. After a few seconds of contemplation, he realized that something about the room caused his vision to distort.

Amidst the sensory overload, Cal spied a small square panel set along the center of the back wall. He leaned in and probed the rectangle. Once his fingers passed over the tiny hole at the center, an aquamarine light flickered from within. Shocked by the unexpected glow that formed above the pane, Cal recoiled.

After a moment, he focused on the floating rows of icon-dotted squares.

And what is this? Oh, wait, I've seen something like this at D'rian Obix. A keypad to keep people out of the counting room. Is this some kind of touchpad, then? I wonder what this opens up. Most places that use a keypad tend to be for secret shit. Or where they hide the good stuff. Safes, vaults, etc. A place this old, it's got to be some kind of ancient treasure.

He shook his head. Something didn't seem quite right. The structures around him were clearly thousands of years old, if not more. The stone walls were aged and worn, and there was a fragility to the upper level that demanded careful handling. This chamber, though, looked immaculate. It felt out of place, which caused a both curiosity and anxiety to well up in Cal's chest.

He redoubled his focus. *Enough of that. I don't have time to piss away on that kinda thinking. All I got to find out what the passcode is. Four digit? Five digit? Hell, I don't even have a clue what these icons even mean. I'm just assuming that punching in a sequence will get it to work. Too bad there ain't nothing lying around, like a note for those people with bad memories. I don't have all the time in the world to figure this out on my own.*

He reached forward and placed his hand against the hovering pane. Immediately, the colored form shifted in tone to an electric orange that throbbed beneath his fingertips. Cal felt warmth against his skin as the tiny beams flickered back and forth. He nudged his palm forward into the pad, threads of illumination reflecting off of the weathered skin. The light formation flashed aquamarine once before changing to orange and eventually to red.

The crimson beams that bounced off of his calloused hand grazed the surface of the nearby wall. As they brushed against the vertical lines, color bled into the etched marks. Before too long, the red flowed into adjacent rows and began to stream away like spilled water towards the corners of the wall.

With his arm still held out, Cal stumbled backwards as his eyes grew wide. Like an infection, the crimson illumination spread and stained the walls a dark violet. He looked frantically from side to side as he watched as the purple discoloration raced along. The buttons that he had pushed were now gone.

"What the bleeding hell are you doing?" Peter's raised voice caused Cal to jump. He spun to find Peter in the doorway. Just behind him waited Oebe, who leaned to look around his outstretched arms. Her gaze only seemed curious about the new spectacle.

Cal stammered, unable to explain the situation. Peter charged into the room.

"What did you do? How did you know—"

"Know what?"

"How did you know how to make this work? I've been studying the Blue Room for months and—"

"Wait a minute! You didn't even know what *that* did?" Cal shot an open hand back to the panel, the border of which now radiated white. The purple glow had now overtaken the entire room.

"No..." Peter trailed off.

"You mean to tell me you never even tried to use it? I guess then you have no idea what this does, then. Right?"

From behind the metal, the hum of gears sounded. Once-invisible seams, from floor to ceiling, suddenly appeared along the back wall. Jets of exhaust spurted from either side as the panel slowly lowered from a hinge at the floor, like some kind of ancient pull-down bed.

The room filled with a cold steam that caused both

men to cough as they attempted to cover their mouths. Oebe curled her nose as she recoiled. For a second, she glanced to her right at the sound of approaching footsteps.

When she turned back, she saw the outline of a metal casket on the floor. Once the white haze began to dissipate, she began to discern the object's details. Though considerably larger, it was shaped much like the sarcophagi of the burial vault above. Instead of limestone, the box was made from interlocking steel plates, larger and more complex in composition than any cist she might have witnessed. The lid was a solid piece of polished metal that was beveled along the edges. From the head of the box, tubes and wires ran back into the newly-revealed opening.

Another light formation, one that glittered in varying shades of green, composed of interlocked triangles appeared above the center of the lid. As the seconds rushed by, the shapes evaporated one by one. When the last faded, the sound of a seal breaking filled the air. The lid rose slightly and glided sideways under its own power. The cover angled down and came to rest vertically beside the sarcophagus.

Wafting like steam off of dry ice, fog rolled out of the open crate, obscuring its contents. Cal took a step forward and craned his neck.

Oebe observed changes in the room itself. The ambient temperature had dropped precipitously. A shiver ran through Peter's body. The red electrical surge had slowly faded, returning the distinctly-tinted walls to their original blue color.

Cal peered at the curiously-packaged contents. Despite anxiety, Peter advanced slowly and joined him. His eyes bulged as he placed a hand over his chest and tried to stifle a gasp.

Laid out within the casket was a human form, covered from head to toe in discolored silver armor plating. From the structure of the figure and the interconnected plates, it was difficult to determine the state of the body, much less its gender. Briefly, Peter wondered if this was some fearsome effigy of the interred. Barring that, it could be another mechanical golem, like the one found in Archenon years ago.

Over its head was an ivory-tinted helm, the metal blackened by a dark patina that accentuated the ornate details of the faceplate. The artisan had carved each facial muscle group. Beneath the permanent scowl of the brow ridge, the eyes were pearlescent orbs. Atop the crown was a pair of horns, curved and swept backwards like the wings of a bat. Running from the base of the helmet along the interior was a collection of bronze-coated tubing.

"Is… is it a body?" Peter inquired. Since there was no sign of breath from beneath the breastplate, he had to assume that the casket was a burial coffer of some kind.

"Hell if I know. I though *you* worked here. Shouldn't you have some kind of idea what's stored in a place like this?" Cal snorted as his hand dropped to his revolver. While he could hear the shuffling of feet behind him, he could not tear himself away from the supine suit of armor.

"How would—" Peter began to bark at Cal when the sound of gas hissing cut him off. One after another, the tubes disconnected and curled away like a den of angry snakes. After a few seconds, the frenzy died down, leaving a haunting stillness in the room.

Both men remained fixed in place, wondering what was about to transpire. Cal had set something in motion and was now left to see what would happen. The growing silence in the room seemed to make time grind to a halt.

The body sat bolt upright as if launched upward. The sudden movement caused Peter to stumble backwards with a horrified groan. The fearsome visage slowly began to rotate back and forth, as if scanning its surroundings. As the glossy pearl eyes met Cal's own, it paused and looked him up and down.

When its gaze stopped on the hand he had resting on his gun, Cal knew in his heart that the proverbial shit was about to hit the proverbial fan. Immediately, he raised both hands in the air in surrender and took a retreating step.

"Whoa, whoa, whoa there, champ. Not lookin' for a fight."

The armored-plated form leapt from the mechanical sarcophagus with surprising agility. It landed square on its feet and immediately went into offensive posture, legs spread, one foot positioned behind the other.

On its left brigandine cuisse was a flat scabbard of metal-plated fabric. In a single fluid motion, it withdrew a stunted slab of metal. With a snap of the wrist, the weapon telescoped to its full length of four feet, the blade squared off at the end. Along the steel's flat edge were a series of geometric patterns.

At this, Peter withdrew to the doorway, where he nudged Oebe aside. Only when a hand gripped his shoulder tightly did he look away.

Without a word, Apello dashed into the chamber, weapons drawn. He crossed the room, fabric flowing behind him as he moved with extraordinary speed for a man his size. The blades slashed through the air, leaving silvery ghosts in their wake.

A clash of swords rang as Apello lunged; his first attack was deftly parried by a flick of the flat blade. The second flurry was also deflected effortlessly, and the third. No matter how fiercely Apello fought, he was unable to force the thing to budge, to even move from its stance.

As his khukuri once more glanced, Apello spun on one heel, pirouetting to catch the dueler off-guard. Before he could complete the maneuver, his opponent surged forward and drove a balled gauntlet into the small of his back. Apello was unprepared for the fierceness of the blow and stumbled to one knee.

His eyes widened; he had the look of one who had never been struck with such force. Before he could rise to his feet, Apello looked up to see Cal, who had drawn both revolvers and leveled them.

"I think we've had enough of that," Cal said as his voice wavered, ever so slightly.

At this, the warrior reached out and extended two fingers. A twist of its wrist produced a six-inch halo of amber light that hovered midair. After a few gestures, the circle filled with angular symbols. As the curiously-detailed nimbus pulsed, it expanded until it became a six-foot-tall barrier which separated the swordsman from the others.

Cal flinched and squeezed the trigger, firing off a round. Even as the copper-jacketed bullet left the gun's barrel, Cal's eyes enlarged. He regretted the decision but could hardly call the projectile back. Time seemed to slow as it crossed the distance and slammed impotently into the barrier. The chunk of metal deformed on impact and dropped harmlessly to the floor.

"Well, shit," Cal mumbled.

"Hold." Though muffled by the helmet, the voice was a husky contralto. After holding its hand out briefly, as if entreating for calm, it waited for both men to lower their weapons. The flat-ended sword was sheathed in its scabbard.

Apello lowered his own blades but chose to keep them close at his sides. Flustered, Cal holstered one of his guns and then wiped the sweat from his cheeks. The other he clasped tightly, but made a show of aiming it away.

Oebe snuck up between the two men and peered inquisitively. Peter remained by the open doorway, his knuckles white as he clutched the frame tightly.

The swordsman reached up behind the fearfully-decorated helm and pulled it forward with a firm yank. From beneath, a headful of copper locks unfurled, which then splayed across the shoulder pads and pauldrons. With a toss of her head, she met the gaze of the quartet on the other side of the illuminated barrier.

Her features were angular, oddly so. The thick bridge of her nose came to a sharp point, the nostrils swept back like the corners of a pyramid. The slant of her brow ridge was severe, as it cut away from the deep valley of her eye sockets, where emerald irises flickered like gemstones in the light. Flat and wide cheekbones extended past the square block of her jaw. Thin lips, colored a light blush, peeled back over ivory teeth. From the edge of her scalp, the thick tawny hair, iridescent with hints of blue and green in the strands, was swept away from her face.

"Okay, now that we're... less hostile," Cal said with a glance at Apello "Can we at least start with some introductions?"

"What year would it be?" she inquired, rudely ignoring his query.

08

"What?" Cal snapped incredulously. For a moment, he felt his head spin, as if the question itself caused mild disassociation. During the brief visit to the Blue Room, he had been besieged by one surprise after another. At this point, if the exotic woman announced that she was a million years old, a demigod or filled with a delicious gelatin treat, he might be inclined to believe her.

"The date and year. Are you capable of providing these?" She pressed, this time with slowly-enunciated words. There was a hum underlying her speech, a vibrating resonance that hid within the spoken syllables. It might have been hypnotic, even soothing, had the situation not begun with such hostility.

"If you have to ask, then maybe it doesn't even matter. Where have you been that you have to ask?"

"Uh, its year 3,220 of the Modern Era Calendar," Peter spoke up as he reentered the room.

She scowled and shook her head. The sullen expression carved deep lines in her pale forehead.

Cal chose to break the uneasy silence. "Not to be rude,

'specially with all the tension in the air, but do they have names from wherever you're from?"

She glared at Cal before relenting. "Centurion Prae Ganvelt."

"Good, good. Prae—may I call you that? No complaints? I'll take silence as acceptance. Okay, well, I go by Cal Reeger." He tapped himself on the chest before motioning to Peter. "The dapper young gentleman is Peter Mathester of the Archaeology Bureau and this is his largely-disgruntled security representative, Apello Satonay. The small lady here is Oebe Nsu-Ogette of the Athenaeum of the An-Sebban."

Her gaze jumped from one person to the next as they were introduced.

"Centurion?" Apello began warily as he shifted his stance. "Does that make you a soldier?" Though he made an effort to keep them behind his back, his khukuri were still grasped tightly.

"Hold up a second," Peter implored as he skipped back to the entrance and glanced down the corridor. "Is this not a conversation we should be having in privacy? We aren't alone and I don't know what kind of commotion this will cause with the others."

"Yeah," Cal was quick to nod. The fewer people who knew of this, the less likely someone would inquire why he'd snuck into the Blue Room. "We probably should see about—"

"Halt." Prae held out a hand. "I'll not be moved from this location until we've come to some kind of peaceful accord, however temporary. I'm woken unceremoniously, and certainly not as planned, to find you lounging about my containment cell, brandishing implements of battle and I'm merely to follow your lead to have discussions elsewhere on your whim? I did not survive this long by being so cavalier."

Cal groaned. He needed to persuade her as quickly as possible.

"Look, Prae, we're all apologies over here," Cal began, making a grand sweeping gesture, holding up his jacket to show her that his weapons were now holstered. He then glanced to Apello, who reluctantly sheathed his own armaments. "Now isn't that right, Apello?"

Apello remained quiet as his eyes narrowed tightly.

"From the way that brawl just played out, do you honestly think you couldn't kick the shit out of us if we came to blows again?" Cal poured on the charm as best as he could. With a few compliments to grease the wheels, he might be able to convince her to acquiesce. Peter was not wrong and Cal knew it; the longer they remained in the Blue Room, the more likely other members of the Bureau might happen upon the new discovery. "Look, we just want to have a sit-down, so to speak, and figure out what's going on. You clearly are confused by all this. As you can imagine, so are we. I mean, put yourself in our shoes. Some lady in full armor pops out of a box and asks us what year it is. The strange tech in this room notwithstanding, that's gonna cause issues any ole day of the week."

"And I should comply so willingly? What do I have to gain from such a conference?"

"Knowledge," Peter spoke up. "If you don't even know the year, I imagine there's a fair bit about the present you don't exactly understand, yet. Unless you're perfectly fine with announcing to everyone of your *unique* situation."

Prae blew a breath through her nose as her jaw clenched tightly. She nodded ever so slightly. "Your entreaties are not without merit. I, too, am in need of some answers. To gain my bearings. Perhaps a discussion in a more *private* setting is in order. If you feel that it's currently the best course of action, I will relent." With a downward sweep of her outstretched hand, Prae dismissed the protective halo. The amber light scattered like embers on the wind.

At that, Cal let out a relieved breath. His shoulders drooped as tension slipped from the muscles. "So, shall we, uh, get the hell outta here? It's only a matter of time before one of the more chatty of Mathester's coworkers decide to come down here and see if they can talk up Oebe some more."

"My tent will have to do," Peter suggested. "If we can sneak her out of the temple, past my associates, we should be able to get her to the Bureau's basecamp. At this time of day, there should be no one present. The challenge will be to get her above ground with minimal contact. Especially with Quillin's team camped out in the mural room not twenty feet from the ladder."

"I can run interference," Apello offered after giving Prae another examining glance. To Cal, he seemed hesitant to leave the others with the new arrival.

"No," Cal objected before Apello could move. He

knew of a more effective diversion. "It's better if Mathester takes Oebe on ahead, has her stop in and speak with anyone who might get in the way. They're all over her like she's some kind of celebrity. She'll provide sufficient distraction." He looked to Oebe, who only dipped her head in agreement.

"It's as good a plan as any," Peter shrugged. He held out a hand to Oebe, which prompted her to join him. "Are you fine with this?"

"I take no issue with the scenario. It is a sound course of action."

At that, Peter ushered her away, only to pause in the doorway. Even with Prae out of sight, he could clearly hear her armor clang with each step. "Um, uh..." he grimaced with a look over his shoulder.

"What now?" Cal groaned.

"Your gear. It would be best if you didn't parade around in it. It makes a god-awful racket and if you're seen in it... As it is, we'll have a time explaining your presence away. The outfit might be a bit much."

Cal glanced back to Prae and looked her over. "Much as I hate to agree, egghead's right," Cal noted with a wry smile. "You'd stick out, well, hell, anywhere like that."

"And what might you suggest as solution?" Prae gave them a look thick with annoyance.

"I should have a canvas sack or two in the crates beneath the desk that you can store it in," Peter suggested. "Are you in need of clothing? I could—"

"I will be fine." She rolled her eyes before removing her armor, piece by piece. A faint flash of blue light crackled in between the plates as each section of her garb was detached. Before Peter and Oebe slipped away, he spied an elastic jumpsuit beneath the steel.

Prae eventually disrobed from her intricate armor and stored it within one of Peter's canvas packs. By the constant glares she shot at both Apello and Cal, it was clear she was not entirely comfortable. Cal couldn't exactly blame her; he didn't feel at ease himself and he had the benefit of not being rudely awoken from a very long slumber.

Prae was dressed in a black bodysuit made from carbon fiber fabric that covered her from neck to feet. While the supple cloth hugged her muscular frame tightly, the onyx color diminished the details and left much to the imagination. As Cal hefted the weighty sack of steel over one shoulder, Prae made a series of hand gestures that sent her sleeping apparatus to its original state, folded up and hidden within the back wall. With Peter and Oebe already out, Apello stood as sentry at the doorway.

I wonder how much this armor is worth, Cal thought as he jiggled the bag's contents. *I bet it would go for a pretty penny on the open market.*

Just as Prae passed into the corridor, Apello stopped her and draped his kaftan across her shoulders. While she briefly curled her nostrils at the rich body odor trapped within the material, she made no comment. Their eyes met and she offered a faint nod of appreciation. Cal trailed close behind as Apello led them away.

Within the hour, they reached Peter's tent north of the temple. Peter and Oebe arrived some time later, only after shaking off a few of the more persistent Bureau members. Peter's residence was simple, with barely enough room for the quintet to move about. An unmade cot and a desk sat in opposite corners, while a circular rug was laid across the center of the living space.

Cal deposited the sack of armor off to the side; it was left partially obscured by an oaken bookcase full of educational tomes and hastily-folded maps. Prae's sheathed weapon was left to rest atop the lumpy rucksack.

Patiently, Prae stood in the center of the room with her feet apart and her hands planted firmly on her hips. As she had on their path though Natx Hollow, Prae took a measure of her surroundings. Her gaze slowly panned over the accoutrements.

Peter eventually broached the first of many questions on his mind. He couldn't explain it, but he felt drawn to Prae, as if her mysterious nature was meant to lure him further in, deeper and deeper. To what, he did not know.

"So, what exactly is, or was, that? The Blue Room, I mean. I've been studying it ever since we unearthed it and until today, I had no clue of the chamber's actual purpose. I-I still don't think I have a clear impression, even now."

"What did you consider it to be?" Prae responded cautiously. At this, Cal moaned to himself. Peter overheard the low grunt. This promised a complicated exchange with a being that may not be entirely forthcoming.

"Natx Hollow is a strange location, archaeologically speaking," Peter began, hoping to elicit some form of reaction. "The upper floors are recent, comparatively. Roughly five thousand years old, despite the weather-beaten exterior. There's a temple, a marketplace and the vestiges of a village. The subterranean structures, though, are a lot older. A lot. And we know this because the construction materials and architectural layout are noticeably dissimilar, as if erected by a different, older society. It's as if someone came by and built their village on top of another, older settlement. By what we've uncovered, the older location features a number of burial chambers. Fewer traditional lodgings. I don't know that people actually lived below, or if they did, it was not by original intent. And with that established, the Blue Room is an even more unique edifice, divergent from either. Even with the time invested poring over every inch of the room, I couldn't begin to place its origins. It's made all the worse by a lack of similarly-featured structures within the Bureau's own records. As far as I'm concerned, it may well be an anomaly."

Prae's head bobbed silently as she listened. When he paused with a pleading look on his face, she drew a breath and began. "What you call the 'Blue Room' is known as an Extended Life Preservation Containment Cell."

"Excuse me? What does that even mean?" Cal raised a hand in the air as if he was a child begging for a teacher's attention.

"Cryogenic stasis or cryopreservation. You are aware

of the concept, correct? If not, then your technological advancement is at an even earlier stage than I would have thought, given the year. Which would only complicate the issue further."

"There it is again," Cal raised his voice as he paced back and forth in the tight confines of the tent. Blocking it with his body, Apello waited by the lone opening. Oebe observed the exchange from the nearby cot. "You making mention of the date. What's so important about what year it is? How long were you sacked out in that containment cell?"

"Longer than expected. Then I should have been." She paused as if to consider how best to proceed. "The last time I saw the sun there were still people living here, taking up residence in what is now a subterranean structure. These above-ground edifices? They did not yet exist."

Peter's face lit up briefly at the implications of Prae's comments. Now was not the time to pester her with additional queries. He sucked down a gulp and continued.

"I'm familiar with the concept of cryogenic stasis from my occasional reading of technical journals and recently-published literature, though it seems the scientific community does not seem to have much success with anything beyond bacteria and fungi. And not for lengthy stretches of time. I can't imagine they're in a position to attempt it with larger entities, much less human beings." He turned to Oebe. "And yourself?"

"I have no such recollection of said topic," Oebe stated bluntly.

"Don't bother trying to pick her brain, Mathester. She doesn't retain that kind of info," Cal interjected. "Trust me on this. I learned a fair bit in the past week what an An-Sebban can and can't remember after the transfer process to the Central Archives."

"Calvin is correct in this regard." Oebe's expression did not change as she concurred.

"Be that as it may," Prae raised her voice to redirect the conversation. "The general concept is not lost on you, correct? That a human can be placed within stasis for an extended period of time? It is such a device that is contained within the area you so casually christened the Blue Room. "

"And, how long were you in said stasis?" Peter asked.

"You will pardon me if I'm not entirely forthcoming on such matters. It's not in our... my nature to provide details about affairs unrelated to your own existence. As I said before, there were no structures here when I went back to the Blue Room. There is a fair amount I'm not entirely certain I should be sharing. There's just as much I'm not privy to myself that is beyond the nature of my own role. Not all of us were at the forefront of our scientific fields."

Cal cleared his throat. "Listen, Ms. Gunbelt—"

"Gan-velt."

"—if I hadn't just seen what I did, I'd just write you off as loony and tell you to hit the bricks, but your little smoke-and-light show bought you a bit of leeway. You could spin pretty much any cock-and-bull story right now and I'd have to consider that it might be possible. With that said, though, there's a whole lot here that don't make sense. You're hidden in a freezer buried well beneath an ancient ruin and come popping out, talking about super-specific intellectual concepts and doing weird magical shit with that barrier that I'm pretty sure no one has ever done before. Maybe if—"

"Forgive me if I don't delve into every little shred of information to appease your curiosities. The answers to most of your questions only spawn additional queries, which then will breed more. At this current point in time, I am not in a position, or mood, to determine what you can, or should, know. Nor do I care. What you've already been privy to is likely more than you should witness."

"You're being awful cryptic about this."

"Make no mistake; I am disinclined to spend my limited time in the Waking State explaining millions of years of history to a handful of people who have the relative lifespan of a fly. People who will be dead within a millennia." There was a growl constrained behind her clenched teeth. Peter noticed that Prae's temperament grew increasingly agitated. He felt empathy for her. He certainly understood how Cal's blunt, unvarnished commentary could be grating.

" 'Millennia?' Don't you mean *century*? No one lives to be a thousand," Cal scoffed.

"Any more."

Before Cal could argue, she raised a finger in warning.

"Let me pose to you a question that would best gauge how little you do, in fact, know. Have you heard mention of Naucilous, Scribe of All? Na-Exetase, the Experimenter? Kayvurim, the Worm of Time? Ruztong, the Black Iron? Belamis, the Last?" At each name she paused and looked into the eyes of each of the quartet present. By the end, Cal had rolled his eyes and turned away, while Apello could only shrug his shoulders. Oebe remained mute.

"Yeah… no. That's a whole bunch of mumbo-jumbo to me," Cal grumbled.

"I have a faint recollection of a reference to the Worm of Time," Peter spoke up tentatively. "I've seen mention of it once in the Bureau's Library."

"And? What do you know of it?"

"Nothing too much. It was part of an inscription carved within the catacombs at the Gul Lyceum in Zehngrad. I don't recall the exact phrasing off the top of my head, mind you. Loosely translated, I think it was something to the effect of 'here resides the Worm of Time, earth dweller, molder of continents.' It was a strange phrase that the report's author seemed to have no explanation for. I'm surprised he noted it at all given its irrelevance to the rest of his documentation."

"And that is all you have?"

"Well, yes." Peter looked away, embarrassed and intimidated.

"That makes the point on my behalf. No matter how educated you believe yourselves to be, it is but a sliver in the mighty forest of knowledge amid which you stand blind."

At this, Cal snapped. "Well, I'm sorry we're not all super

smart and that we don't know every damn thing like you do. Maybe if you'd like to bring us up to speed. Or maybe just keep being a haughty bitch about it. That seems to be what you're best at."

With a wave, she brushed his vitriol aside. "I don't have the time to invest in such an undertaking. With events as they are, I have far more pressing needs. I must head to Ala'ydin. It is only there I may gain the answers I seek."

"Well, sure, just scarper on as you please. Have yourself a fine little outing then. I mean, I don't even know where this place you're talking about is. It's like you're just making up words to mess with us now. So feel free to walk on out to who-knows-where. I mean, since we only have your word to go on."

"Of course, your kind would not be familiar with Ala'ydin," Prae mentioned under her breath. In the tight confines, all could hear her clear as day. The low hum of wind blowing through the canvas tent did little to mask her words. Cal's eyes narrowed as his face flushed.

Before Cal could launch into what would surely be a tirade, Peter interrupted. "Why do you need to head off to Ala'ydin? What is there that would help you? Perhaps we could be of some assistance."

Apello straightened ever so slightly.

"Ala'ydin is the center. Where all known record of my kind is kept. It is there I hope to uncover why the cycle was broken. Why I had to be brought into the Waking State millennia off schedule, no less."

"Okay, I'm officially lost," Cal barked as he threw his

hands up in the air. He turned to Oebe, who appeared to be staring into the distance. In an ordinary human, this might have signaled that she was mulling over something. As an An–Sebban, it could be a sign of intense observation.

"Well, can you at least direct me to the city of Guilwhite?" Prae inquired. "From there I can find my way."

"Uh," Peter replied with a dull stare. He'd never heard of such a place before.

"The Halls of Severdohn?"

"Yeah, no." He shook his head.

Prae's lips pursed tightly.

"But, uh, let me get a couple of maps together and we'll see if you can figure out where Ala'ydin is, nowadays. Or, uh, any of those other places, I guess." Peter stepped over to the bookcase to retrieve slips of folded paper, many yellowed with age. He paused more than once and flipped through the documents against his arm as he mumbled to himself about whether any of the maps would be up-to-date. "Perhaps we can even help you get where you need to go," he offered. At this, Prae narrowed her eyes.

"I will be joining you," Oebe announced, which caused Cal to spin and give her a stern look.

"How's that?" he asked her.

"It is my intent to travel to Ala'ydin. The opportunity presented is invaluable. As An–Sebban, it is my purpose to record data not present in the Central Archive."

"But w-wait a minute," Cal sputtered. "You were supposed to just—I was hired to bring you to Natx Hollow and back."

"I will return to the Central Archive when I am done observing. This is non-negotiable," she proclaimed. "If you are in conflict with your contracted employment, please address your concerns with Grande Dame Hru-Gatta when next you speak with her."

This knocked the wind out of Cal's lungs.

The others looked at her silently. Apello crossed his arms and glanced sideways to Cal, who had slumped with a sigh.

"Well, I guess she *told* me. Makes the decision all the easier for me, I guess" Cal groaned. He uttered a thin laugh, rich with resignation. "I still am under contract to be Oebe's escort. Someone would literally have my hide if I didn't tag along."

Could still find something of value if I tag along long enough, he thought to himself. *'cause this place has been a bust so far when it comes to saving my skin.*

Exasperated, Cal headed for the tent's entrance. As Peter began to share the maps with Prae, Oebe watched from the comfort of her seat. Before Cal could disappear, Apello grabbed him by the sleeve. They shared a stare before Apello quietly escorted him outside.

As the sun began to drop in the west, Cal noticed a handful of the younger Bureau members trickle their way back to camp. Before too long, most of the on-site staff would return and dash any chance he might have to sneak around to find something.

"I guess you want to have words?" Cal looked over

Apello's shoulder to ensure that they were alone. The heat of the setting sun was still enough to cause Cal to break out in a sudden perspiration. At least it would help hide any nervous sweat if the conversation got tense.

Apello reached up and tugged him by the collar. "So, is it always standard procedure for League members to abandon their charges when convenient?"

"I, well—"

"Save your fabrications for those prone to being duped. I am aware you slipped away once the opportunity availed you."

Cal opened his mouth to protest. Before he could defend himself, Apello leaned in close.

"I care not for your justifications. Whether you thought to steal from the dig site or not is the least of my current concerns." Apello's voice dropped an octave as he spoke slowly. "You have set in motion events far beyond your ability to manage. Since I hold no faith in your capacity to tend to your own charge, much less Mathester or Ganvelt, I have little choice but to keep watch over you."

"Oh, goodie. The more the merrier."

For a moment, it seemed Apello struggled with the urge to strike Cal. Apello looked to the approaching archaeologists. With a long sigh of exasperation, he released Cal's shirt.

"Watch yourself." Apello's parting shot was delivered coldly and made Cal think that one wrong move would find him bleeding out in a back alley somewhere.

Cal took a moment to straighten his shirt and compose himself. After a few deep breaths, he was able to lower his heart rate before nudging the canvas flap aside. Upon re-entering the tent, Cal's gaze fell to the armor-filled sack resting in the back corner. That little window of opportunity had now shut. He was going to have to stick it out by Oebe's side and see where Prae led them.

By the time night fell, a course of action was decided upon. In two days' time, they planned to depart for Attis Grove, a village on the border between the Quartewuste and Vilfdonum Steepe. It was from there that they would set out for Viisibourg. With some time spent looking at Peter's maps, Prae determined that Ala'ydin was in the Seitsweald to the east, before they reached the Siamsoth Mountains.

Before permitting her to mingle with the rest of the Bureau associates, Apello provided Prae a change of clothes in return for his kaftan. Draped over her jumpsuit was a tan linen knee-length robe and, on top of that, a brown striped kibr. While the rest of her armor remained packed away, Prae strapped the scabbard to her hip, where it remained hidden beneath the folds of fabric.

With the story that Prae was also on contract to escort Oebe, she was free to roam about the camp. Since Peter was the only person to witness Cal and Oebe upon their arrival, it proved a simple enough solution. Still, she was rarely left alone. From time to time, either Peter or Oebe would keep her company. Cal made a few attempts, though their conversations were brief.

After a while spent socializing, Peter escorted the new arrivals to a pair of guest tents. As he slowly made his way back to his own quarters, he stumbled upon Apello, who was waiting patiently in the shadows cast by hanging lanterns along the interior of the camp.

"Lord alive, Apello" Peter gasped as he placed a hand on his chest. "You've scared a year off of my life."

"I do not feel good about this situation," Apello said, his tone grave.

"It'll be fine. You're too fretful over this," Peter replied. Ever since Oebe and Cal's arrival, Peter had noticed growing tension in Apello. It was subtle, but Peter noticed the strain in his eyes and the tight clenching of his jaw. "I'll just escort them east to Ala'ydin. Prae has no knowledge of the modern world. She needs someone to get her across the grasslands without incident."

"With the An-Sebban and her handler, she doesn't exactly need you to play tour guide."

"Do you really trust Reeger to get her to where she needs to go?"

Apello snorted as he shot Peter a look. Peter felt relief at the comment that both men knew was the truth. Before Apello could raise further objections, Peter continued.

"She needs our help. Not in the traditional sense, per se, but still."

"Do not mistake your desire for her to be a damsel in

distress for the truth of it. Prae strikes me as a person with little need from the likes of us. Whether 'tis factual or just a construct of her ego is up for debate."

"She's also a person who has limited understanding about how the world, as it currently is, functions." At that point, Peter's tone was almost pleading.

"And she relented to this? She does not strike me as one to graciously take offered help."

Peter sighed as he bit at his lower lip. "Eventually. Don't know whether it was because she agreed that we could help her get to her destination more easily or not. Don't care as long as it lets us tag along."

"What do you get out of this? Why would you throw yourself at such an undertaking? This is not the career you signed up for. To be an escort, a tour guide. At best, this ends up being a diversion. At worst, the Bureau reconsiders the tenure of your membership for abandoning Natx Hollow."

"*Why?* Did you not hear her say that the last time she saw light, these buildings were not even here? When she stepped out of that containment cell–hell, before that when Cal stumbled on how to open it–everything I've ever done for the Bureau up to that point became irrelevant. All of my time and effort spent scribbling assumptions based on clues thousands of years old was made worthless. Out strode someone who could tell me whether *any* of my presumptions, my theories, were with merit. And when she tells me I'm wrong, I'll hopefully begin to understand why. Even if I can never reveal to the greater populace her existence, her impact on our understanding of mankind's history could prove immeasurable."

"And Ala'ydin?"

"If it's truthfully a previously unrecorded location, as far as the Bureau knows? I won't lie—won't feign at nobler intents—the thought had occurred to me. If Ala'ydin lies beneath somewhere the Bureau hasn't established an expedition…" Peter grinned at the thought. He didn't have to explain it to Apello. Even if Ala'ydin was merely a handful of interconnected crumbling structures, his career would be set for life, as long as it remained undiscovered by his contemporaries.

"Your course of travel?"

"Prae places Ala'ydin in the northern Seitsweald. We'll first head east to Attis Grove, get ourselves free of the Quartewuste. From there, we'll pick up the Nria Highway and head on to Viisibourg. Pick it up on the eastern side until we reach Righan's Path. We'd take that north as far as we could."

At the mention of Viisibourg, Apello shifted. Peter noticed the slight change in the bodyguard but chose not to comment.

"And you will be telling Master Contrell…"

"That I'll be escorting Ms. Nsu-Ogette and her minder out of the Quartewuste and ensuring that their arrangements to return to Greater Decedistadt are secured. From there, I may find myself detained, or not. Usually, many days pass before I find myself in Master Contrell's company. It may be weeks before he actually notices I'm not here."

At that, Apello snorted humorously. "You'll not be going alone. Not with Cal and Prae," he eventually stated. "I do not trust your safety or that of the An-Sebban with *either of them*."

Peter opened his mouth to protest but quickly decided against it. Apello was not one to argue if his mind was set.

"Reeger was correct about one thing: there isn't anything here at Natx Hollow for me to be concerned with. The only creature I can deem truly dangerous is heading east with us."

09

One-by-one, the components spread out across Erudatta's work table were removed and mounted in their appropriate place along the skeletal framework. With the golem's mechanical brain in working order, the rest of the process proved simple enough. Though it was time-consuming, Erudatta constructed the complex interior one section at a time before he affixed the exoskeleton of polished brass and iron plates.

While the procedure consumed the span of a week, it only took a few hours to complete the clockwork mechanisms that now clicked and clacked behind the curved casing of its upper torso. From time to time, he paused to rest his tired hand. Even with liberal use of the tools in his prosthetic and the metal supports that surrounded his thin digits, his joints would ache after tending the miniature components and wiring.

In these brief respites, Erudatta wished he hadn't been forced to give up smoking tobacco. At least then the downtime might be consumed with something he relished. He enjoyed the flavor, the numb sensation that warmed his perception in the afterglow and even the smell that lingered. The activity itself was meditational and settled his mind enough to focus. Without regular access to the outside world, though, he had long expended his limited stores. Even worse, his favorite strain of leaf went extinct at some point, a victim of sudden shifts in climate and topography over the eons. Erudatta was convinced that certain tectonic shifts initiated long ago had been the culprit for the loss.

After the ache began to subside, he returned. He leaned over the nearly-finished mechanism and quickly recalled where he had left off.

Erudatta's mechanical man was similar in design to the lorica segmentata of eras long past. The galea-shaped headpiece, with a mostly-featureless faceplate, rested atop a torso composed of segmented metal plates assembled in curved bands around the trunk. Matching shelves of arcing, layered steel extended over the shoulder joints. Both arms and legs were covered in molded plates fashioned to approximate the musculature of a well-developed male.

While Erudatta took great pleasure in the artistry of the build, he was disinclined to forge matching gold icons in the traditional forms of lions or eagles for the chest plate. That would require foraging for materials he may not own.

He took a half-step back and for a moment wished he could dust off his hands. Now accustomed to the prosthesis, he still found that he missed simple, almost instinctual, habits. He knew he could just brush the dust and grime off against the robe with the same result, but there was a finality about the feeling of his palms rubbing together that was gone forever.

He reached out, with thumb and pinky finger extended and made a quick waggle, which produced a pair of yellow circles, one inside the other. After a few additional finger movements, the glowing mid-air ring filled with geometric symbols. Erudatta examined the halo for a second before flicking his open hand and brushing it towards the seated android. The energy quickly disappeared, appearing to pass through the breastplate.

Erudatta stood patiently as he watched and waited. He knew it would require a few minutes before the energies took root within the major systems inside the chest cavity. Such knowledge never made the wait easier.

"Any day now."

As the vermillion bulbs behind the eye slits lit up, its head rolled back. Gears spun to life and the mechanical man lurched out of its seated position with a clanking of metal boots on the concrete floor. With the golem standing at attention, Erudatta leaned in and performed a cursory examination. After a few moments of poking around, as he tested the spring in the joints and the sturdiness of the armored exterior, he stepped back and rubbed at the stubble along his jaw.

"Nomenclature assignment. Self-recognize as Masina."

The colored lights flickered twice. The name had taken root. Erudatta was relieved that his work on the machine's brain was successful. The mechanisms never really needed to be named. It was a convenience for Erudatta, especially in older days when he had more than one under his supervision.

"Masina, cognitive test, Protocol Promoveo. Response string."

Its reply came in the form of a series of clicks, none longer than a second. Erudatta listened and occasionally nodded from time to time.

"Good, good," he muttered after the tones completed. He knew the android would never be able to think critically, that it would only follow encoded orders. He had worked long and hard to program for most scenarios that it would encounter. "Masina, geolocation test, Protocol Promoveo. Response string."

Another series of chirps filled the air.

"Masina, stride mobility and dexterity display, full string, single cycle."

Pleased with his success, Erudatta took a step back and watched as the android strode around. Its movements were stiff, but with the appropriate cloth covering, it would appear to be a man in the dark of night. The jerky gait would be hidden both by the cover of darkness and the brown cloth strewn across the nearby table. Erudatta knew this was the only way. He had established a series of protocols that would force his creation to only travel in populated areas by night and to avoid most settlements when possible.

"Now to see the time of day," he announced with a gentle pat on Masina's bronze head as it came to rest.

As he shuffled to the nearby console, Erudatta's attention went to the display. The column of LEDs was a constant presence in his workroom, something he largely ignored during the routine of his day. He lived with the certainty that they would never change. There would always be a single vertical line of ten white rectangles, only broken by one left unlit and another that blazed bright green.

Now he noticed that nine were white and two glowed green.

10

As a granular spray kicked up, the thick rubber treads of the four-wheel transport carved a swath through the shifting sands. Weaving between the desert ridges, the automotive laid down a serpentine trail; one that would slowly be concealed by the blowing winds before sunrise of the following day.

Within the passenger cabin, the restless passengers weathered the baking heat, which only began to relent as the landscape transitioned to arid grasslands. A canvas tarp tacked over the metal-frame roll cage provided only the barest shelter from the scorching sun as it arced overhead. In time, they passed through a barren stretch of earthen canyon that dumped them out onto the edge of the Vilfdonum Steepe.

Peter knew that the trip across the Quartewuste would take almost the entire day. Since he had traversed it months before on a supply run, he drove it like a seasoned professional. Even with the rugged auto, the journey proved grueling and ultimately exhausting. With no established trade routes through the expanse of desert, he had to rely on memory to retrace his earlier trip. It wasn't until they bypassed the eastern boundary that he caught sight of signage which pointed them in the direction of Attis Grove.

The sun was setting behind them when they rolled up to the outskirts of Attis Grove.

With the Bureau-owned transport parked at the western edge of the antiquated village, they proceeded on foot. While Apello did not care to leave the automotive unattended, it proved necessary if they were to find lodgings for the night. The interior of Attis Grove was composed of winding, cobble-stone lanes between groupings of quaint cottages that fed into a central public courtyard. At the heart of the square was a marble fountain, flanked on all sides by larger public-use buildings, including the community's lone inn.

Much to Cal's chagrin, the small township was lacking many of his preferred diversions. There were no bright lights glaring blindingly and the local citizenry weren't crammed in shoulder to shoulder. He spotted no short skirts, visibly-alluring cleavage or painted faces, thick with enticing hues. He wondered where Attis Grove hid its taverns and brothels. Even a church-run bingo parlor would suffice. While Peter and Apello discussed sleeping arrangements, Cal grew surly over the lack of entertainment.

As they crossed through the courtyard, Prae's pace slowed. Though her emerald eyes passed over the town folk, they never paused for more than a second before moving on to the next. For the most part, the citizenry drew no visible reactions. It wasn't until her gaze fell on a nearby alleyway, darkened by shadows from the setting sun, that she showed interest. Her face reddened and her brow creased as she halted mid-step.

"Look at this," Prae snarled. She flashed an open hand at a huddled man propped against the side of the general store. He was pale and sickly, dressed shabbily in long-unwashed apparel and looked to be in the midst of a drug-induced haze. Customers who passed through the nearby open doorway paid him little heed. "How barbaric you must be to *still* have such waste littering your city streets. Are there no public services to tend to such ills?"

This triggered Cal's temper.

"My apologies, Madame," Cal sniped. "Unlike you, our society didn't manage to cure the evils of addiction, poverty and depression on day one."

Peter groaned. He could feel the tension. Cal was predisposed to bite at any off-hand comment made by Prae. It was as if he couldn't resist the urge to look for a fight in every conversation.

Prae glared as she blew a sharp breath through her nose. "You! Scoundrel!" Her words came from behind clenched teeth with the ferocity of a lion's roar. Before she could continue, Cal interrupted her.

"I *have* a name, you know. I'm sure you've heard it a few times by now. You'll get a more positive response from me by using it."

She stepped in and violently took him by the collar. "Names are for people I have an interest in knowing."

His head craned back; he made no attempt to extricate himself. A cockeyed grin creased his lips. There was mischief in his eyes. "Aw, don't be like that, hot stuff. Maybe you could do us all a big favor and cool down before you make judgment calls about people you don't know?"

"Enough." His voice heavy with caution, Apello boomed as he placed a hand on Prae's arm. She shot a fierce look his way, which only met his own cold stare. When he refused to budge, she eventually relented and released her grip on Cal.

"You need to sort your shit out, lady," Cal barked as straightened his shirt. "Maybe you can figure out that you ain't queen shit of the world before it's too late." At that, he stormed off.

"Hey! Where are you going?" Peter called out.

Without looking back, Cal hollered. "Somewhere to unwind. Don't wait up for me."

As they watched him disappear, Peter turned to Apello.

"I wonder if he realizes that Attis Grove is a dry town."

Apello cracked a smile so faint, Peter wondered if it had been a trick of the light.

After checking in to the room he shared with Apello and Cal, Peter excused himself to visit with the females of their group. Cal had not turned up and it was just as likely he wouldn't before late in the evening, if at all. Though Apello kept to himself as Peter slipped from the room, Peter was convinced he had something on his mind. Apello's stern expression was enough to dissuade him from prying.

As he trotted the short distance between the two rooms, Peter mulled over Apello's apprehension. He had never thought the Thosan was one for over-thinking, which left Peter with two obvious options. Firstly was certainly frustration with Cal's abandonment of his charge. Even in the presence of others who could stand watch over the An-Sebban, it was not League protocol to walk away from contracted duty.

Secondly, he believed that Apello may prefer Peter to leave Prae to her own devices. That it would be better for both of their livelihoods to point her in the right direction and head back to Natx Hollow. Peter knew it would take all his fortitude to fend off the imposing man's arguments. If worse came to worse, he might have to part ways with Apello. The promise of greater opportunities was something on which he should risk his career prospects.

Peter paused by the entryway, marked with a brass number seven, and knocked. For a moment, he wondered if whether Prae would understand the traditional beckoning. *How else would one get the attention of people inside a room? Yelling through the door? Well, okay, with as forward as Prae is, maybe so. Or, perhaps they just know when visitors are there. Maybe, if Oebe's inside, she'll answer.*

Before he could rap his knuckles on the stained maple a second time, the door swung open to reveal Prae, who was still dressed in the sun-bleached robe and striped kibr.

"Is there an issue?" Prae inquired. By the tension in her stance, she appeared ready to strike at an instant. Peter wondered if there would ever be a moment in which she might unwind. Her constant vigilance must be an exhausting way to experience life.

"No. Not at all. I just wanted to see if things were satisfactory. If the accommodations were sufficient for you and Oebe."

"Yes," she responded as she stepped aside and let Peter into the room. With a sweep of her hand, she motioned to the meager furnishings: a quartet of beds barely wide enough for a single person, a bedside table and a chest of drawers. Loosely covered by a set of curtains hung at the back of the room was a pair of glass doors that led out onto an adjoining balcony. The chambers Peter shared with Apello and Cal was similar. "They are adequate for a temporary rest. Unquestionably an upgrade to the lodgings at Natx Hollow. Though I am not certain why you would be concerned. You are not the owner of this structure and have no monetary gain in the opinion of your customers."

If he had an ounce of Cal's surliness, he might have made a sarcastic response to her about polite inquires. Instead, he moved the conversation along. "How fares Oebe?"

"Asleep," Prae responded, nodding in the direction of the small woman on top of the furthest bed. Still dressed in her robes, her eyes were closed and her hands were placed atop her chest. "The heat and travel took their toll. She reclined without a word only a few minutes after we entered. Despite her disinterest in being fawned over, she is the frailest thing."

"Indeed."

As Peter shifted his weight nervously, Prae narrowed

her eyes.

"You have a query you wish to pose."

Peter let out a long sigh before nodding. "Yeah, I guess I do. So, uh, what was with that little trick you pulled off back at Natx Hollow? In the Blue Room? With the bulletproof circle of light."

"You mean you—oh, pardon, I forgot your level of biomechanical... technological advancement may have not reached such a point, as of yet. It's a practice once known as semanifesture, a technique developed in our later years. It would be, well, I'm not entirely sure how far along... Well, that's a conversation for a later date."

Peter frowned at the ambiguity. At this sign of displeasure, Prae shrugged. He wanted to press her further, but some part of him understood her need for discretion. Peter regarded her as he would a modern man reluctant to hand over the secret to fire to a tribe of prehistoric cavemen. Any additional inquiries were held at bay by the looming opportunity for revelation once they arrived at Ala'ydin.

"My apologies for being so obtuse. I have to remind myself what may be present or not in terms of advancements among your people. It's difficult to know what to explain, or how. Or whether I should."

"Well, to be honest, it's not wholly alien," Peter admitted. "In the major cities, like Greater Decedistadt, a similar form of technology exists, though it's primarily used as business signage, advertising, street lamps in some of the more upscale sectors. Light projections that manifest

as neon displays on every street corner in the more…
ostentatious parts of town. I've never seen it employed in quite such a fashion, especially by a person, independent of some form of portable device."

"I can imagine." She nodded as she looked to her boots for a moment. After a few seconds of silence, she met Peter's peering eyes. "Would you happen to know how those that developed it came by this advance?"

"Unsure. Sorry, that's not exactly my field of expertise," Peter replied.

"Understood. Wasn't mine either, but after you get trained in it and used to the process, you become fairly experienced in the matter."

"What was—is your field of expertise?"

"Soldier. While many of the others were deeply entrenched in fields of science, law, research, I was the sword. The shield. The lone member of the military retained."

Peter nodded, grateful for the rare unguarded moment. It felt like the first real interaction between the two. He knew there were still volumes left unsaid, but this was at least a start.

Peter could hear the faint breaths of Oebe's deep slumber. "Well, since you seem to be doing well, I'll leave you two be."

Before Peter could turn away, Prae motioned for him to wait with a flick of her fingers.

"Hold a minute."

"Yes?"

Prae placed her hand over Peter's face, fingers spread. Her palm hovered only inches from the tip of his nose.

"Uh, can I ask what it is you're doing?" Peter nervously cocked his brow.

"There is a semanifesture technique that can, well, they say it gauges a man's character. How much of that is truth is up in the air, but by the colors, one can supposedly determine certain qualities of moral fiber."

Before Peter could protest, she made a quick twist of her wrist which created a toneless circle of light. Two vertical slashes of her fingers were followed by a trio of curling arcs. As the icons solidified within the halo, she retreated with a single step.

Peter's eyes focused on the glowing circle as he waited for something to occur. He began to notice slight fluctuations along the edges, as if the energy was undulating. After a few seconds, the formation began to fill with peach and cream colors. Small threads of red, green and blue flickered, but were quickly lost in the overall softer hue.

"So, uh, what does this mean?" Peter's eyelashes fluttered as the brilliant formation began to slowly dissipate.

"Purportedly that you're a man of earnest character."

"You don't sound entirely convinced about that."

"As I said previously: not my field of experience. I learned of this technique and what the results *should* mean. Doesn't mean I can consider it wholly reliable. The human heart is complex and not so easy to place into simple categories."

"And you needed to do this... why?" Peter continued to blink as his pupils returned to normal.

"If I'm to take you to Ala'ydin, I need to know you can be trusted with what you see there. What you discover. That you can make the appropriate decisions on what to keep to yourself. What to make public." The gravity of her tone struck home. She was potentially leading him to something rife with complications. That what he learned may need to be evaluated for both its value and its danger to society before publication.

"I-I think I get your meaning."

"I must ask you—can your man, Apello, be trusted? I know he works for your business as an independent for-hire. Those kinds tend to be pliable for the right amount of gold."

"He's a good man. Keeps to himself and probably doesn't rightly care for anything other than tending to his responsibilities. If I'm honest, he scares the shit out of me, but I don't think I've ever seen him spend his earnings irresponsibly. I think he keeps the bulk of it in some form of savings, though I've not been able to discover for what."

Peter's words seemed to temporarily appease Prae. His own vocation was a more immediate concern than Apello's nature. It was his job to report findings and he had come along with the hope of discovery.

"What of Oebe?" Peter asked as his gaze turned to the sleeping woman.

"She has not an ounce of guile within her. That much I can already see. Whatever this Athenaeum did to bend her into this form, it has made her pure in intent. She is witness without judgment. That she was lashed to such a puerile man-child is an unfortunate occurrence. Perhaps this Merced League would do well to review its personnel files."

Peter snorted with a wry smile. "So, I take you're not a fan of Cal? I mean, it's not that hard to understand."

"He reeks of thievery, booze, whores and lies. You would do well not to rely upon him."

"I'm sure that's exactly why Apello came along."

With what remained of Jaefor's stipend burning a hole in his pocket, Cal was distraught to find no seedy entertainment in the hamlet. After a lengthy walk to cool off, he returned to the main square and began a tour of the local establishments, hoping to find even the smallest bar hidden amongst the businesses and public facilities.

Eventually, he stopped in front of the same general store they had passed, outside of which he and Prae had aired their public disagreement. The seemingly-homeless addict had disappeared since then and left only a few pieces of garbage in his place. As he entered the still-open doorway, the aroma of dried meats, tanned hides and tobacco overwhelmed him.

With a long, slow scan of the retailer's stock, Cal became quickly disillusioned. There were no bottles of booze on the shelves; not even a limited stock tucked behind the counter. The shop owner seemed content to sell basic wares for those living within or nearby Attis Grove.

Cal let out a sigh. He would have to head for the inn at some point. He only hoped that he wouldn't run across Prae.

Their interactions had started off merely at-odds, like two people on different wavelengths, but grew incendiary over their time together. He was unsure what rubbed him the wrong way about her. Part of him wanted to blame it on a her aura of superiority. Even with that in mind, he wasn't entirely certain why it crawled under his skin so much. Jaefor and his cronies had always acted in an arrogant fashion, but it never seemed to bother Cal all that much. *Yeah, well, I can't exactly lump Prae in with the likes of Jaefor. I got a fair idea of the crimes he's been a part of. Prae, not so much.*

"Can I help you, son?" the shopkeeper called out. Cal knew that the older gentleman, with ruddy, wrinkled skin and a headful of white hair, had been eyeing him since his entry. Cal could guess that the man considered he was there to shoplift, or worse, rob him. With that in mind, he stepped up to the counter and pointed to a glass jar by the register.

"Actually, how about a half-dozen of the sarsaparilla candy sticks." He pulled out a few notes and placed them on the counter as the shop owner removed six of the brown-colored sugar rods and placed them in a small paper bag. *I wonder if Oebe has ever had something like this,* Cal pondered as the man made change for the purchase. *Or, rather, I wonder if she recalls the experience.*

"Here you are." With his change and candy, Cal turned to leave, only to come to a stop when the shopkeeper cleared his throat.

"Yes?" Cal looked back over his shoulder.

"Sorry to be nosey…"

"But?" Cal was short with the man. Adding apologies to curiosity never made the inquiries seem less intrusive.

"You came into town with that group earlier, right? With the Thosan and that guy from the Archaeology Bureau. Uh, Mathester, I think was his name."

At first Cal was a bit disturbed that the man knew Peter. It quickly dawned on him that Peter had been to Attis Grove previously for supplies. "Uh, yeah, we came in from the Quartewuste. What of it?"

"Well, that little girl…"

Cal found himself relieved. Oebe he could explain away. Prae, on the other hand, would be difficult, since he himself hadn't the faintest idea of who she was. "An-Sebban," he replied with a nod.

"That's what I thought. Never seen one before. Only read about them."

"I imagine they don't have much occasion to send one of their own out here," Cal said as he tossed the storekeeper a half-hearted wave and departed.

Oebe woke to find herself alone in the dark room.

It took a few seconds of staring into the darkness before she recalled where she was and how she had arrived. The remnants of the long, hard nap still fogged her senses and, only once she heard the shuffling of footsteps behind the curtains to her right, did she move from the bed.

She dropped to the floor and opened the cloth, which allowed the cold glow of moon light to spill across the carpeted floor. On the other side of the glass doors stood Prae, who leaned over the metal railing of the balcony, facing away from the bedroom.

Oebe opened one of the doors and slipped through the crack as she joined her roommate. With inquisitive eyes, she followed Prae's own gaze to the waning gibbous moon above. The lunar orb hung high as wisps of cloud slowly migrated eastward across the sky. Below, the town was faintly lit by streetlamps that outlined the quiet hamlet. There was only the faintest noise of wind as it rustled through the winding lanes, which left Oebe to assume that it was late, and that most of the citizenry had gone home for the evening.

"There used to be mountains here," Prae announced without provocation. She reached out with one arm and drew a line along the darkened horizon. "A massive chain that cut through the land, a wall that separated the desert from the prairies. It was there at the end of the second era, before I departed the Waking State, and when I awoke again, sometime during the beginning of the third era, they were gone. Certainly a whim of one of my kind. I… enjoyed climbing them from time to time."

Oebe cocked her head to the side, as Prae shifted her

stance.

"You have little to interject, I see," Prae commented.

"You asked no questions. There was no impetus to respond."

At this, Prae let out a small snort of laughter. "You are truly a unique creature among mankind."

"I am not unique. There are other An-Sebban who share my condition."

"Ah, yes. In speaking previously with Peter, I have come to some understanding about the nature of your mind, or rather your memory, the process of your ability to recollect. I've also noticed a certain emotional distance in how you interact with the world. With others, as well, including those with whom you travel. Am I safe to assume that these are related?"

Oebe nodded once. "With An-Sebban, emotional expression is stored in lower layers of our memory. This is because the topmost layer is reaped during the transferral process. If emotional data is stored there, it would be lost, erased during the filtering methodology as unnecessary noise. For that reason, it becomes accumulated deeper, but because of the nature of the procedure, these processes become inactive. Without attached memories to give them context, the emotions are without form."

Prae frowned and, just as she seemed about to ask an additional question, Oebe continued.

"Imagine plants growing in soil. The more recent recollections are the organic layer, or humus, that is constantly being tilled. Below that are the topsoil and subsoil layers. This is where the brain chemicals attached to a network of largely-dormant neurons resides. Plants left to flourish, whose roots reach the deeper layers are healthier and develop. By this clumsy example, information or memories that are retained over longer periods eventually attach to emotions stored deeper. The neurons awaken and emotional attachment has the opportunity for growth."

"So, the longer you go between... transferrals, the more like the others you become."

"If that helps you understand the nature of An-Sebban, then yes, that is a fair comparison."

"Does it bother you that you are different than other people?"

"No. Does it you?"

The comment was innocuous enough, though Prae's eyelids flickered for a moment as she reflected.

"I guess I hadn't considered it," Prae said. She turned her gaze back to the moon just as a bank of clouds moved across its face.

11

Though Jaefor made his fortune from businesses of
questionable legality and morality throughout Urigo
Sector, he actually held residence in Locuple Sector, two
districts to the north. The three-story townhome was one
of the many gray-brick buildings spread across the upscale
neighborhood. Visitors could reach the granite front steps
via a central avenue that funneled traffic through the ward
and into the heart of the city.

Many of the local residents were politicians, legitimate
businessmen, or self-professed descendants of the founding
fathers, whose own wealth was earned almost entirely
through inheritance. None bothered to inquire how their
neighbor had jostled his way into the community; the lavish
lifestyle on display was enough to justify his residence.

The interior of his abode was teeming with excesses
seemingly required of the well-to-do. Between marble
columns that lined the vaulted entry and gold leaf trim
on every wall, visitors often mistook Jaefor as one of the
'old rich.' To this end, each room was decorated with pricy
artwork and curios of varying age.

At the top of the main staircase, which had steps

fashioned from ivory and obsidian slate, was a set of double doors that led into the sitting room. The salon was furnished with plush, velvet chairs and lit by a fire that had been roaring for some time in the white-marble fireplace. Jaefor chose to meet Illgosses, who had arrived earlier for an impromptu conference, in the cozy room.

As the two men shared a snifter of aged bourbon, from Jaefor's collection in a nearby liquor cabinet, he shifted in his seat. After some gossip, he set his gaze on the man with whom he entrusted his finances. Though Illgosses had been a reliable employee and confidant for decades, Jaefor could not recall a time when he had not looked weathered and greasy. Thin graying hair, unfortunately parted by a scar that intersected his scalp, was brushed out of his pasty face. The flickering fire sparkled in his green spectacles as he sipped at the beverage.

After a few minutes of chatter about financial returns on local investments, Jaefor set his jaw and cleared his throat. "That's all well and good," he began with thinly-veiled impatience. "But I'm certain you did not make the trip all this way to cover matters easily discussed the next time I'm in Urigo."

"Yes, yes," Illgosses said with a cockeyed grin. "I was of a mind to inquire on a specific person who so cavalierly asked for a stipend of cash over a week ago. One who, according to my ledgers, lacks an ounce of credit to his name and yet had the appropriate papers providing him with an additional loan."

"Cal Reeger," Jaefor stated without a change in expression. "I had a need to provide for him so he could procure something of value with the sole intent of wiping his debt clean."

"You sent him to perform the Natx Hollow job, didn't you?" Illgosses' tone bordered on insolent.

Jaefor nodded before finishing the last sip from his glass.

"Would you care to educate me as to why you would send Reeger? We have far more capable employees that could have handled that assignment. Reeger's the constant butt of jokes amongst the populace of Urigo. No one thinks he can manage to piss without spraying his boots, and you thought it a good idea to send him, on his own, to pick the place clean for you?"

Jaefor leaned forward as his brow furrowed. His fingers gripped the glass tightly. "Firstly, the kind of man you would have dispatched would have lacked the subtlety needed for such a delicate matter. Someone like Raxus? He would have killed the entire expedition to bring back a single canopic jar. It's that kind of trouble we don't need to court. No amount of profit would be enough to keep the Magistrates or Central Judicia from sniffing around, focusing their attention on our day-to-days. Secondly, Reeger is in arrears and this solves two problems for us. If successful, he settles his debt. If not, we disavow any association with him. He takes the fall if he bungles it."

"I guess you'll have to forgive me for being a bit dubious of his odds at success."

"Cal Reeger is that special kind of dumb that can't keep himself out of trouble. He's mouthy when he shouldn't be, bets on poker hands he has no chance of winning, and flirts with women well out of his league. And, yet, he manages to survive. He has the fool's luck. On top of that, he's so downtrodden that he fails to recognize his own talents. He has an eye for quality and a strong sense of self-preservation when the need arises. Where he lacks at guile when it comes to extricating himself from debt, he's curiously able to string a phantom existence from the scraps of other people's lives. A smarter, more capable man would have disappeared, run off to Zehngrad or the Siamsoth Mountains by now. Reeger, on the other hand, keeps coming back to try and claw his way out. It's almost perversely honorable."

"And you thought that this was a good combination of character traits to exploit? We worked hard to get that League contract so we could sneak our own man inside. To waste it on such a man—"

"The secret to Reeger is that you can't ever let him know he's better than the trash among which he sleeps," Jaefor stated coldly, placing a hand on his knee and craning his neck forward. "For him to succeed, you have to push him down, having him scraping the bottom to get the best from him. You see, you have to take everything from the man and place him at the nadir of his existence. Then, and only then, will he either chose to wallow or act in such a manner as to better himself."

Illgosses snorted as he rolled his eyes.

"Is there a problem with this decision?" Jaefor's question was loaded; only one response would be acceptable.

"No, not at all," Illgosses shook his head. "I have to say

that I don't think Reeger really deserves this much thought. Certainly not this much philosophizing." He set the half-finished glass down.

Jaefor was silent for a moment.

"I think we're done," Jaefor dismissed him. At that, Illgosses excused himself and departed.

Illgosses' transit to Urigo Sector was a slow, introspective march. He left the posh neighborhood behind as he weaved his way back through the increasingly less-affluent areas. Along his journey, he paused briefly to watch a pair of Magistrates in the midst of arresting an accused pickpocket. Once batons were brandished and the public flogging of the young man commenced, Illgosses hurried onward.

Illgosses also resided away from the hustle and bustle of D'rian Obix. His own personal chambers were part of a converted office space just outside of the garish, sordid ward. The three-story building had once been owned by a moneylender who went out of business years ago. Illgosses acquired the property for a pittance, but saw no reason to renovate.

The ground floor was abandoned and littered with discarded furniture and equipment. The exterior windows that weren't yet boarded up were cloudy with unwashed filth. Up a set of metal steps at the back of the building was an adjoining office and bedroom that he called home.

As he climbed the stairs with a hand on the railing, he overheard a door in the building slam shut. He paused until he recognized the echoing of boots on tile. He nodded in relief before resuming. The visitor was not unexpected, even if the arrival was before the appointed time.

At the landing, he hung an immediate right and nudged his way into the office. Beside the doorframe was a bronze placard that had once proudly named the original business' owner. A series of furious scratches across the surface marred the block letters, which made them illegible.

Leaving the entrance cracked, Illgosses' shoes shuffled across the aging rug that had once been a vibrant red with green accents. Time and sunlight through the lone window had dulled the hues. What remained was a dust-encrusted field of dried fibers that kicked lint into the air as he walked to the chair at his desk.

As Illgosses settled, the door to his office swung open. A man fully dressed in slate-colored armor over snakeskin charged in. As he came to stop in front of the seated Illgosses, he reached up and placed both hands on either side of his bronze helm. The helmet's polished faceplate was expressionless, with two slits for eyes and another for its mouth.

With a single fluid motion, he pulled it from his head, set it in his lap, and dropped into the armchair across from Illgosses. As his skin was blistered red and covered in scars, Raxus often chose to hide beneath the ornate helm. There was not a strand of hair on his head, not even eyebrows or facial hair. The crystal blue of his eyes stood in stark contrast to the ruddy hue of his face.

In all his years, Illgosses had never heard how Raxus had become this way. As far as he knew, no one was privy to the information and Raxus' dour temperament did not welcome personal inquiries.

"You said you wanted to speak with me earlier. What's this over?" Raxus began as he leaned back into his seat. The wood creaked under his armored weight.

"What do you know of Cal Reeger?"

"Irresponsible with his money. Unliked by every piece of tail in Urigo. Prone to running his mouth, whether drunk or not. Bit of a lecher. He seems like the kinda guy who would keep a diary and at the top of every entry would be 'Dear Journal, I am soooo horny right now.' "

While Illgosses enjoyed a hearty chortle, Raxus sat grimly.

"Yes, well, then I guess you have no clue as to his current whereabouts. More to the point is that Jaefor dispatched him to Natx Hollow to burgle the site. Said it was to clear his outstanding debt."

Raxus seemed unmoved. He sat quietly with his hands clasping the side of his headgear.

"This is, as you might think, a gross misuse of resources. Someone far more trustworthy—in so much as we employ people who can be trusted—should have been sent to handle such a delicate matter. At lot of time and money went into procuring that League contract only for Jaefor to hand it off to someone of Reeger's nature."

"So, what do you have in mind?" Raxus asked as he drummed his fingers across the top of his helmet.

"I want you to post a handful of men you can rely on in Ilgyngate to see if he comes back through. Men who can grasp the concept of necessary discretion. At the Langspur Northern Station should do. If he's foolish enough to see things through to the end, he'll have to pass through there to return to Urigo."

"And I assume that you wish for me to follow his trail?" The raspy quality in Raxus' voice made his words rattle.

"Theoretically, he should have headed on to Natx Hollow. We have eyes on the ground that confirmed he left the city with the An-Sebban in tow, so unless he's truly stupid, he had to escort his ward west. The fact that he went to the Athenaeum is, frankly, unexpected. Perhaps he considered dumping the dead weight once he got to Ilgyngate and made a break for it. Jaefor seems to think well enough of Cal to expect that he'll reach the Quartewuste and maybe even come back like an obedient dog playing fetch."

"Foolish," Raxus grunted.

"Yes, the man is far too much of a wildcard to safely assume anything. The fact that he followed through on picking up the An-Sebban is curious enough. Perhaps, he knew he would be watched as he left the city. Perhaps, he intends on seeing it through to the end. Won't that be a deliciously unexpected twist."

"Your angle in all this?"

Illgosses chuckled for a moment. "Always one to cut to the heart of the matter, eh?"

"You're not one to piss away money unless you think it'll reap rewards. You didn't invite me to a private sit-down unless you had something in mind. Hiring me and a few of my associates to do side work, 'specially on the hush-hush from Jaefor, isn't gonna come cheap and we both know it."

"True. Jaefor seems to hold out hope that Reeger will waltz into town, hands full of treasure. He's surprisingly optimistic on his investment. I, on the other hand, have considered that he's already ditched and headed for the darkest hole in which he can hide."

"Let's get down to brass tacks. What do you want me to do when I find him?"

"If he actually has something of value, kill him and take it. If it's anything that can be bartered, I'll arrange for the sale. Field offers through my own network of resellers. Certainly a number of interested parties could be roused with the right inquiries. If you find him empty-handed, bring him back and let Jaefor do what he pleases with him. Then, I can lord it over Jaefor that I was right all along not to trust him. When I point it out that he's been far too capricious as of late, I can leverage it for more control of the books. More control of the day to day business."

"So, your plan is to swipe the treasure out from beneath Jaefor's nose? Isn't he gonna take issue with that?"

"Only if you can't be trusted to remain quiet in the matter," Illgosses grinned. "And to that effect, I'm sure a bonus can be attached to your usual fees. Ultimately, Reeger has accrued a sizeable debt. I would rather flip his finds for money than to pay off the red in his register. Jaefor may fancy one or two of the baubles for his own collection, which doesn't exactly put coin in the bank. Sometimes, someone has to be the responsible one when it comes to balancing the books. Reeger will be dead at the end of it all."

12

"I knew we shouldn't have allowed Cal to arrange for the lodgings," Peter muttered sourly as he settled into his place at the table. The tavern's din alone was enough to set him on edge. A thick atmosphere of booze, smoke, and fried foods made the air something one might consume rather than breathe. He grew progressively more uncomfortable by the minute. Certain he would need to bathe after the night was over, Peter let out a sigh and tried to make the best of it.

On their arrival to Viisibourg, Peter openly admitted that he'd never been so far east, much less to the bustling city. So when Cal gleefully offered to coordinate room and board for the night, he was receptive, assuming that Cal was familiar with the locale.

It wasn't until they were checking into the inn, a dank hovel situated near what was most certainly the red-light district, that Peter realized that Cal's selection of the establishment was based solely on the attached tavern. Now seated for a quick meal before turning in, he knew it was too late to issue a complaint. He would suffer though the questionable accommodations until their departure the following morning.

Founded at the heart of the Vilfdonum Steepe, the city of Viisibourg was an older settlement, established early in the previous millennium. The skyline, dotted with factories and warehouses wedged uncomfortably in between blocks of apartment complexes, was unbroken, except for the occasional tower or steeple.

The self-governing township had long ago been dubbed 'the Clockwork City' after early technological advances during the industrial revolution of the late 2800s. Before the turn of the 30th century, Viisibourg was known for producing clockwork mechanisms, including the earliest recorded timepieces and the first automated ground transport. While the heart of modern scientific advancement migrated south to the more affluent Greater Decedistadt, Viisibourg was still home to a number of specialized artisans, due in large part to various unions that considered the city home.

Though Peter acquired a table that would seat five comfortably, only Prae and Oebe joined him to dine on the limited menu options. Cal had arrived at the tavern earlier, but was roaming the bar area, trying to engage with the local women, with diminishing degrees of success. Already into his third drink, he was growing brash and annoying to the other patrons. From time to time, he would stop by their table. A half-full glass of beer was placed before his empty seat.

On one such stopover, he sauntered up beside Oebe and casually placed a hand on her shoulder, which caused her to cock her head to the side.

"Hey short-stack," Cal slurred as he plopped a mug of ale in front of her. Some of the golden liquid splashed up over the rim and spilled onto the table. "Have this one on me."

"What is it? Specifically."

"Something to loosen you right up," he responded over his shoulder, weaving his way back to the bar.

Peter bit his tongue as he watched Cal flag down the bartender. To Peter, it seemed as if Cal was making up for lost time. His sullen attitude had given way to giddy indulgence.

Peter shook his head and turned to his tablemates. Oebe had a hand on the tankard as she leaned in and cautiously sniffed at the beverage. Prae was quietly eating her own meal as she eyed the clientele. Peter noticed that Prae sat at attention, as if expecting trouble. Any interest in the room she exhibited was done in an effort to make threat assessments.

"Did either of you see where Apello ran off to?" Peter spoke up as he picked at the last of the food on his plate. The meal was serviceable, though lacking in flavor. If he had been a fan of alcohol, he might have imbibed to cover up the aftertaste.

"Did he not inform you?" Prae inquired as she pushed her plate away. "One would think with the nature of your arrangement that he would have communicated his plans."

"No, he was out the door before I was done getting cleaned up. Said nary a word."

"He conversed with me," Oebe volunteered after

taking a sip, much to the surprise of the other two. "I might have stated that I spoke with him, but I did not, in fact, have reason to utter a word. So, rather, I listened to his announcement."

"What did he say?"

"That he, and I quote, 'would be away for most of the evening as I have personal business to attend to in town.' He did not expound upon it beyond that." With a curious look on her face, Oebe leaned in and took another nip. To Peter, it seemed as though she was attempting to evaluate the nature of the beverage, both in its taste and her physical reaction to it.

"Odd. He made no earlier mention of a personal connection to Viisibourg," Peter said with a frown. "I wasn't aware he knew anyone in town."

"The man does keep to himself," Prae offered. "Understandable as not everyone so readily desires to have their private business made public."

At this, Peter shook his head. Between the mood, the raucous clamor, and the less-than-savory flavor of his meal, he was strongly considering excusing himself for the evening. Before he could push away from the table, he caught sight of Oebe as she rose to her feet.

"What is Cal doing?" Oebe inquired with an almost childlike curiosity. Her tiny frame seemed to waver as she stood with the glass held tightly between her hands.

Peter located Cal by the bar attempting to flirt with a busty redhead who wore the raiment of a call girl. After a moment, she shook her head and dismissed him with the flip of her hand. Undaunted, Cal shrugged and moved down the bar to the next female in line. The display struck Peter as wantonly pathetic.

Peter would admit that Cal was not an unattractive man, though he was in desperate need of a change of style. The leather jacket and suspenders combined with the frumpy unwashed mass of hair atop his head was doing him no favors.

"Looks like he's trying to make a new friend for the evening," Prae snarled before taking a swig of her beverage.

"But, I was under the impression he already has friends," Oebe turned back to the table. For the first time since meeting her, Peter noticed her features slacken. Curiously, she seemed relaxed, as if the endless duty of observation was temporarily suspended.

"Not as many as you might think," Peter groaned. "And not of the kind he's looking for tonight." The general impression he got from Cal through their time together painted the picture of an unreliable, and somewhat unrepentant, degenerate. Considering how readily Cal seemed to fall back into salacious habits, Peter had misgivings about his reliability.

Once dismissed by the next questionably-attired female, Cal peeled away from the bar area and returned to their table. He picked up the half-empty beer and downed it before he gave the room another scan.

"On the prowl tonight?" Prae offered a barbed inquiry without even looking at Cal.

He made a clicking noise with his tongue as he

fashioned a gun from one hand and pointed it playfully at Prae. Without saying anything else, he slipped away and back into the crowd; his attention was drawn by a brunette on the other side of the room that appeared to be a few too many drinks along.

"Prowl?" Oebe inquired as she looked back and forth between Prae and Peter.

"Uh, he's looking—"

"Sorry, I wasn't certain if such terminology was reintroduced." In the poor light, it was hard to tell if Prae was blushing. "It means… to look for a dance partner," Prae offered, hoping to end the subject.

"Yeah, *dance*. The one with no pants," Peter commented under his breath. He scratched at his scalp as he looked from Oebe's inquisitive gaze.

"I don't understand."

Before Peter could fashion a response, Prae held out a hand, asking him to hold off. "I say let Reeger explain this to her. It's his fault we're in this situation."

Oebe shrugged as she took a mouthful of the drink. Peter cleared his throat as he turned to Prae.

"One thing comes to mind," he began quickly. "It occurred to me as we were checking in. You were on the receiving end of a few inquiring eyes on our arrival. Are you taking steps to hide your… bundle?" He lowered his voice and leaned in. "Your armor. Did you hide the duffle somewhere in your room?"

"The thought did not occur to me."

"Well, let's just say that I've heard Viisibourg is not a place you'd want to leave anything of value lying about. There are rumors about unsavory elements in the town. Travelers being robbed of their possessions and such. I've heard tales of a group of fences working out of the city, funneling stolen goods to associates in other locales. Should you not be concerned about someone stealing your armor? For all we know, someone is breaking into your room as we speak. Maybe even an employee."

"Let them try," Prae said with a smug smile. "Upon its completion, my gear was attuned to me via biometric authentication before I even donned it. Anyone foolish enough to take it for their own will find themselves unable to wear it. Imbedded semanifesture techniques would make it very *unpleasant* to dress themselves up in their ill-gotten prize."

"Or they could just be looking into selling it to a collector. Which is all the more likely. Small time crooks looking to flip for a quick profit. You won't be finding too many people stealing to upgrade their apparel. A quick payday is the more likely outcome."

"A similarly unwise option. It's simply a matter of creating a tracking semanifesture that would point me in the direction of any lost pieces. Anything stolen would be easily located."

"Well, isn't that convenient," Oebe commented in a strange bubbly tone. If she was anyone else, the upbeat, almost chirpy statement would not have seemed out of place. Peter cocked a brow as he slowly turned to face her.

"I think you've had enough," Prae announced as

she took the partially-consumed beverage from Oebe's possession. Oebe frowned. "And I think it's high time we got you to bed."

"I can see why Cal enjoys the drink so much. It's like liquid relaxation."

Peter offered her a hand as he stood. "Yes, let's get you settled in before the more *unpleasant* effects manifest. I fear you won't find this drink so appealing come morning."

Over the next few hours, the events of the evening melted into a booze-fueled flurry of interactions. Faces became indistinguishable and conversations were nothing more than a staccato of noises that incited responsive nods. Cal's enjoyment had degraded most of his senses, which left him to wander the establishment in a drunken loop of self-induced foolishness. Before long, Cal was able to focus long enough to register that his compatriots had left him on his own. To this, he only shrugged before trying to talk up yet another female. Having lost track of time, it wasn't until the crowd in the room began to thin that he finally paid off his tab and departed.

Under the influence of six glasses of ale and a few too many shots of brown liquor, Cal stumbled into his room and eventually flopped onto the bed, still draped in his clothes. For a fleeting moment, it crossed his mind to wonder where Apello or Peter were. If he had been even remotely sober, he might have recalled his optimistic splurge for a single-occupancy.

Splayed across the down-filled comforter, Cal let out a long sigh as his breathing grew lethargic. As he started to drift into sleep, he felt a weight on the mattress that caused it to shift slightly. Moments later, something soft and warm crawled on top of him. Even half asleep, he grinned. *Looks like one of the dames decided to join me after all.*

As the feminine body lay prone across his torso with her head resting on his chest, he grunted with a growing pleasure. His alcohol-tainted blood slowly headed southward as his mind focused on the soft frame against him. He reached up an arm and placed his hand on her back as his thoughts remained on the pair of soft breasts pressed against his ribs. Drawing in a long breath through his nose, he caught a whiff of vanilla and powder.

With his fingers, he caressed the ridge of her spine.

"Oh that feels good," she uttered. Somewhere in the back of his brain, neurons attempted to fire off.

"So good you could join—"

Once the relevant information solidified in the part of his consciousness that was not besieged by arousal or drunkenness, his eyes shot open. A surge of adrenaline immediately pushed all sensations to the periphery. Looking down, he immediately recognized the mop of pale hair beneath his chin.

"Oebe! What are you doing?" he cried out, which caused her to lean up and meet his gaze.

"I wanted to get closer to you," she announced matter-of-factly. "I observed as you attempted to get closer to other women downstairs and wanted to experience why you were so interested in making new friends."

"But—"

"I was led to believe that people acquired intimacy by lying with one another. Or, so that is the beginning of the process as I can piece together. I was not provided more details as Prae and Peter chose to avoid the conversation. I assumed that if anyone knew the procedure in its entirety, it would be you."

"Hey, wait a minute! Are you…" Cal moaned as he rose, picked up the diminutive woman underneath her armpits and moved her to the side. "You know what… Forget it. I'm not sure what you mean by 'getting closer.'"

"I was led to believe that friends become closer by sharing physical events, up to lying with one another."

"Well… it isn't just lying *with*… oh, what the devil am I saying?"

"Do you not want to be closer to me?" In the room's limited light, her hazel eyes seemed to glitter, as if moisture was collecting along their surface.

"It's, well, that's not the thing. Friends can be closer without, well, *that*." With the sudden turn of events, Cal had largely sobered up and any arousal he felt was gone. "Friends can just talk and learn about one another to be closer."

"Then why were you trying to touch and kiss those women? Did you not want to be friends with them?"

"I, uh, well, you could say that I wanted to be *more* than friends."

"I'm not entirely sure what that means. Would not being more than friends also require being friends?"

Cal grumbled. Without waiting for a response, Oebe continued. "Peter said that you wanted to dance. A dance I am not familiar with. What is the 'dance with no pants?' Do I need to take your pants off? I am not wearing pants, so yours would be the only one we need to remove."

"Nononononono!" He held out a hand.

"Why? Would this not make me your friend?" A pained look crossed her face.

"You're already a good friend, Oebe." *I'm gonna kill Peter and Prae for this,* he thought to himself. "But, what you're thinking about is, well, sex."

"Sex? What does anatomy have to do with this?"

"Not, just the body parts. Intercourse. You do know what that is, right? Oh, god, why are we *really* having this conversation?"

"Prae said 'I say let Reeger explain this to her. It's his fault we're in this situation.' That is why we are having this conversation." Her imitation of Prae's cadence was spot-on.

"Sounds about right." Cal got up from the bed and offered a hand to Oebe, which she took. "Let me get you back to your room."

"No need. I am only three doors down the hall." Once on her feet, she tugged at her robe to straighten out the creases.

Cal escorted her from his room and watched from the open doorway as she trotted away. Once she disappeared, he rubbed at his temples and stumbled back to bed.

A heavy cloud cover lingered over the skyline and obscured any sign of moonlight. Only the streetlamps at major intersections offered a faint radiance. Moisture in the air grew palpable as the temperature slowly dropped; a mounting chill forced those loitering outside to seek shelter. Though Viisibourg's nightlife was known for its rollicking nature, the bitter shift in seasonal weather proved enough to clear the streets.

By the time Sert Egeto had finished with an extended round of drinking and gambling, he found himself staggering through the familiar deserted alleyways. While he was not one to usually head home straight from work, tonight had been an unexpectedly-long evening. After a few successful bets on cards, by which he tripled his pocket cash, Sert felt charitable and ordered an extra round of drinks for his table-mates.

Though he knew he should return to the warm meal and expectant wife that waited for him, he just couldn't pull himself away. Not with the drunken delusion that luck was on his side. It wasn't until he overplayed his hands and lost the next two rounds that he knew it was time to depart. To make the best of a night gone sour, he thought to enjoy that meal and then his spouse, whether she was interested in her duties or not.

Sert eventually arrived at the A-frame, single-story cottage that he shared with his wife of four years. The trip from the bar was not long, but in the cloudy night and through the haze of one too many drinks, it took him longer than expected. Even then, he cocked his head to one side when he noticed that none of the lights were lit.

With a disgruntled shake, he pawed at his pockets for almost a minute until he unearthed his keychain. He jammed a key into the lock and gave it a turn. After a nudge of his shoulder, he barged into the house. As the door slammed behind him, he began to grope about for the toggle on the nearby wall.

"Gelhda!" His words slurred as he bellowed. "Gelhda! Where'n the hell is the light switch? Woman, get out here and help me find the light! Why'n the hell is it so dark in here? Bitch, have you already gone to bed? Best get your—"

"Gelhda is no longer here," a deep male voice spoke up from the darkness, which quickly cut off his diatribe. Shocked, Sert stood upright as a lamp on the other side of the room flickered and cast a sallow glow on the sitting room. His keys slipped from his hand and dropped to the ground with a clang of metal on wood.

Seated in Sert's favorite armchair was a large man of Thosan descent, dressed in a cashmere kaftan, reclining casually as his hands rested on the arms. He looked curiously familiar with his dark skin tone and coarse facial features.

"Who'n the hell're you?" Sert spat out as he lurched forward. Despite his elevated adrenaline, the extra drinks were doing a number on his sense of balance. "What'n the hell'r you doing here? I'mma call the law on you if'n you don't get outta here."

"You might have occasion to recall my given name. Apello Satonay."

As the words sunk in, Sert's eyes widened.

Apello launched from the chair and lunged forward. As Sert tripped over his own feet and spilled backwards, Apello caught him by the sleeve of his shirt. With a sharp tug, Apello yanked him upwards, only to drive a fist into Sert's face before dropping him to the floor with a thud.

Sert could feel the blood oozing from his nose as he lay flat on his back. The coldness of the wood tiles felt comforting against the buzzing in his skull. Before he could gather himself, Sert was unceremoniously hauled back to his feet.

Instead of striking him again, Apello spun the man about and flung him into the recently-vacated armchair. As he slammed into the seat, Sert could feel the frame of pine beams beneath the upholstery groan against the impact.

"Wha-what is this about?" Sert sputtered.

"I think you know well enough," Apello leaned in and glared at the smaller man.

"Gelhda? B-but I was always a go—"

Apello backhanded Sert across the cheek before he could finish.

"Good to her?" At that point, Apello's teeth were clenched. He snarled his words like a wolf snapping at prey. "By what metric do you measure that? Tell me, from the moment she became yours, how many times did you beat on her? Over the span of four years? How many times did you lash out at her? Give her a black eye? Bloody her nose? I take you for the kind of man who cannot get an erection without hitting a woman beforehand. Prove your mastery over her with violence before you can get the blood flowing to your vile member. Two, three violent events a week. You drink a lot, so maybe even more. Perhaps you only hit her once, perhaps three or four times if you were feeling particularly vicious. Let's call it two blows at a time, four to six in a week. I'm probably giving you the benefit of the doubt here, but I figure you've managed to rack up a sizable tally. Gelhda would never confirm the breadth of your crimes, as if she was protecting me from the truth. Or, that she was protecting you. Want to make a guess as to what your final count comes to?"

"What? Are you mad?"

As Apello towered over him, Sert's only thought was to clench the plush arms of his chair tightly.

"There is always the possibility that I am." Apello cracked a smile more sinister than humorous. "Not going to hazard a guess? Not a betting man? That seems so unlike you. Well, in my estimation—and mind you I'm not good with numbers—that comes out to twenty-five a month, rounded down for your benefit. Never say that I wasn't fair. Over a year, that number grows to three hundred. Over the span of your marriage? Roughly twelve hundred."

"What's the point in all this?" Sert blurted. While agitated at the unexpected situation, Apello's imposing figure kept him locked in his seat.

"Your magic number, *my friend*. It's twelve hundred."

"What does that even mean?"

"It's the number of strikes you're due. And it's time to pay up." Apello leaned in and drove his armored elbow into Sert's forehead, which bounced his skull off of the top of the chair. "Three."

"W-wait a m-minute," Sert stammered as he held a hand out. The other quickly went to the burgeoning welt on his forehead. "Y-you know you won't get away with this. I'll g-go to the constables. If-if you stop now and tell me where my wife is, I'll forget this ever happened."

"Four." Apello stomped on his foot. Sert tried to hold back a scream as the heel of Apello's boot broke two toes. He then grabbed him by the collar and again dragged him to his feet. With his face only inches from Sert's, Apello spoke in hushed tones. "I've sent Gelhda away. She will return to Thosa Prathvi. She will return to being Gelhda Satonay. And, maybe, one day she won't be haunted by the memories of her time in your presence."

"You can't! She's my wi—"

"Five." Apello lifted a knee to his stomach. The blow was vicious enough that Sert was briefly raised off of the ground. Before Sert could even recover from the attack, Apello was speaking again. "Do not think I don't know by what means you came into possession of my sister. You lack the capacity to find a woman all your own, so you paid for her. You scraped together what little money you had to your name and you paid a visit to the slave markets of Geinnburg. She was fresh off the boat, having been abducted from her native land, and you spent money with the sole purpose of owning a life. She is not your wife. She is only a possession to you."

Before Sert could respond to the accusation, Apello flung him to the ground. Apello then straddled him, with his knees jammed into Sert's shoulders, and withdrew one of his blades. As he bent over and grabbed the downed man by the jaw, he spoke coldly.

"I need you silent for what's about to come."

Except for Gelhda, Sert's quiet wife who was now missing, no one knew of Apello or his nightly visit.

13

Ever since the An-Sebban and her entourage had departed from Natx Hollow, Quillin was confident about his fortunes, almost cocky. Between his own thesis and the eventual upload of supporting data to the Athenaeum's Central Archives, he felt sure about a pending promotion within the Bureau. Maybe he would even be allowed to head his own expedition.

The decision to focus on the aged fresco had been a relatively easy one to make. The mural room was one of the first discoveries once they descended to the subterranean structure. Rather than gamble on something undiscovered, he had jumped at the opportunity. It was a sure bet. Now, with so many of his fellows flocking around him, most of whom he knew hoped to garner some degree of success merely through association, he was almost giddy.

The one thing that soured the experience was the recent departure of Mathester. Quillin had always enjoyed the competition between himself and Peter. Without the ability to rub his victory in Peter's face, it didn't feel completely realized. With Mathester's sudden leave, where he curiously departed to escort the An-Sebban to Attis

Grove, Quillin's celebration felt suspended.

He took breaks in the temple's entryway, pensively watching the empty courtyard for any sign of life. The occasional lizard scuttled across the sand-blasted stone from one sliver of shade to the next. He had never been one to remain above-ground during the day as the blistering heat wore on him. Even now, he was sweating profusely and wished that he had shaved the peach fuzz along his jawline before starting his day.

As he squinted through the midday light, Quillin picked out a dark form on the distant ridge. Delight quickly faded as Quillin realized that it was not Peter. While he watched the robes flutter in the wind, Quillin wondered if the visitor was one of the Harenas. The hood draped over the visitor's face was unlike the traditional red-and-white checkered kufeya, and he had never seen Harenas travel alone.

"Walk away," Quillin pleaded under his breath.

When the hooded form began to descend the steps of the distant wooden scaffolding, he swore to himself. If Apello was around instead of off with Peter, Quillin would've been on his way to retrieve the paid muscle. This was the exact reason the Thosan was under contract. Instead, Quillin leaned against the archway and waited for the visitor to reach the valley floor.

The draped transient finally stepped foot on the dusty ground and made a bee-line for the temple entrance. Quillin drew in a long breath, mustered his best smile and accepted that he could not avoid the interaction.

"Can I help you?" Quillin called out. With cautious steps, he slowly approached the unexpected visitor, who came to a halt in the center of the courtyard.

"I hope so," a muffled voice replied, the consonants raspy.

"My apologies," Quillin continued. "I guess introductions are in order. Edward Quillin of the Archaeology Bureau."

"Raxus." The response was terse.

Quillin placed a hand over his brow to block the worst of the sun as he drew within a few paces of the visitor. His breath caught as he saw the expressionless faceplate hidden in the hood's shadow. Even obstructed by the cowl, sunlight reflected from the glossy nose and chin that jutted out beneath the fabric.

"What brings you out to the middle of the Quartewuste?" Quillin asked as he tried to distract himself from the man's mask. "Not many come out here if they don't have to."

"Looking for someone. Said to be heading to Natx Hollow. I was pointed this way. Wanted to see if anyone here spotted him."

"Oh, certainly, we don't usually get visitors but we did have an emissary from the An-Sebban out here not long ago. She left not a week past, at the most."

There was a brief pause, filled with raspy breathing muffled by the metal. "Was she with someone? A man by the name of Reeger?"

"She had a retinue. A pair of bodyguards. One of them was a guy, but I didn't catch his name. Sorry, but when an An-Sebban arrives, we in the Bureau tend to forget anything else." Quillin grinned sheepishly.

"A pair?"

"Yes," Quillin responded with a nod. "A man and a woman. The woman looked to be the more intimidating of the two. Not sure why the Athenaeum hired out two people unless they thought the An-Sebban was in danger. Not my money, not my concern I say."

"And you say they're already gone?"

"Yes, one of my co-workers, Peter Mathester, borrowed a transport and took them east to Attis Grove. Wanted to see about coordinating their transit back to Greater Decedistadt. He headed out on one of our Arhkady G-12s, no more than a week ago. In fact, he probably should be back already. Likely got delayed waiting for supplies before his return. Sometimes the general store in Attis Grove doesn't have everything in town and the poor lad dispatched for the pickup has to wait for a special shipment to arrive before they can get away."

"An Arhkady G-12?"

"Oh, yeah, the Bureau rented out a couple for our use while we were here. Big tires with deep treads and a heavy steel frame seem pretty good for navigating the desert. You can see one of them right… over… there."

As he torqued his torso to direct Raxus' attention, Quillin motioned to the north. Through cracks between the decaying structures, Raxus picked out a four-wheel craft a few yards up the slope that led up out of the valley.

Once Quillin's attention was drawn away, his head bobbing back and forth as he tried to spy between crumbling edifices, Raxus reached within his robes and produced a curled blade; anyone familiar with the region would have recognized it as one employed by the Harenas. The aged weapon showed years of use: the steel was nicked in a few places along the front curve and the leather-wrapped handle was darkened and discolored from its owner's sweaty grip. With a flick of his gloved hand, the knife swept wide and cut across Quillin's throat.

Raxus stepped aside as an arc of blood spurted into the air and splattered on the sand-dusted tiles. As his eyes widened, Quillin placed his hands across his throat in a vain attempt to staunch the bleeding. In less than a minute, he wavered and fell to his knees.

Without a word, Raxus dropped the blade and departed the way he came, leaving a single set of footprints in the shifting sands.

Quillin's body would be discovered hours later with the knife left on the ground by his feet. The on-site Bureau members eventually identified it as a ceremonial hunting weapon of the Harenas. This only served to generate a terrified gossip that spread like disease amongst the crew. Once advised of the situation, Master Contrell began to contemplate plans of prematurely ending the expedition. Even if Apello was there to serve his duties, any unprovoked attack from the Harenas was enough sign that their stay was overlong.

Raxus would eventually arrive in Attis Grove late in

the evening with an eye for the owner of the local general store.

14

Central to the sweeping plains of the Vilfdonum Steepe, there were many transit routes that led in and out of Viisibourg. Originating from Attis Grove, the Nria Highway looped around the Clockwork City before progressing on a rolling eastward track through the hilly plains toward the distant Siamsoth Mountains. Bearing south was the Nairt Rail Line, which served as a major connection for supply distribution between Viisibourg and Ilgyngate.

As they travelled east, the sight of the looming mountain range drew Prae's attention. The Siamsoth was a sprawling chain that partitioned the lush timberlands of the Seitsweald from the eastern coast and surrounding Haitwilds. Running well over two thousand miles in length from the austral shores of the Ninse Moors, the range eventually curled westward as it crossed the N'tirna Lakes and Zevent Bay, as they eventually terminated along the southernmost edge of Zehngrad's frost-bitten savannahs.

Much of the trip was spent in relative peace and quiet. While Prae was focused on their destination, both Cal and Apello seemed absorbed on where they had been. With his attention on the road, Peter only managed small glimpses of his travel-mates. One time he saw Cal and Oebe's gazes meet. Immediately, the pair looked away, both blushing.

After a meal break at a rest stop just off of the highway, they passed into the lush forest of the Seitsweald and picked up the winding trade route of Righan's Path. Swallowed up by the overgrown woodlands that spread for hundreds of miles, the two-lane road led northward where it would eventually meet the Pontam-Petram, a stretch of land that connected the Seitsweald to Zehngrad.

After scouring the maps Peter had brought, Prae advised that their destination would be in an unpopulated stretch of the forest to the north. During their trek from Viisibourg, Prae had pored over the regional charts as she constantly provided directions that would lead them to Ala'ydin. Peter often nodded appreciatively; he had long ago given up on explaining that it was best to remain on major motorways as long as possible.

It was clear to Peter as he patiently listened that Prae had an idea of where Ala'ydin should be, as she often referenced the geographical coordinates right down to the minute. Since there were no major cities or marked courses in the vicinity of their destination, Peter expected to eventually be forced off-road. When they were almost 100 miles south of the jagged mountain tops that marked the entrance of the Pontam-Petram, they left the paved roadway and forged a path across the dense woodlands.

Progress through the wilds became slow, even more so as the copses became thick and tangled. Sunlight came at a premium as the canopy grew thicker, the trees merging into a mass of leafy branches. The transport was sturdy enough to handle the dirt pathways, but once the woods became too thick to pass, they were obliged to continue on foot. This decision came with dissent from Cal, but when assurances were made by Prae that they were only a few miles away, he begrudgingly agreed.

As they left the vehicle behind, the jingle of steel caught Peter's attention. Slung over Prae's shoulder was the canvas sack, filled to bursting with her armor. He wondered why she brought it with her, but knew better than to ask. Peter hoped that their arrival at Ala'ydin would somehow loosen her tongue.

Except for the occasional fauna, including a deer that was scared out of the underbrush as they drew near, there were few signs of life within the forest. He had heard that, except for the occasional recluse, isolationist or naturalist on expedition, the Seitsweald was largely uninhabited. That any of the sprawling sixteen million acres was mapped served as a testament to those dedicated to such a task. Except for Dirx Gardens in the south, there was few civilized structures in the timberlands that abutted the distant mountain range.

Hours into their hike, they happened upon a winding gorge carved by a dwindling river. After a pause to discuss their course, the group descended into the lush ravine, which was no less than twenty meters deep at its shallowest point. While the stream snaked through the valley, signs along the canyon walls indicated that this had once been a much larger tributary, maybe as recently as a few dozen years ago. Except for a few tense moments when the loose soil gave underfoot, the group made it to the riverside safely.

As they hiked along the rocky edge of the river, Prae motioned to a rise in the distance. Beyond a bend in the valley appeared a sharp peak above the surrounding earthen ledges. Nearly camouflaged by a dense layer of foliage, the diminutive hilltop seemed to rise straight out of the riverbed. The surrounding tree-line was that of an old-growth forest which soared hundreds of meters into the air.

"By all accounts it should be up ahead," Prae announced as she picked up her pace, emboldened by the discovery. "Our best bet would be to start a more comprehensive search over there. The entrance is sure to be hidden amongst the brush."

At this, Cal spoke up. "So, you guys left this place out in the middle of nowhere with the hopes no one would walk across it? Did it not occur to the greatest minds of your time that someone might stumble across this place? 'cause camping in the great outdoors is a thing that people do. Like there's gear and all for it. It's an industry in which people make a living. Hiking, backpacking, spelunking and all that outdoorsy shit. Or so I hear. Consider it second-hand info as I'm not one for a bed made of dirt and rocks."

"Shan't be an issue," Prae responded tersely without looking to him. "You'll have to trust me on this."

"We've been doing a lot of that recently," Cal said under his breath. Out of the corner of his eye, he spotted Apello as the man nodded. The two men shared a brief smile.

"Have you been here before?" Peter inquired aloud as he struggled to keep up. His breathing was ragged and his hair was pasted to his scalp. He had already removed his vest, which was now over one shoulder.

"Ala'ydin? Twice, but the last visit was some time ago. I know of where the entrance *should* be, but the topography has undergone a severe transition since then. This forest? It's grown up around the region since my last foray. My recollection was that this all used to be farmland, far as the eye could see, but that no longer seems to be true."

"How long ago was 'since then'?" Peter asked as he labored. Every stumble on loose soil caused him to fall even further behind.

"Not entirely certain. Once I gain access to the Repository within Ala'ydin, I'll be able to better gauge the date and place how long it's been since then."

"Sounds like a deflection to me," Cal sniped as he rolled his eyes. "And, trust me, I know what a deflection is. You know, at some point, you might consider giving us a sliver of something that might be mistaken for information. We did follow you all the way out here."

Prae shot Cal a look that caused a chill to run down Peter's spine. After a few seconds, she drew a breath and softly shook her head.

Peter tripped as his boot slipped on a patch of wet stones along the riverbed. With a clumsy waggle of his arms he was able to maintain his balance. Once he wiped the sweat from his eyes, he caught sight of his party as they pressed on without him.

"Wait up for a moment!" Peter called, placing his hands on his hips. When neither Prae nor Apello even paused, he groaned. "Or not."

He threw a dismissive wave before he kneeled down and scooped a palm-full of water from the creek. He took a long sip, which felt especially refreshing. On some level, he knew that the water itself wasn't special, but in his parched state, it was the most pleasant thing he could imagine. A second handful was splashed up into his flushed face.

As he remained hunched over with the water dripping from the tip of his nose and lips, he began to draw in long breaths. Unlike Prae, who appeared to have limitless energy, the trek had worn him out and left him badly in need of a break. Apello and, to a lesser degree, Cal managed to keep in step with her. Oebe showed no signs of exhaustion, even despite her smaller frame.

"Peter," Oebe unexpectedly spoke from behind him, which caused him to flinch.

"Yes, Oebe?" He slowly stood upright and brushed the damp strands of hair out of his face. His aching muscles made him wish for a long cool dip in the river.

"These markings are familiar," she announced, which drew his eye to her outstretched hand. A few yards away stood a solid cliff face, mostly hidden beneath the thick growth that bounded the meandering stream. Between the leafy boughs was a flat surface, etched with vertical marks, none longer than three inches. Peter's brow creased until he made the connection.

"The lines!" he blurted.

"They are analogous in pattern and dimension as the ones at—"

"Yes! The Blue Room in Natx Hollow? Certainly." Peter cupped his hands, turned upriver, and yelled with what strength he had left. "Over here! I think we've found something!"

For a second, he considered shouting again, but once the distant forms came to a stop along the rocky banks, he dropped his hands. Instead of waiting for their return, Peter pressed on through the brush, pausing a few feet from the wall of stone. As he leaned in to examine the markings, he felt Oebe sidle up beside him.

"These are of a similar chirography as the markings at Natx Hollow. The assumption that this is some form of written language is wholly with merit," she announced unprovoked. "Translation, though, would require additional data and theoretically some form of cipher. It would be in our interest to see if Prae has access to such information, or if something of this nature can be accessed within Ala'ydin."

At this, Peter turned his head and looked to Oebe. He cocked a brow and began to say something when he was interrupted by the rustling of nearing footsteps. Prae burst through the underbrush and approached where they stood waiting. Apello and Cal were not far behind.

"What is it…" Prae trailed off. "Oh, how fortuitous."

Peter graciously moved aside as Prae marched up to the cliff face and held out her left arm. She hummed with a note that, to Peter's ears, implied relief.

With a spin of her open hand, a violet circle, barely a

foot across in diameter, formed midair. Even though he had no idea how she could perform the act, Peter was no longer shocked by the act of semanifesture.

A few flicks of her fingertips created a pair of crooked lines, immediately accented by a trio of dots and a sharply-angled curve. After a few seconds of hovering, the light flickered as it sank into the wall. The rows of etched lines now glowed with the same purplish-red hue.

As the seconds passed, a rectangular outline, roughly 100 inches tall by 50 wide, began to appear along the surface.

"I'm getting some kinda déjà vu about this," Cal spoke as he huddled by a tree trunk a few yards away. One of his hands rested on the handle of his revolver as if the weapon would help him. "Is some kinda futuristic stow-away bed gonna flop down here any second?"

"Not exactly, though the process of semanifesture energies for both are not dissimilar."

With a blinding flash, the once-glowing section disappeared. Beyond the opening was a vaulted corridor that descended into the darkness. Except for the sunlight, which splayed across the tile floor, the interior seemed to be lit by a faint blue glow that emanated from within. The details of the passageway itself remained obscured.

"I, uh…" Cal stammered as he stepped forward. "I got a feeling I don't even want an explanation about what just happened. Like you could say 'Poof, magic!' and I'd be okay with that."

"Well then," Prae began as she looked back with a grin

on her lips. "Poof, magic! Or whatever that means. Shall we continue?"

"Rather than fret over things you cannot control, you could always remain out here," Apello suggested as he moved forward to join Peter and Prae at the opening. "I have the distinct feeling things will not become more comprehensible the further in we traverse."

Cal shrugged his shoulders before he sullenly followed.

Beyond the doorway was a staircase that descended a few dozen meters to an arched hallway. The surfaces of the corridor had the reflective quality of tarnished metal. Geometric shapes of various sizes and shapes lined the walls in a pattern of columns so complex that at first it seemed like random decoration.

Once away from the brilliance of the outside light, cerulean radiance leaked from cracks between the sections of wall. Peter paused every now and then to look in closer, but without a firm understanding of how the construction had been created, he came away even more confused. It was as if the walls themselves were built over the light source.

As he was about to pose a query to Prae, Cal interrupted his train of thought as he called out. His voice echoed in the vaulted hall tinnily. "I know this is probably a loaded question, but do you know how any of this works? The weird architecture, the magical disappearing door, the… semanifestures, was it?"

"Not really."

"But I thought you was all better than us savages?" Cal spit the barbed comment her way.

"Do you know how everything in your world works?" she fired back.

Cal bit at his lip as he fell silent.

Before too long, the corridor terminated at a circular, domed court, only a dozen yards in diameter. On the other side of the room was an alcove set into the far wall. With space for a lone person to stand, the recess was circular, like a tube of metal attached to the main room.

"Hold a moment," Prae requested, opposite the empty cubicle.

"What is it?" Peter inquired as he studied the surfaces. Though he had to squint, he found the area curiously blank. The odd design of the corridor walls was abandoned for a simpler, more utilitarian design.

"I'll need to change into my suit to enable entrance." She set the duffle on the ground as she slipped out of the kibr and robe, which left only the black bodysuit on.

"What? Got your employee badge attached to the breastplate?" Cal cracked.

After letting out another sigh, she only commented "Something to that effect," before she knelt to strap the greaves across her legs. As each piece was laid over the next, small sparks of azure light flashed.

Without pulling up her hair, Prae slipped the ornate helmet over her head. Strands of her copper mane stuck out from the bottom edge as it flowed halfway down her back. She gave the terrifying faceplate a tug before moving on.

She strapped the scabbard to her hip and withdrew the

weapon. A flick of her wrist caused the blade to extend. With her free hand, she produced a circle of red light above the blade's forte. Prae then folded her thumb into her palm, extended her fingers and drew four diagonal lines across the halo. She swept her hand downward, forcing the energy to sink into the steel as it drifted away from the crossguard. A series of symbols, composed of interconnected angular lines, pulsed to life as they burned in varying shades of scarlet.

With her weapon prepared, she strode forward and passed her open palm over an adjacent wall panel. A familiar aquamarine shape quickly appeared midair. Prae ran her fingers over the pane and tapped at illuminated symbols with certainty. Once finished, she stepped back, as sapphire and gray vapors began to fill the alcove.

Pinprick lasers from a tiny hole atop the archway came to life. As they crisscrossed her armored form, Prae stood still until the thin crimson beams ceased their inspection.

Without so much as a word, she faced her waiting travel-mates.

"So, who shall go first? Due to the nature of the procedure, I must be the last." Her head turned slightly. Even though he could not see her eyes, Peter could tell she was gazing directly at Oebe, who stood quietly with her arms behind her back, enthralled by the spectacle.

"I shall," Apello announced as he strode forward. With a hand placed on one of the blades beneath his clothes, he charged into the soft blue mist and spun about to face his compatriots. After a pulse of white light filled the alcove, filaments of color began to permeate the air, like sparks of lighting jumping from cloud to cloud. Within seconds, the room was awash in hues of coral, orange and tan that throbbed with a life of their own. Swaths of blue spun like threads in the weave of vapor. Another flash of white sparked, for seconds longer than the first, which obscured all detail from within.

Once the brightness dissipated, Apello no longer stood in the alcove.

"Do I even want to ask where he went?" Cal's kvetching was even starting to wear on Oebe, who shot him a glare. Peter struggled to keep a burst of laughter contained.

"Be patient," was Prae's response. She reached over and nudged Oebe by the shoulder. "Go on ahead. Apello will be waiting for you on the other side."

Oebe looked up and nodded before she followed Apello's lead. After the initial sparkle, she was surrounded by a mélange of silver, white, cream and turquoise before she, too, was gone.

"Cal?" Prae beckoned.

"Okay..." Cal groaned as he slowly marched inside the alcove. He closed his eyes as the first burst went off. As colors began to clarify from the muddled mass, Prae stepped forward and raised her sword.

Noticing the shift in her stance, Peter recoiled.

The colors within the chamber eventually coalesced into sharply-defined strands of mauve, dark blue and coral. Prae let out an uncertain hum and lowered her blade. Her posture softened. After another blinding flare, Cal was missing from the cubicle.

Prae seemed to let out a breath as her shoulders sagged. With a flick of her arm, the glowing symbols along the face dissolved, like embers dashed to the wind, and the blade withdrew to its original state. She slid it back into the scabbard and looked to Peter, who eyed her warily.

"What was *that* about?" Peter inquired. "Your so-called security measures?"

"Yes. It's the same as what I did to you in Attis Grove."

"Yeah, not exactly the same, I see. And if you didn't like what you saw?" He cast a glance to the sheathed weapon at her side.

Without a pause to temper her response, she replied. "I would be forced to strike them down. For the safety of us all. When you see what is on the other side, you'll understand."

Where Peter had been excited about coming to Ala'ydin, he was now beginning to understand some of Cal's pessimism. Prae's cavalier attitude about killing one of their party made his flesh crawl. "And Oebe? You sent her through, no fuss, no muss."

"I didn't want her to witness what I might have to do to Cal."

"And Apello before her? You assumed he was fine?"

"No, he caught me off-guard. I was not expecting him to charge in like he did."

"Then you don't know him like I do," Peter said as he shook his head. "So, I'm not certain why I should step into the light. What's to say you don't strike me down when I'm not looking."

"You've already come this far. I know it wasn't done completely out of the kindness of your heart. I saw the threads of color in the semanifesture. While there is plenty of good within you, there is a flash of desire for success in there. The hope that within Ala'ydin lies something to be leveraged for your own personal gain. Would you really stop when you're so close to your perceived goal?"

Embarrassed by having his motives addressed so bluntly, Peter looked away. Even though he could not see her eyes from behind the glossy pearl orbs, he tried to avoid her stare. "So, at some point, are you going to explain why you're even allowing me within such an important location? It doesn't seem congruent with keeping this secret. Especially considering you're not deluding yourself about mine, or anyone else's, motives."

"Yes, but not at this instant. Let's hurry up. The others have waited long enough." With a wave of her hand, she ushered him along.

After a few seconds, Peter relented and stepped into the alcove. He wondered if he should turn around. Perhaps if he did, he would see Prae withdrawing her weapon yet again. Instead, he just stared at the wall as the colored vapors began to shift. Even though he expected it, the bright flare of white light still caused him to flinch.

15

As the overpowering brilliance dispelled and Peter's vision began to clear, his entire body was overcome by paresthesia. It was as if every inch of his skin had fallen asleep all at once and now the blood was returning. The sensation, though brief, proved maddening as his muscles locked up tightly. Nerve endings flared to life, providing a sensory rush that his mind struggled to process.

"Here you go," Apello's words were a beacon to the disoriented Peter. The Thosan reached into the alcove and seized him by the arm. Apello's tight grip sent a shockwave to his brain. As if expecting the reaction, Apello held firm. Even with Apello's support, Peter stumbled as he stepped onto an octagonal platform.

"Thank you. I didn't expect… well, I don't think I *had* any expectations." Peter's hand went to his forehead, which was clammy and dotted with sweat. "But it certainly wasn't that."

"It will take a few seconds to pass," Apello noted.

"And the others?"

Apello gestured to the other side of the entrance, where

Oebe and Cal waited. Oebe appeared unaffected. Cal, on the other hand, looked a bit green, as if his morning meal was considering making an unwanted reappearance.

As Peter began to gain his bearings, the details of his surroundings came into focus. He now found himself in a man-made facility within a vast cavern of indeterminate dimensions. The quartet waited on one of a series of raised platforms connected by walkways of hexagonal brass-plated tiles. Flanking the elevated pathways were mill-finished steel railings arranged in diagonal patterns that reminded Peter of Prae's earlier displays of semanifesture.

Much like the entryway, the vast chamber's light radiated from between creases in the panels of the exterior walls.

Mounted to the stage were four identical alcoves. Within each tube of stone and steel stood ancient mechanical constructs fashioned in the likeness of man. Just over seven feet in height, the statue-like machines were layered in bulky segmented plates, like a pill bug molded from hammered bronze. Their exteriors were tarnished and coated in a dense layer of dust from ages of disuse. Between the sections of armor was a complex series of gears interlinked to a skeleton of metal rods. Mounted atop each torso was a head, cast in the fearsome visage of a falcon topped with a pschent of gold. The backwards-swept crown of feathers was molded from oval strips of iridescent brass.

"Well, that's, uh, certainly terrifying," Peter commented, unable to look away from the immobile guardians that loomed over him.

Having taken notice of Peter's fear, Cal spoke up. "Yeah,

seeing them the first time's either a life-affirming moment or a pants-shitting one. Guess it depends on the type of person you are."

"Then, I take it you'll be in need of new trousers?" Peter replied sharply. He glanced at Apello and assured him with a nod that he was fine on his own.

Cal's response was a bark of laughter.

Peter gazed beyond his immediate surroundings to the vast cavern about them. Multiple pathways angled away from the central aisle. This caused Peter to postulate that there were several chambers deeper within. Between the darkened haze in the air and the dim illumination, he could not ascertain where these avenues led. For a moment, he contemplated the scale of Ala'ydin.

As he gazed over the side of the nearby railing, he observed a faint mist that swirled in the almost-imperceptible flow of air throughout the site. Peter struggled to name the specific colors contained within the vapors, though there were flickers of iridescent copper and bronze that shimmered before being lost in the murky haze.

Peter shivered as a chill ran through his body. The air itself was thick with a cool moisture that almost adhered to his skin. Peter also noticed metallic odors in the air.

From the whistling breeze below them, Peter wondered how deep the cavern was. He patted at his pockets for a coin; the delay before impact would allow him to make a fair estimate of how far it fell.

A brilliant spark of white caused him to glance over his shoulder. Prae strode from the alcove and met the others as they gathered on the far side of the platform. As she came to a halt before Cal and Oebe, who remained propped against the railing, Prae removed her helmet and tossed her hair with a flip of her head.

"Where to now, chief?" Cal inquired.

"Further in." Her attention quickly turned to the walkway. Without a pause to catch her breath, she charged forward, forcing the others to give chase. Cal swore under his breath as he prodded Oebe along with a hand on her shoulder. After a wary glance at the statues, Apello followed, one hand tucked carefully behind his back.

"So, what exactly *is* Ala'ydin?" Peter inquired. His focus was split between the wholly unique atmosphere of their surroundings and the path on which Prae led them. "I know you said it was a central location where vital information was stored, but beyond that, I cannot place the original intent of this site. The architecture is by and large alien to structures and sites currently on record."

Prae hesitated, as if reluctant to answer. "This was our final habitat. Where the last of us took refuge in the final years. And as such, to my knowledge, it is now the only locale that remains standing. Over the eons, the other sites were lost to the elements or time, or to the machinations of those whose judgment can be called into doubt. The Tower of Noth, the Coastal Atlesdotor, the Aerie at Celentia. All evidence of these once-grand city-states no longer exists, erased as future civilizations rose to power and claimed the land as their own."

"How long ago would you estimate that it was first established?" The follow-up was purely instinctual, a habit born from his schooling and time with the Bureau.

There was a pause. "Long before I was born. Well prior to the establishment of the house of Ganvelt."

Without missing a beat, Peter continued. "How old would you be?"

"Ugh. Man, even I know not to ask a woman that!" Cal's groan was loud.

"I think this one time, such common courtesies can be waived," Apello interjected, to which Peter nodded appreciatively.

"I won't be able to firmly state such details until we've reached the Repository. Until I've had an opportunity to run specific queries. I'm not entirely certain how much time has elapsed since my last foray in the Waking State. And even then, I did not openly traverse amongst the living since the early days of the third era."

"You mentioned that before. The phrase 'third era,' that is. What do you mean by that, exactly?"

"In due time. It will be easier to explain once we arrive at the Repository."

"Deflect, deflect, deflect," Cal scoffed with a snort.

Prae glared at him over her shoulder. "Fine… by a rough estimate of my time spent in the Waking State, I would guess I'm somewhere around three hundred and eighty, give or take a decade. The time invested in hibernation on top of that would prove a far more challenging task to nail down off the top of my head. Information within the Repository would allow for more accurate estimates."

At this, Peter gasped as he placed a hand over his mouth. Cal frowned before continuing.

"What-what are you? I mean, no one lives that long."

"Not anymore," she responded matter-of-factly. "We were once called Progenitors by those in the third era who became aware of our existence. Not sure how they were enlightened, but it was recorded by Naucilous that we were known of and worshipped as demi-gods. I can't imagine that went over too well with some of my kind. There was evidence that our existence became known during the end of the second era as well, but it wasn't until the third era that such revelations became an issue."

"What name *did* your people go by?" Peter asked.

"Scientifically? Homo sapiens. Humans."

Beyond the towering guardians that welcomed them, Peter saw no unique sculpture or artistry. The architectural choices present hinted that the location had not been intended for public use. As best as he could determine, it was an installation for a specific purpose, be it military or administrative.

Already tired from the long day of travel, Peter's feet began to drag as they continued. The path had stretched two miles before a destination came into view. In the distance, he could make out a lone archway in the far wall.

Once through the doorway, Peter hesitated; the path

broke off in opposite directions. To their left was a meeting chamber that featured a steel-framed, u-shaped table with a marble top. After a moment, Peter felt an absence by his side; Prae had already guided the others to the right and descended a circular staircase.

With a hand against the railing, Peter hurried down the concrete steps. At the bottom of the stairwell was a corridor, roughly fifty yards in length, which led directly to a lone room. There were no other doorways. The lack of ornamentation or artistry gave him an uneasy feeling.

"We've arrived," Prae announced as she looked over her shoulder.

"The Repository?"

She nodded once before entering. Through the doorless entrance they followed her, coming to a stop only a few steps inside. Prae strode across the chamber until she reached a massive control center along the far wall. Metal-covered consoles featuring angular desktops in a curious juxtaposition were connected to one another via wires and bronze-coated tubing.

A faint pulse of illumination, soft and cold in hue, began to throb from the creases where the walls met the ceiling. As this light grew in intensity, they noticed four metallic structures arranged like step pyramids, each of which stood almost ten feet in height and occupied the four corners of the room. Except for a metal chair beside the central console, there was no sign that the chamber had seen use. Both ceiling and floor were flat, unbroken surfaces that lacked detail. In all the years that Peter had studied ancient locations of one kind or another, the distinct lack of ornamentation struck him as strange, almost off-putting.

Mounted above the complex machinery was a slab of matte black stone enclosed in a thin alloy frame. Across the face of the obsidian board were a series of pinprick holes, arranged in staggered rows from end to end.

Prae dragged the chair to the console as she sat down. Without a word, she swept both palms across the surfaces. For a second, nothing reacted. Prae's countenance never wavered. After she repeated the motion, a flicker of red brushed her hands and the device sprang to life, rattled from slumber.

As a series of light formations flashed, Peter held up a defensive hand over his eyes. Once his vision adjusted, he recognized familiar forms in the configurations. Across the desktop was a pair of matching keyboards and row upon row of toggle switches and buttons composed of warm colors. Above the blackened rectangle, an oversized viewscreen displayed a flurry of lines which scrawled from left to right in what he had come to assume was Prae's written language.

Ignoring curious noises issued, Prae began to diligently tap at the control panels, causing a long string of characters to scroll across the massive display. After a few seconds, she tapped a red icon and leaned back in her seat as if pleased.

"So, is everything as you expected?" Peter asked after the moment of silence. He glanced just as Oebe reached out to run her fingers along the wall. She met his curious eyes and offered a sheepish smile in return.

"Nothing appears out of order," Prae noted without

turning away from the garish spectacle. "I've set the database to run a query. Considering the volume of records to delve into, it might be an investment in time before we have an answer."

"Time seems to be something you have experience with," Apello spoke with a pointed tone.

"Yes, that is truer than you might know." She drew in a long breath with resignation before she ran her fingers across the rubicund keys. "I suppose I owe you some manner of explanation as to how this all came to be. How this situation became what it is today. It's the least I can do for your assistance thus far."

There was a murmur of agreement among the trio of men. Prae swiped her hand across the board, which brought up a timeline that extended for what appeared to be millions of years. Peter could not decipher the minute increments; even if he could translate Prae's written language, he would have been unable to accurately gauge the entire span.

"Let us start at the beginning. We were the first to settle the earth," she began as the screen zoomed to the left-hand side of the chart. As a green marker moved to the right, a crooked line began to waver as it slowly angled upwards. "The first humans to rise from the genetic soup that was the formation of all life on this planet. As expected, it would be hundreds of thousands of years before our people would make all the requisite advances—fire, the wheel, electricity, and eventually semanifestures—to become what we were towards the end. I won't bore you with the finer details; I assume you have some understanding about societal development."

As the marker reached a specific point along the timeline, the peak turned from green to red. It angled downward sharply and plummeted to the zero point along the Y-axis.

"By the year 48,435 of our formal calendar, we as a race had become sterile. Those of us able to breed slowly began to die out as the years grew long. I don't know whether it was the generations of genetic alteration, the modified foodstuffs or the overdependence on highly-specialized medication, but we had done it to ourselves. We exchanged our ability to reproduce for a vastly-extended life span. And it wasn't even a sudden occurrence; more and more of us couldn't breed as the generations passed. Procreation became an anomaly, a miracle of genetic confluence, the duplication of which proved evasive to even the greatest minds. The science community's fight against the looming disaster merely ran out of time."

She paused, as if the revelation weighed heavy.

"I was one of the last generation born among our kind. Both of my parents died young; neither lived to be two hundred. It, uh, it was not unexpected as many of those who were able to breed did so at the cost of their own life span. Medical treatments for expectancy extension were denied to those who could reproduce… well… As the years progressed, our numbers dwindled. At the end, there were only twelve of us."

There was a hitch in her voice, something that Peter had never heard before.

"Before we became so few, our leaders concocted a plan. One that I came to understand had been in the works for generations. They had become resigned to our fate, as if they knew where we were headed and found themselves unable to alter our genetic course. A select few were to enter extended stasis, not unlike cryogenic hibernation, though far less harmful or traumatic than earlier attempts at the technology. Only one of us would be allowed to remain in the Waking State at any given time and only for short intervals. When done, the next person in the cycle would then be awoken from the Dormant State. Out of a hundred thousand, there were twelve chosen. Each of us had a role. Some would observe, record, theorize; others would tinker, prod their projects along. Even on the edge of extinction, there were those of us still toiling over their lifelong projects."

She paused for a moment, before adding "I expect that they first posed the strategy in hopes that a solution could be discovered while we were in stasis. That we would eventually be able to return to a perpetual Waking State. I doubt there was a contingency for the eventuality that we would never be cured. I wonder how many of my kind gave up on any experiments that entailed such a scenario, only to focus on their own preferred distractions."

Peter cleared his throat. "I don't understand. If you said that there was only twelve of you, how did—"

"Mankind repopulate?" Prae interrupted. "Between Na-Exetase and Scroturea, there were concerted efforts to reseed the planet with samples of the genetic material that were stored on record. As I understand it, eugenic historians had recorded earlier genome data along our own evolution. Samples of which were used to seed the gene pool, nudge it in what they deemed was the right direction. From time to time, they would look in to see that the process was making the requisite progress."

She tapped at the keys again, which caused a new entry to appear. As it rose from zero, the blue stroke slowly arced upward, only to dip on occasion before leveling out.

"The second era of man," Prae announced. "As expected, the earth repopulated and began to progress in a manner not unlike our own. From time to time, there were noticeable leaps in their scientific development, as if aided, whether by the intent of my fellows or by their own discovery of our technology. Those potentially responsible never admitted to such actions, likely for their own sake. I was always left to ponder that few of my kind so desired repopulation, a return to our halcyon days, that they ignored the dangers of such interference."

"How so?" As the words left Peter's lips, the wavering blue dropped to near zero, in what would have only been a few centuries.

"Ultimately, I fear one of us handed them the means to their own destruction. Whether it was hubris or carelessness, they were given unearned knowledge that brought themselves to their conclusion." After that, the line eventually trembled as the years passed until it eventually hit zero. The chart progressed for almost a hundred thousand years until an entry, this time green, popped up.

"The third era. It was the last time I walked among man for any length of time. Let us see how they fared."

With a flick of her palm on a circular icon, Prae caused the timeline to zip forward. The jade stroke vacillated, never rising above a few hundred thousand lives before it too crashed. Next was a yellow record, whose span was far shorter than the last. This likewise failed to sustain longevity before its collapse.

"I'm confused. Are these full civilizations being founded and eventually dying... or, uh, rather falling into decline?" While Peter had known that it was possible, seeing it displayed so clearly proved unnerving. During his time at Natx Hollow, he had seen clear evidence of one civilization that sprung up on the ruins of an older one, but he always assumed that there was some overlap. That mankind went extinct on more than one occasion only to be resurrected was a concept he struggled to grasp.

"Yes. You are witnessing the extinction, the failure to survive, of previous cultures. I was not aware that a fourth era had commenced. Or that it, too, had passed so quickly." A fifth entry, this one a light blue, began as it slowly angled upwards. Prae watched silently until the timeline came to a stop, which indicated that it reached the current date. She tapped at a few buttons, which caused a string of marks to generate. "The fifth era... the year, it appears, would be 2,451,231."

"Two million..." Peter placed a hand on his forehead. His head spun as he tried to process the implications.

The group stood still, lit by the glow of the display. Prae reclined casually, waiting for inquiries. The silence was broken by Apello's deep voice.

"Why did they not place the containment cells

together? Would it not be easier to have everyone in a central location? Within the halls of Ala'ydin, no less. There appears ample space here."

"There was a theory—a possibility—that extended periods in the cells could possibly lead to dementia. We were to be interred in separate locations, hidden throughout the world, with as little evidence available as to the whereabouts of others. As one of the many scenarios postulated before our eventual hibernation, it was thought that a madness could set in, potentially infecting the afflicted with a desire to kill the others while they slept. Be it a perverse yearning to be the last of our kind, or madness-driven revenge for perceived slights over the lengthy span of time, the theory was enough impetus to cause such a decision to be agreed upon. So, each cell was concealed from the others, the coordinates only known to the occupant. Only at Ala'ydin would one even be able to begin the effort in tracking down the others. Which is why the cycle was intended for each man or woman to be in the Waking State for a short period of time. To provide a needed break from the effects of the Dormant State while they performed their duties."

"If you all knew where Ala'ydin was, what was to keep you from coming here and tracking down the rest? One would think such an effort within your abilities."

"Nothing. Nothing at all. Those of my kind, as you saw, could enter as they wished. Though, the Repository isn't what one might call entirely forthcoming with such specific information."

"Shocking, I tell you," Cal sneered.

"Our best opportunity is to see what information has been stored, to see if a trail of evidence exists that would give me an inkling of why things have transpired as they have. Why I was not woken on schedule. There will be no easy listing of coordinates to dial up for cells still in the Dormant State. It was by specific intent that such data would not be gathered."

"And if one of your kind goes around the bend and *really* wants to get at the rest of you?"

"There are countermeasures. I'm sure you witnessed them on our way in."

Cal opened his mouth. After a moment's pause, he shook his head and shrugged his shoulders.

It was then that a thought occurred to Peter. "And you're telling us this all… why?"

"Because someone must know. This can't all be lost. I fear that something has happened to one, or maybe many, of my kind. Ever since the extinction of those living in the second era, decisions have been made—questionable at times—that concern me greatly. Kayvurim, the one colloquially known as the Worm of Time, was adept in terraforming, shifting earth in massive quantities, even so much as to alter tectonic plates. After the loss of the second era of man, I awoke to a world massively altered by Kayvurim. Records indicate that he may have done the act in a fit of rage. Overturned the metaphorical table, so to speak. Continents were shattered and reformed. If anyone was alive beforehand, they certainly perished during the process. It was so catastrophic that the count of species wiped out was stunning to behold. On top of that, the shift caused one of the containment cells to end up on the bottom of the ocean, many miles below the surface. Maer Vinctum was lost to us, his cell prematurely removed from the cycle."

Despite the heavy mood, Cal spoke up. "Well the history lesson is nice and all—well, for Peter and Oebe, I'm sure, for me it was boring as shit—but where are we at in terms of finding out these answers you wanted? I mean we did leg it halfway across the continent to find this place and so far, we don't seem like we're all that closer to your goal."

"Like I stated previously, this kind of information isn't exactly sitting out in the open. It takes time and patience. I'm running a few queries and hopefully those will provide evidence that can—"

Prae broke off her response as bright orange flickered in the top left-hand corner of the screen. A shrill klaxon issued from a speaker buried somewhere deep within the room. Though he could not read the writing, Peter assumed it represented some warning or notification.

"What is that?"

Prae rose as she reached down and withdrew her weapon. When she turned, her look held apprehension the others had never seen in her before.

"Prae?"

"We have a visitor."

"Well, that's either the most convenient thing ever, or we've got us some trouble." Cal placed a hand on one revolver as he looked at Oebe. He was surprised to see her brow furrowed as her eyes bulged. For the first time since they had met, she looked concerned at the development.

16

Not one for sprinting, Cal struggled to keep up as Prae rushed from the Repository back to the entrance. She moved as if wholly unencumbered by fatigue. Not even the weight of her armor, which was roughly a hundred pounds in the canvas sack, seemed to impede her. By the time they covered half the distance, Cal was starting to feel discomfort in his ribs and a growing wheeze in his breathing.

At his side ran Apello. While he wasn't rasping like Cal, there was perspiration streaming down his face in rivulets. From the echo of footfalls throughout the vast cavern, Cal assumed that Peter and Oebe, though some distance behind, had also followed.

As she drew near the courtyard, Prae slowed. With her eyes narrowed, she picked out the recent arrival through the darkened haze. Standing alone at the center of the platform was a male draped in a tan hooded robe. The ragged and soiled hem of the woolen cloth dragged along the floor. The unexpected guest stood at attention, as if waiting for orders before progressing. Even beneath the weather-beaten cloth, the visitor's movements seemed jerky.

"Friend of yours?" Cal inquired as he withdrew his

revolvers, one at a time. Though he was accustomed to it, the sound of steel scraping against leather caused a chill to run down his spine. Apello moved up beside him.

Prae replied. "I'm quite aware that you're attempting to be sarcastic, but the answer is, in fact, no. I'm not currently familiar with whoever this might be."

"So, not of one of your fellow *Progenitors*, eh?"

"That remains to be seen. All the same, it would be in our best interest to remain cautious. He did manage to arrive unscathed through the transport."

With her sword at her side, Prae advanced a handful of guarded steps. The robed visitor's torso jerked, as if its attention was drawn to Prae's presence.

Without a word, Apello stepped forward, leaving Cal by himself on the bridge. His hands still behind his back, Apello covered the short distance between themselves and Prae.

Peter skidded to a halt as he came up behind Cal. As Oebe had kept pace the entire run, he reached over and took her by the arm. If their encounter devolved into violence, he would have to look out for the An-Sebban. The raised walkway wasn't particularly wide and if the fight abandoned the platform, there was the distinct possibility of someone being knocked over the railing.

"Patience, please," Prae requested with an open hand. After a few seconds of stillness, she proceeded warily.

As the visitor remained in place, Prae cocked her head to the side. Just as Cal was about to inquire, he noticed that a series of tones issued from beneath the cowl.

"What the hell is that?" Cal's voice raised an octave. There was no musical quality to the sound, but a strange, convoluted pattern of varied clicks that developed. To his right, Apello's body tensed up. A sick feeling began to develop in the pit of his stomach that preceded certain trouble

"It's attempting to speak—Oh, my!" The shock in Prae's voice caused Cal to flinch.

Apello took this signal to spring into action. Ignoring Prae's earlier plea for caution, he launched headlong as his blades slid free of their sheaths. With a shift of his weight mid-stride, he dashed past her and lunged at the cloaked form, who, despite the incoming attack, refused to budge from its place.

Apello struck at it with two crossing slashes. The curved steel glanced impotently off of its chest. A pair of dull clangs rang out as Apello's forward movement halted abruptly with a skid of boots on tile.

The fierce gashes opened ragged seams. One of the blades had cut through the straps that held the robe around the throat. As the fabric unfurled, it slipped free, dropped to the floor, and revealed the nature of the new arrival.

Standing before them was the effigy of a man in bronze and iron. While the limbs appeared to be modeled after the human form, with mock musculature and bone structure, the bulky chest was layered in segmented metal plates and topped with curved spaulders of steel. Except for light from behind the eye slits, there was no sign of life in the galea-shaped cranial unit.

"What in the holy hell is *that*?" Cal blurted.

"A mechanized golem," Prae stated matter-of-factly.

Stunned, Apello found himself feebly gawking at the steel and bronze. It was only when the vermillion lights behind the rectangular openings turned on him that he shook off the daze. As he fell back into a defensive posture, the golem spun its left arm upward. The balled fist caught him under the chin with a sharp crunch of metal on bone, made all the worse by his half-open mouth. The blow sent him to the ground. His weapons fell with a clatter as he slumped against the nearby alcove.

The golem's right arm elevated sideways at a ninety degree angle as the palm faced the nearby bay and pointed at the ancient statue within. A glint of red shimmered from a pinprick hole at the center of its hand and began to flit along the machine's surface. Red dots scoured the dulled metal in a manic display of erratic rays.

Prae's eyes widened. Her muscles tensed before she kicked off the dusty surface.

"No!" Prae barked. With an almost inhuman speed, she advanced. She was almost on top of the metal humanoid as her weapon rose in an upward sweep.

With a spin of her shoulders, she slung her sword in a diagonal arc, only to have it deflected as the android shifted in anticipation. Certain joints only managed strict angular movements, but articulation from the shoulders allowed for a strange array of motions as the machine-man went on the defensive.

As the attack pulled her forward, the golem followed

its parry with an immediate counterattack. In the simple piston-like motion of its arm, it delivered an almost-effortless blow to her back that drove Prae forward. The impact was violent enough that Prae lost her weapon, which dropped to the ground with a clang.

Driven to her knees, Prae rolled and attempted to right herself. As it spun its right arm in a vicious arc, the open palm struck her solidly across the chest. The force of the impact flung her against the railing. Prae grimaced as her lower back hit the bannister. The echo of metal on metal rang in her ears.

Before she could recover, the machine-man lunged towards her with its arms out. Prae managed to jab a free hand into the assailant's chestplate at the last moment, which barely stunted the incoming attack. Prae grunted through clenched teeth as she struggled to keep it at bay. The force radiated along the bones in her arm, sending a searing pain into her shoulder.

The sound of Apello's rage-fueled war cry cut through the air. He leapt at the machine and delivered slashes to the plates that formed its back. Each strike deflected off of the armor, leaving only faint scratches.

Its left arm disengaged and swiveled backwards in a 180-degree horizontal turn. The open hand struck Apello across the shoulder with the flat edge. The blow spun him like a top. As he dropped to the floor, he instinctively clasped a hand to his arm. An embarrassing grunt spilled from his mouth as he tumbled a few feet away.

In the brief window of opportunity, Prae mustered her strength and drove the palm of her free hand into its throat.

This only forced the android to recoil a half-step before it hammered both arms into Prae's chest. Once again, her lower back was thrust against the steel railing, which sent a spike of agony along her spine. Her vision blurred for a moment.

As it pressed her shoulders, Prae struggled to maintain her balance. Though she made no effort to look, she could hear the faint wind blowing through the kaleidoscopic mists below her.

It almost didn't register when the air cracked with the sound of gunshots. The first round hit the base of its skull, which caused the head to jerk. The next two shots pierced the tangle of mechanics tucked between the helmet and the adjacent pauldron. Sparks spit from split wires and gears began to click from within.

Taking advantage, Prae lurched forward with a coarse grunt. Her feet planted squarely against the balustrade, she mustered her strength to force the discombobulated android off of her. Once free, she wasted no time as it bobbled and staggered backwards. She scrambled to scoop up her blade in one hand. As she rose, with the weapon out in front of her, she was able to gauge her opponent's condition.

The armored entity wavered. A shower of sparks continued to pour from its head and torso. A pair of matching dents was visible along the jawline, evidence of two shots that had failed to find their mark. Rivulets of fluids leaked from the spinal area down the armor.

Prae spread her feet, one behind the other, and hefted the flat-bladed sword above her shoulder as she gripped the hilt. Her opponent failed to move either in retreat or attack. Its arms began to flail erratically as chirps issued from behind the faceplate.

"Is that so?" Prae said under her breath as she raised the weapon, held in place for only a second, and drove it downward in a ferocious arc. The edge slammed into the helmet and split the molded metal with a bell-tower toll that sounded deep into the recesses of the cavern.

She yanked back, causing the weapon to jerk away. The jagged crease in the steel ran almost a foot in length down the brow.

The overhead blow landed with such a brutal impact that it sent flakes of bronze into the air. Broken internal machinery began a screeching cacophony of grinding steel that assaulted the ear. The torso began to heave back and forth in a spasmodic spiral of what could only be described as death throes. The golem collapsed to the ground, a heap of distorted angles. While the right arm and left foot continued to twitch, the rest of the contraption rested limply.

Once the disturbing tremors dwindled to a few pulses along the limbs, like the faint twitches of a fading heartbeat, Prae relaxed. She drew in a deep breath as her features slackened.

"Is–is it safe?" Peter peeked around Cal, who remained in place with both revolvers aimed at the carcass.

"It is… disabled." With that pronouncement, Prae snapped her wrist upward, causing the blade to retract, before she returned it to the scabbard. She looked over the synthetic man for any sign of life, and then turned to where Apello sat on the floor with his back against the railing.

She opened her mouth to chastise him, but once she saw his face, she held her tongue. He scowled in discomfort and avoided her gaze.

While Prae stood above him and said very little, Peter knelt by his side and began to grill him about his injuries. After a few pats and prods at tender spots along his shoulder, arm and jaw, it was clear that nothing was broken; at worst, he had a muscle strain or deep bruise. He spit blood from a split lip, but there was no worse damage to his mouth.

Though Oebe stood obediently behind Peter, her attention was on the android at the other side of the platform.

Leaving the others to tend to Apello, Cal snuck up beside the mass of damaged metal.

"So, this one belong to one of yours?" Cal asked aloud as he nudged as the limp leg with the tip of his shoe.

"Pardon?"

"Is this something that one of your Progenitors built? I only ask because it looks like a more modern version of these other ones." He made a sweeping motion to the inert guardians that flanked them.

"Oh, yes, it would not be a stretch for you to assume that. I have a pretty good idea of who's responsible for our friend here."

"Oh, goodie." Cal rolled his eyes.

"And it was sent to kill us?" Apello spoke up, rubbing at the swelling along his lower jaw. Blood had dribbled from his mouth and down into his beard.

"No, it was not. It likely didn't even know of us until we attacked." Prae's eyes lingered on Apello, who snorted as he looked down.

"But, you—" Apello interjected before Prae cut him off.

"I was shocked by the content of its message, not its *intent*. If you had let it finish, I might have discovered more. Maybe even prevented our skirmish." She turned back to Cal and continued. By now, Cal had joined them by Apello's side. "I would assume that it was dispatched here for similar purposes as our own visit. Information gathering."

Relieved that Apello was not badly injured, Peter offered him a handkerchief before he stood up and dusted off his palms on his pants. "What was it doing with its hand? You know, with the red lights? You seemed fine to let it be until it started what I can only assume was an examination of the ancient sentries."

"It was *trying* to activate the other guardians. To use them to aid in its defense. If you thought our friend was a challenge, these behemoths would have certainly forced us to flee."

Apello groaned. Prae offered a hand to help him to his feet.

Oebe left Peter's side and walked over to where the automaton now rested. For a few seconds, she stood over the limp remains as her eyes scanned the surface. She absorbed every detail lit in the cavern's soft blue radiance. Design elements were familiar, though the particular details seemed like phantoms in the shadows of dormant memories.

She knelt and ran her fingers over the delicately-molded exterior of its forearm. When she reached its hand, she rolled the joint around until the palm was turned upwards. Oebe leaned in and peered over the intricate work of not only the exoskeleton itself, but the complex components that lie beneath.

With the nail of her index finger, she flicked the tiny hole on the uneven surface. A beam of red light flashed from the opening for only an instant, but it was enough to catch Oebe in the left eye. Her eyelids fluttered. Oebe opened her mouth when the sounds of whirling gears caught her notice.

Her eyes grew wide as she sat upright. The once-lifeless extremity straightened. The hand spun 180 degrees as the arm twisted in her direction. Out of survival instinct alone, Oebe rolled backwards as the fingers clawed at her and managed to grab her by the collar of her robe.

Oebe screamed as she was violently jerked back.

Frantically, she gripped the bronze-covered digits to pull herself free. As a wave of fear overwhelmed Oebe, her senses immediately shut down.

As gossamer-like data flicked along her vision, she barely noticed Cal, who skidded up as he clasped her shoulder. His terrified yells sounded like dull thuds that beat impotently against her ears. It wasn't until she saw the light reflected from his revolver that rational thoughts began to surface through the ocean of terror.

The gun went off with a disorienting clap that caused her to flinch. Even though the bullet pierced the elbow joint, she found herself still trapped within its clutch. Though Cal continued to press against her shoulders, she was being drawn ever closer. A searing discomfort was growing across her chest. The sensory overload, plus the spike of self-preservation–fueled fear, exceeded her ability to process.

Her head lulled backwards as Oebe's hazel eyes rolled back in their sockets. Cal's plaintive cries fell on deaf ears.

"Aside!" Prae barked sharply as she grabbed Cal and tossed him sideways. Cal lost his balance as he tumbled the ground a few feet away. Prae brought down her sword along the elbow.

The first strike snapped wires and tubing, which caused an arc of gray fluid to spurt from between the metal plates. The viscous liquid splattered up the artificial limb and splashed against the front of Oebe's robes. If she had been conscious, the acrid smell might have turned her stomach.

Ignoring the rank odor, Prae delivered another strike. This time, the blade shattered gears and support rods. A third blow severed the appendage from the rest of the body. The fingers slackened and released Oebe. She slumped lifelessly to the ground.

As Prae focused on what remained of the golem, Cal clambered across the platform and dragged Oebe away by her limp shoulders. He placed her head in his lap and checked her breathing and heart rate. Once it seemed that both were fine, Cal let out a relieved sigh.

Prae delivered one final strike to the head for good measure. Cal was certain he could hear the metal plating crack under the weight of the blow.

Peter gave Prae and the android wide berth as he scurried to where Cal sat with Oebe across his lap.

"Is Oebe okay?" Peter inquired. There was a shrill quality to his voice, as he struggled with a surging panic.

"I think she'll make it just fine," Cal announced, letting out a long breath.

Peter leaned forward and ran fingers along her throat. There was some irritation, but the skin appeared unbroken. "She seems relatively unharmed. Perhaps the shock, the sensory overload was too much for her. She's appears to have shut down as a defensive mechanism."

"Fainted," Cal interjected as he narrowed his eyes. "She fainted. Machines shut down. Don't talk about her like she's some kinda appliance. Just 'cause they messed with her head to make her an An-Sebban doesn't mean she ain't a little girl underneath."

"I…" Peter sputtered as he looked away. "You-you're right. Such a scare would cause anyone of her constitution to faint."

"You would've passed out, too. Perhaps pissed yourself in the process."

"True."

Her jaw tightly set, Prae observed the unconscious An-Sebban for a moment. Without a word, she knelt down briefly, only long enough to take the ruined android by one of its legs. As she began to walk away, she dragged the metallic corpse behind her. A dwindling trail of fluids was left in her wake.

"What are you doing?"

"Our friend here has some answers to provide. I need to hook him up to the database in the Repository."

17

Cal marched down the empty corridor.

He liked to think he was one to roll with the punches. In light of the path his life took, he considered this a fine philosophy that served him well. It allowed him to shrug off the unpleasantness of his daily interactions throughout Urigo Sector.

With that in mind, though, he now found himself seething with anger. His balled fists, which swung at his sides in time with his stride, were white across the knuckles. He was going to give Prae a piece of his mind. Whether she dignified his tirade or not remained to be seen. There were certain social conventions, like inquiring after an injured compatriot, of which Prae clearly needed to be made aware.

Keeping the Repository's entrance and its kaleidoscope of colors in his sights, he didn't want his anger to lose its edge. A string of muttered swears slipped out as he reached the entry.

Once he barged into the chamber, now awash in the glow of the viewscreen, Cal skidded to a halt. Prae knelt over the golem's remains; the damaged automaton was beside one of the pyramids as if prepared for a funeral. Her hands quickly flitted about as she created iridescent silver semanifestures between its mangled head and the nearby structure. She paused briefly and looked at the device, which now lit with pulsing icons that raced along the surface.

With a subtle bob of her head, she moved to the chair left caddy-corner by the main console. Without looking back to Cal, she spoke up as her hands dashed across the keyboard.

"How fares Oebe?"

Still mystified by Prae's gestures, the question did more to diffuse his anger than he expected. The diatribe in his head began to unravel. In seconds, it was almost completely forgotten. He cursed his own unreliability.

"Uh, she's appears to be okay, but she's still out like a light. Peter located what looks like a barracks on the west end, not too far from where we came in. When I left, he was laying her down. Between the exhaustion and the stress, I figured she's gonna be out for some time."

Prae nodded silently as she continued her efforts.

"So, uh… you mind me asking what in the hell you're doing?"

"Attempting to establish an information bridge between Masina and the Repository. I fig—"

Even though he knew she couldn't see him, Cal still held out a hand to Prae. "Whoa, whoa, whoa. Wait a minute. You don't just get to slip that right by me like it ain't nothing. Masina? What in the blue blazes is *that*?"

"Its nomenclature assignment, or rather, its name. Before we were so rudely interrupted earlier, it was attempting to establish a line of communications with us. Or possibly just myself. I'm not certain it had fully captured the nature of the situation." She concentrated on the scrolling text. Cal quickly scanned the room and noticed that Prae's helmet was set on one pyramid-shaped structure. On the floor was the now-deflated canvas sack that had once been used to transport her gear.

"So, I wasn't hearing you speak crazy earlier. You *did* state that it was trying to chat you up. All I got from it was a bunch of clicks and beeps. I'm gonna assume that it was some form of robot language. Boop, beep, boop, etc."

"Not exactly. Masina was communicating via a tone-based approximation of the written word. You've seen evidence of it earlier, whether you realize it or not."

Cal knew exactly to what she was referring: the walls of the Blue Room and the outside barrier were covered in row upon row of vertical marks. He hadn't really considered their purpose. It just wasn't something he cared about. Still, with Prae's comments, it began to make some degree of sense.

"Well, then, what was it attempting to say? I mean, it did take you by surprise for a second there. Pretty sure I've never heard you respond like that before."

"It was in the process of establishing its identity, as well as the name of its manufacturer and time and date of origin. What caused me alarm was the nature of its purpose. It had been dispatched to Ala'ydin to discover why a second containment cell was activated. I can only assume that its maker is aware of my awakening."

"Hmm. Guess that gives you a pretty good idea of what's been going on, right?"

Prae nodded in response.

"Have you been able to make any progress?"

"As much as I assumed I would. Slivers of information here and there. Not enough to give us a clear picture of the entire sequence of events. That not one but two containment cells are open has gone unrecorded, though that may be by intent. Those who programmed the Repository did so in a manner that even eludes me. Still, it appears no one has visited Ala'ydin in some time. The last recorded arrival predates the fifth era."

"I can tell," he added sardonically. "This place is in dire need of a cleaning staff. So, that leaves us screwed, right?"

"Not as much as one might think. Our recently-arrived friend here—" She playfully twirled her wrist in a mock introductory wave. "—may give us all the information we seek. I'm attempting to connect its internal workings to the Repository. Let the machines scour its programming. If they aren't beyond salvaging, we should be able to retrace its course back to the location of origin."

"You busted up its head pretty good. You sure there's anything to be recovered?"

"There appear to be redundancies contained within the torso. Data backups and low-level systems that can act in case of emergencies. Its creator was no amateur and this was not his first effort."

"You mentioned that it named its maker? Do you know the person? Oh, who am I kidding—of course you do."

"Erudatta, the Plotter."

"That's… that's not the kinda inspiring nickname I'm thinking I wanted to hear. Maybe Erudatta, the Puppy-Petter would be better."

Prae uttered a bark of laughter as she turned away, which caused the chair legs to scratch along the floor.

Their eyes met for a moment as they fell silent. In the polychromatic aura from the surrounding mechanics, her iridescent hair briefly bewitched Cal. Not even the low din of electronics at their task was enough to distract him from the sense of uneasiness that crawled across his chest.

"Cal," Prae began. "Thank you."

He cocked his brow and gave her a curious glance. "For? Oh, oh, that, out… well, out there. Think nothing of it."

"You likely saved my life."

"Ah, you would've been fine." He turned away to hide the blush. "You're a big girl."

"Still…"

Overwhelmed with awkwardness, Cal scurried frantically for a topic. "So, what is it that you're supposed to do? I mean, I know you said you were a Centurion, but what exactly is that? You'll forgive me as that's not currently a job description that one applies for nowadays. Not something that easily goes on a résumé."

"It's a flowery label for soldier."

"Ah, well, that makes sense, I guess. And your purpose? In the grand scheme of things, I mean. You said the others all had jobs, right? Recording, doing science shit, messing with people's mailing addresses."

A smile curled at the edges of Prae's lips. "To say I was the last remnant of the military division would be an understatement. We were the enforcers, protectors. While they could make golems—like this one and those posted at the entrance—to defend, they still needed someone to operate independently when the need arose. Someone to act as judge or executioner if one of us did indeed go mad." She hesitated with a downcast look. "They were the Intelligencia: the thinkers, documenters, experimenters, schemers. Everything they performed was intended to be a part of a larger machination."

"You make it sound like they didn't even need you. They didn't even let you fight in a few wars? In the eras that came after, I mean. You know, just to keep your skills sharp."

"It was agreed upon long ago that the Progenitors were never to be directly involved. I could never draw my blade and be an active participant in the events of those who followed. Instead, from time to time, my fellows would gently nudge affairs in an attempt to 'redirect' the flow of human evolution, to tweak mankind's history. The line between what should and should not be done was always indistinct. In the later years, rather than chance crossing it, I stayed my hand."

"So, getting involved with conflicts behind the scenes?

Sounds a bit more sinister, if you ask me."

"Presented without the knowledge that it was deemed a vital necessity for the growth of mankind, I'm certain it does. War, sadly, has its place. How else would you convince mankind to willingly readjust its own population density? Without such enticement, one might have to introduce a virulent pathogen which, if unchecked, might end up as an extinction event."

"So I guess it never occurred to your fellow people to go in and tweak mankind's genetic makeup? Or did it? I'm little fuzzy on what you guys would or wouldn't do. Maybe make us a little more resistant to disease, immune to cancer? I mean there are a lot of people who died prematurely that maybe could have been saved with a little interference by one of your more intelligent scientists. Assuming that's what you guys can or want to do."

"I'm sure such experiments had, at some point, been theorized or perhaps even developed in a laboratory setting. Whether introduced in live testing is another thing. If such a scenario had occurred, I doubt such findings would have been published. After what we did to ourselves, I imagine there was some reluctance to chance such a thing again. Even the risk of censure from the rest of my kind would be enough to steer one away from such a controversial experiment."

"I-I guess that makes some sense."

"And on top of that, our most experienced virologist, Magromous, seemingly became more interested in studying disease, making them stronger rather than developing cures for them. From the records I gleaned, left within the

Repository eons ago, it appears he became more interested in the lives of microscopic entities. The demise of the second era of man disillusioned him to the more complex forms of life."

In that moment, Cal was reminded of something that had occurred to him earlier. Cal snorted with a roll of his eyes. "You know, it occurs to me for someone who claims they're 'just a soldier,' you can do an awful lot. I don't think the average Magistrate has the same kind of talents that I've seen you use."

"When you're one of a handful remaining, one is expected to have a baseline knowledge of most topics. I never thought, in all my years, that I would need to create a data bridge semanifesture. Yet, here we are." She pointed to the silver halos between the shattered metal cranium and the machines.

After a quick glance at the viewscreen, Prae turned back to Cal. "Enough about me. What about yourself? What of your family? Parents?"

Cal's response came swiftly. "Child of a broken home. Father left mother before I was even ten. Last I heard, he became a merchant marine out of Nachtport. Mother eventually settled in a small little hamlet by the name of Leewar Cliffs up in Einnlande. I haven't seen—spoken to her in some time." He paused for a while, turned away from Prae. After a minute of awkward silence, he spoke up again. "But at least I can still see them, if I want. If I make the time to travel. You, well…"

He grimaced. Prae nodded before continuing.

"Yes, both of my parents passed well before I went into hibernation. Before the initial stages of the final plan was set into motion. Mother was a scientist, a geologist. Father, well, let's just say that I took after my father."

Cal nodded. Prae cleared her throat and spoke up.

"Cal, I feel I must come clean with you about something."

"Okay…" Cal leaned back as he cocked a single brow. "That's not usually how I like to hear topics started."

"Back at the entrance. When you passed through the portal. It was a complex series of semanifestures intended to gauge the qualities of your character. Or something along those lines. Your emotional state of mind, as it was. Your intentions and ulterior motives. If what was displayed showed malice, or immediate ill-intent, I would have been duty-bound to kill you."

Cal gasped with melodramatic exaggeration.

"I know it's not what you want to hear, but it would have been for the best. If you had gone through unmolested, the guardians would have activated. They would have surely killed you and probably the remainder of the group. I don't think that even I would have been able to fend off one of them, much less all four."

Once the gravity set in, Cal bit at his lower lip as he remained quiet. Eventually he spoke up. "So, those are the countermeasures you were talking about earlier."

Prae nodded without meeting his gaze.

"And you're telling me this now, why?"

"I figured it was owed to you after your earlier actions."

"Uh, thanks, I guess. And the others? Did they know?"

"I only recently revealed it to Peter before he passed through. I had performed a similar technique on him earlier, during our layover in Attis Grove, so I was assured he would not trigger the defense systems."

"And you just assumed Apello was okay? I must say that hurts a little."

"I did not expect him to charge on ahead. When the semanifesture did not set off an alert, I knew it was safe to send Oebe on through. A bit of good fortune, I guess."

Before Cal could decide on a droll retort, an alarm immediately set his nerves on edge. Prae turned her attention back to the screen. A few flickering blue icons appeared along the right side, which goaded Prae into tapping at the keyboards before she depressed an adjacent red circle.

"More trouble?"

"Nothing of the sort. It looks like we've uncovered the navigational history data. Let me run a trace on its course. Authorize the Repository to reconstruct the path it took to arrive here."

As she entered a string of commands that caused the display to construct a rudimentary map of line segments, Cal stepped up beside her.

"Well, since we're being honest… It was a lucky shot. Or two. I'm actually not that good with my guns. Or anything, if we're being brutally candid."

"Seriously?" There was unvarnished surprise in her voice.

"Yeah, I've only had to fire them a handful of times and most of the time it's just a scare tactic. Most people tend to run from gunfire as a reflex. The ones that don't kinda don't take to being shot at all that kindly."

"And yet you brandish them so readily."

"They're pretty much the only thing I can call my own." He patted at the matching handles affectionately.

When Prae looked at him, Cal found himself surprised by the warm glow in her usually cold green eyes. Chalking it up as a trick of the light, he immediately dismissed it.

She spoke up. "I must say... It strikes me odd that you're so inquisitive. This seems unlike you."

"More like something Peter would do, right? Talk your ear off, eh? I could say I was bored. Well, not really if I'm being honest. I did come down here to blast you out about Oebe, but I guess I got distracted."

"Really? How so?"

"Look. No offense meant, but you're kinda a cold woman, Prae."

"How do you mean?"

"I mean, you didn't seem to give two shits about Oebe's condition."

"She showed no evidence of being mortally wounded. No bleeding from open wounds. No marks from broken bones. As I am not one to have any substantial medical education, my efforts were best invested elsewhere."

Cal scoffed with an eye roll. "Don't know if it was because of the long nap, your military training, or just how your people—the Progenitors, right? Well, how they were. Are. I mean, I don't know that I really want to know what your people were like at the end. By the way you guys decorate a place, I can't say that you were good entertainers."

Prae let a thin smile slip. "No, we were not ones for entertainment towards the end."

Another series of mechanical notes drew her attention. She hummed to herself before running her fingers along the keyboard again.

As Prae's concentration was on the android's remains and the data she could extract from them, Cal's gaze returned to her helmet. The aged white exterior was lit in radiating hues that flashed in erratic patterns from the bordering façades.

He reached out with one hand and began to run his thumb and forefinger along the surface. The metal was cold to the touch and the hand-carved features felt rough against the pads of his fingertips.

When the sound of footsteps caught his ear, Cal's arm swiftly recoiled.

"I've got her settled in," Peter announced as he appeared in the doorway. "She's still out of it, which can be attributed to exhaustion, but she seems fine. Nothing broken and no external wounds."

"Good to hear," Prae said. She remained focused on the oddly-structured map slowly taking form. Though the topographical aspects were largely unfamiliar to her, the cartographical data points were of far greater interest.

"How are the accommodations?" Cal asked.

"Sufficient," Peter replied with a strained look. "On another, somewhat-related topic, Cal, did she bring any additional luggage with her? A change of clothes, perhaps?"

"Nothing but the fineries on her back."

"Yeah, that's specifically the issue."

"How you mean?"

"Her clothes are worn thin in places and, well…" Peter hemmed and hawed for a moment. "They could use a good washing due in large part to the gunk our mechanical friend sprayed on her. I disrobed her from all but her undergarments before laying her down. She could use a change."

"Oh, uh, yeah," Cal sputtered through his clenched teeth. "Uh, well, take my jacket and see if that'll do until we get back to civilization. I'm sure we can buy something to tide her over in Viisibourg on the way back through. Assuming that we're heading back that way, I guess." He motioned to the leather jacket hung haphazardly on a piece of equipment.

Peter reached over and collected the garment. "Okay, between that, my vest and Apello's kaftan—"

"Dig into the duffle," Prae waved to the nearby bag, which was almost lost in the shadows of the desktop. "The one we used to store my gear. I should only need the robe until our return, so use the overcoat Apello leant as you deem fit."

"Good, good. That should give me enough to work with. Thank you."

Cal stepped aside as Peter knelt and quickly withdrew the striped vestment. As he rose to his feet, his gaze was drawn to the display. Before he could utter the question that was plain on his face, another notification rang out.

"What is that?" Peter inquired as he glanced back and forth between Cal and Prae. Cal offered him a wordless shrug.

"It's the course our friend here took to arrive at Ala'ydin." She reached up and ran her index finger along the southern-most endpoint.

Initially, to Cal the display seemed like a chaotic arrangement of line segments that overlapped, like a pile of glowing rods. The longer he looked at it, though, the clearer the picture became. He began to notice familiar topographic features. When his eyes followed the ragged coastline that ran southwest from the end of what was certainly a mountain range, he knew where the android had originated.

"Oh, shit," he groaned as his eyes traced the path along a narrow land bridge to a circular peninsula, back to its source. "Greater Decedistadt."

"Oof," Peter joined in. "That's a needle in haystack."

Oebe awoke from her sleep with a peculiar look

of bewilderment on her face. It was not caused by the unfamiliar surroundings that took shape as her vision cleared.

As was the nature of the An-Sebban, Oebe's rest cycles often went unbroken. They were periods of time during which her eyes sealed shut, only to reopen some time later with a feeling of refreshment. The concept of dreams was one that she understood, though she had little recollection of experience with them.

Still, she found herself besieged by vaguely-interconnected images that had visited her. If she had experience with psychology, she might have pondered at length over their meaning. Instead, she reminded herself that she had been away from the Athenaeum's Archives for an extended period of time. Without a regular transferral, the collected information was beginning to affect her personally.

With a shake of her head, she sat upright. She was draped in a piece of woolen cloth that had been hastily converted into a makeshift cover. It fell off and collected about her waist. The chill that permeated the installation caused gooseflesh to rise along her bare skin. She looked down and noticed she was no longer dressed in her traditional garb. Instead, she wore a thin sleeveless shirt and her underwear.

After a moment to gain her bearings, she slipped off of the bunk. Her bare feet touched down on the icy flooring. The room about her was a plain rectangle that featured two matching rows of bunks of limestone. The walls were etched with a similar pattern as others throughout the site;

this led her to conclude that they had not yet departed Ala'ydin.

Atop the adjacent bed was a pile of folded fabric. From the colors and patterns, she recognized most as clothing previously worn by her allies. Set atop the stack was a slip of paper with a handwritten message.

"Your clothes are ruined. Try these on until we return to civilization. – Peter"

She paused for a moment. As Oebe thought back on recent history, she recalled the attack and how the golem had latched onto her. That was when her memories began to grow hazy. That her recollection of recent events was unreliable began to concern her. What good was she to the An-Sebban if she failed to record observations?

Eventually, she picked through the stack of garments and dressed herself. Between the striped woolen overcoat, Peter's gingham vest and the weathered leather jacket, she assembled a hodgepodge outfit that kept her reasonably warm. She stepped into her black leather slippers, which appeared no worse for wear. She collected the kaftan that served as blanket and headed for the entrance on the far side of the room.

Beyond was an octagonal atrium, with a pair of connecting pathways leading away in opposite directions. On the other side was a stairwell that descended into the darkness. Oebe stepped up to the bannister and looked over the side.

Oebe thought she had seen something similar before, maybe of limestone or marble, though she could not recall specific details. This architectural arrangement was more ornate in composition. She recalled no prior experience with hexagonal brass-plated tiles, and the balustrades were oddly simple.

She slipped away and passed into the right-hand corridor. A few paces along the curling hall, Oebe picked out echoes of conversation. Familiar voices confirmed that Peter and Apello were not too far off. She followed the snippets of conversation to their source. She trod along the hall until it reached an antechamber for the vaulted bridges which led back to the Repository.

Oebe paused in the shadows of the open entryway and listened. She quickly noticed a certain change in Apello's disposition. He often looked away from Peter and stood with a softness in his stance. Briefly, she wondered what had transpired that would have made the stalwart protector so submissive.

"It's odd," Peter admitted. "It's like there is no sign that anyone ever lived here before. There's not a stitch of fabric to be found in the place. No paper or books. No furniture beyond the basics, and nothing is made of wood, so we won't be lighting a fire to warm the place up. Though, considering the assumed age of the location, I guess I should be surprised that anything is left standing."

"The sleeping arrangements?"

"Limestone bunks with mattresses composed of a viscoelastic silicone polymer. I'd read of its like before, in scientific journals, but to see it used in a practical application was… strange. Oebe seemed to rest upon it without problem, though maybe fainting into unconsciousness removed any complaints she might have offered."

Apello nodded quietly as he leaned against the nearby wall.

Just as Oebe was about to make her presence known, Peter drew in a long breath.

"Are… are you well? I am generally loathe to pry in personal matters, but it seems that you have been on edge as of late. I mean, what with—"

"I am *fine*." Apello cut Peter off before he could finish the statement. The sharpness caused Peter to raise his hands in a defensive posture. "What happened earlier was a bit of rashness that won't be repeated. Perhaps… I am willing to admit I have been distracted. This excursion has gone on longer than expected and…"

"Yes, I'm well aware of it. Master Contrell is most likely put out by now. I-I'm not looking forward to our inevitable return." Instead of pressing the matter, Peter nodded before continuing. "Well, it appears our path will eventually lead us south to Greater Decedistadt. If you feel it best that you return to Natx Hollow, by all means feel free to. I will certainly understand. Myself, I feel compelled to see this to its end."

"Greater Decedistadt?"

"Prae was able to trace the golem back to its place of origin. Somewhere in the northern sectors. She mentioned specific co-ordinates, but since I left the maps back in the transport, I couldn't point exactly where. Cal made mention he was from the city so he can assuredly prove sufficient guide once we arrive."

Though Peter had no clue as to why, this revelation seemed to raise Apello's interest. His eyes widened as he shifted.

"I will be joining you." His tone brooked no debate. "I have other matters to be tended to within the city."

"Well, then..." Peter eyed him warily and bit at his lower lip. Instead of prodding, he turned away. Once he spied Oebe in the doorway, Peter waved for her to join them.

With heartfelt thanks, she returned Apello's robe and inquired about their dining arrangements. It wasn't the topic she wanted to investigate, but in light of the tense mood in the air, she felt it best to change the subject. The innocent question was enough to lighten the mood; Peter offered to escort Oebe back to the Repository, hoping that they could convince Prae to quit Ala'ydin altogether.

18

The remains of Masina attached to the Repository via Prae's semanifestures were the only sign that the group had ever visited Ala'ydin. Upon their exit by the riverbed, Prae restored the cliff-face façade to its original state. By this time, the others paid little attention to the mannerisms and gestures of the art; despite a lack of understanding of its nature, they grew used to her application of the techniques.

Following a protracted hike through the underbrush, they located their transport and began their return. The trip to Viisibourg was long and quiet. Despite a number of nagging questions, Peter kept mostly to himself as he navigated back to the Nria Highway. They arrived in the city to find it much as they had left it; Viisibourg was bustling with commerce as the populace was largely unconcerned about events that transpired beyond its borders.

After securing lodgings, in an establishment far more upscale than that of their previous stay, the party departed to procure apparel for Oebe. With assurances that he would meet up with the others later in the evening, Apello slipped away. Peter warily watched the Thosan depart. Eventually, the rest of the travelers strolled into the northern shopping district a few blocks to the east.

The corner of the bazaar in which they stopped was a quaint circle of cottages converted into boutiques and storefronts. Garish décor was aimed to convert walking traffic into customers. Mock thatch roofs hung over wooden eaves and the alleyways between buildings were hidden with colorful silk and wool awnings. At the center of the plaza rose an obelisk of stone topped with a silver and obsidian clock face.

Despite the open-air nature of the district, the air was thick with incense; vanilla and floral scents floated in the breeze that slithered between the tightly-packed shops. While Cal was used to the overbearing public aromas, Peter's nose itched as his breath felt artificially stifled. He immediately longed for the cleaner air of his field work. Even the suffocating heat of the Quartewuste was tolerable as long it as it remained uncontaminated.

When they stumbled across a turquoise-and-pink A-frame that promised a "variety of ladies fineries," Prae and Oebe looked at each other and slipped inside. Peter lingered by the doorway, unsure of whether he should follow. Since Cal chose to lean against a nearby streetlamp with his arms folded, he decided to remain outside.

While both Cal and Peter eschewed the daintiness of their surroundings, they stayed put despite the opportunity to slip away.

The pair spent some time in idle chatter as they waited. They watched the throng of shoppers that milled through the district. More than once, Cal's gaze stayed on an appealing passerby, which drew Peter's judgmental sneer. Eventually, Peter nudged Cal in the side and pointed to the boutique's entrance.

With a warm smile on her face, Oebe stepped out of the open doorway, dressed in a gray-and-white striped tent dress. Her hair was tied in a ponytail that ran down her back. Draped across her shoulders was a navy knit shawl. Clutched in her hands was a leather rucksack, which appeared to be laden. Peter could only assume that the clothing she wore into town was now stored inside.

"So, does it suit you?" Peter inquired, to which she immediately nodded. Wordlessly, she reached out and offered the sack to him. Peter took it and peeked inside. At the top of the stack of folded fabric was his gingham vest. "I'll be sure to return your bag once we get back to the inn and returned everyone's garments." Just as he was about the sling the rucksack's strap over his shoulder, he turned to Cal. "Would you care for your jacket?"

Cal tilted his head and took a measure of the weather. "Naw, it's nice out. I think I'll enjoy the day while I can." When he looked back to the storefront, he was stunned to find Prae waiting in the doorframe. Instead of her usual black bodysuit and tan robe, she was dressed in a red linen tunic and olive slacks. Without the camouflaging bodysuit, Cal was finally able to examine Prae's physique.

Though she sported wide shoulders and muscular frame, Prae exhibited the lean curves of a woman who had spent a life of vigilant fitness. What the decoratively-stitched elbow-length sleeves did not cover revealed defined muscles that might have put even Apello to shame.

Except for a pair of scars that ran just below the crook of her arm, her pearlescent skin seemed flawless.

Despite a floundering attempt to disguise it, Cal's stare first fell on the curvature of her hips and then lifted to the diminutive rise of her breasts. When their eyes eventually locked, the curious scowl that creased her forehead caused Cal to look away.

Prae let out a snort as a smile curled her lips. With a pair of long strides, she joined Oebe along the cobblestone pathway. She looked down to Oebe, who was giddy. Now, dressed as she was, the An-Sebban was as ecstatic as her conditioning allowed. As Oebe's head turned at the sound of conversation in the distance, the swath of hair that was tied back swayed to the side. Out of the corner of her eye, Prae caught sight of something unexpected. Located just below the base of her skull, squarely in the middle of her neck, was a quartet of circular metal holes.

"And yourself?" Peter posed to Prae.

"It fits well," she replied. "It's been some time. I forgot what casual apparel felt like against the skin." She lightly ran her fingers along her arm before she recalled something. "Oh, the shopkeeper did inquire as to how we would pay for these. You will understand that neither I nor Oebe have the occasion to carry money."

Peter turned to Cal, who only shrugged his shoulders. "Man, all I got left is enough for food and transit passes for the Langspur line for Oebe and myself. Being in the League ain't exactly profitable. Not rolling in the cash, as one might say." He patted at his pockets to drive home the point.

Peter let out a groan before he crossed to the shopkeeper who waited in the doorway. Peter reluctantly paid the bill before rejoining to the group.

"So, Prae, you seem to have let your hair down, metaphorically," Peter stated.

"It has been some time since I've walked among others. Partook of the comforts of camaraderie."

"Well, then, why not enjoy yourself? Go out for the night? On a date, I mean. I'm sure someone would love to be your escort. Cal even." Though Peter had meant to be playful, Prae's expression darkened. After a pause that grew uncomfortable, she spoke up.

"I can't be romantically involved with Cal."

"That goes without saying," Peter said under his breath, much to Cal's displeasure.

Cal glared at Peter before objecting. "Hey, now. I'm a perfectly—"

"No, you're not. You're a lech and a crook."

"That's not the point," Prae raised her voice to disrupt the looming argument. "I can't be involved with any of your kind. Your lifespans are too short. You would be gone in the blink of an eye. And that's not to mention the fact that at some point in the near future, I will have to return to hibernation. The next time I am scheduled to awaken, you would have been dead for many millennia."

With that said, the group fell silent. The gaiety was gone and Peter felt embarrassed. Prae avoided making eye contact as she observed the ebb and flow of the crowd.

As she placed a balled fist over her mouth, Oebe tried to stifle a yawn. Instead, she made a high-pitched squeak that was barely muffled behind her hand.

"Tuckered out?" Cal inquired as he lightly grasped her shoulder.

"Yes, I could use some recuperation." The redness in her eyes did as much to confirm her exhaustion.

At this, Cal turned to Peter and wordlessly offered to take the rucksack with a flick of his fingers. "I'll take Oebe back to her room and see about letting her get some rest."

"Sounds good."

The pair made their way through the throng of shoppers. With the bag slung over one shoulder, Cal made certain Oebe was never out of arm's reach. When they vanished around the distant street corner, Prae shifted and faced Peter. She found his brow furrowed as he looked off to nowhere in particular.

"There is something on your mind." Her statement broke his concentration.

He shook his head. "H-how did you—"

"There's a crease along your forehead that deepens when you want to pose a query but are looking for either the opportunity or courage to ask it." She pointed at his face.

Rather than wait for him to muster the courage, Prae took him by the sleeve and led him into a nearby alley, the entrance of which was loosely covered in silk tapestries. Once they became hidden within the shaded lane, she motioned with a turn of her hand to continue. The aggressive maneuver seemed enough to dissuade Peter from hemming and hawing.

After a brief glance through the cracks in the cloth, he lowered his voice and began. "Well, I was mulling over the numbers you provided us earlier. About your Waking State age and the number of years that have passed since your birth. You stated you were three hundred and eighty, but that the year itself was 2,451,231 by your calendar."

"I was young when I went into stasis."

"So, does that mean that the others would be noticeably older?"

"It stands to reason. But not as old as you might be calculating in your head."

"Ah, I see you grasp what was causing my issue with the calculations."

"Certainly. You must understand that moving forward in the cycle is not an instantaneous progression by design. That, when next I return to my containment cell, the processes will begin anew and sometime in the following millennium, the next in the cycle will be released for their time in the Waking State. Even if I chose to stay among mankind for a decade, it would be nearly eleven thousand years before my next opportunity." She paused for a moment, as if contemplating over whether she should continue on the particular tangent. "After the third era, I spent less and less time in the Waking State. Sometimes only long enough to grab a breath of fresh air before retiring."

Well aware that he was treading a tender subject, Peter's

voice softened. "This is not the first time you've mentioned that. What happened that caused you such distress? I mean, if you don't mind me prying."

There was unmistakable pain in her eyes. "Loss. On a grand scale. I grew attached to those of the second era. With so little time spent amongst my own, I adopted those who came after as my kin. When the end came for them, I lost more than a kinship with those who came after us. I woke at the beginning of the third era and found a world unlike what I was used to. Many of my favorite vistas were gone, replaced with an alien landscape I no longer recognized or wanted anything to do with."

"I-I'm sorry," was all Peter could muster.

For what felt like minutes, they stood there. Just when Prae moved to exit the alley, Peter spoke again.

"How did you know?"

"Excuse me?" With a hand still grasping the silk curtain, she looked over her shoulder.

"That things were not right? In Natx Hollow. That you hadn't been awoken on time?"

"Firstly, I found myself in a chamber with four other individuals. I should have awoken as a natural part of the process, without the interference of outside influences. Secondly, no such complex existed when last I went into the Dormant State. And, on top of that was the above-ground structure which was clearly of a different origin. Far too much time had passed for such a natural occurrence."

Peter only nodded at the explanation. If he had any further questions, he kept them to himself. Prae's distressed mood was sign enough that he had prodded as far as he should.

"Oh, Peter?"

"Yes."

"One question of my own: what is up, to use the modern parlance, with your man Apello? His rash actions forced us into a melee that might not have needed to occur. Is he always so prone to violence?"

Peter considered the matter. "I've never known him to be so hasty. Though, we aren't exactly fast friends. Perhaps the events of the previous few weeks have got him out-of-sorts. He *was* hired by the Bureau as protection. Perhaps he just takes his role a bit too stringently."

"Perhaps you don't know him as well as you think." With that, Prae stepped out into the street.

The closer Cal and Oebe drew to the quaint inn, a two-story building of stark white paneling and decorated in lush greenery, the quieter she grew. He noticed the signs, clear as day. The more exhausted she became, the more she seemed to shut down unnecessary interactions. Cal wondered if she was still able to observe at a full capacity when she was like that.

It did not surprise Cal that Oebe was fast asleep as soon as her head hit the pillow. He envied her ability to fall deep into slumber as soon as she was supine. He wondered how late it would be before he finally succumbed to his exhaustion. In light of his tight financial situation, he would have to do it sober, an undesirable prospect even in the best of times.

Not wanting to disturb her, Cal placed the rucksack on the bedside table and withdrew his jacket. With a shake to knock out the worst of the wrinkles, he slipped it on and peered into the bag. He pulled out the vest and overcoat and draped both across his folded arm. At the bottom was a pile of black cloth that he recognized as Prae's. He removed this as well, leaving the opened bag.

Cal took a few strides to the room's second bed, where he dropped the striped kibr and bodysuit beside the sack that contained Prae's armor. On the other side were Oebe's An-Sebban garments, still soiled from the spray of Masina's lubricants.

Cal reached out a hand for the tie-string that bound the luggage. He began to mull over their return to Greater Decedistadt. Technically he could not admit that he had, in his possession, something of merit. The wealth of information and the experience gained from the trip were vital, even life-altering, but both lacked what he might call a tangible worth. The location of Ala'ydin might prove to be a bartering chip if he thought that there was anything at the location that Jaefor wanted.

With all other avenues seemingly closed, he considered the value of Prae's armor. Despite his dire situation, he struggled with the idea of stealing from her. The repellent nature of the thought churned his stomach.

No matter how his homecoming played out, he knew he had to deliver Oebe back to the Athenaeum. If his fate was tied to whatever Jaefor planned to do with him, the least he could do was see the An-Sebban safely home.

When his fingers brushed along the surface, something within shifted. The sound of metal as it bumped against metal crashed through the room's quiet.

Cal shot a glance at Oebe, who remained immobile, her hands across her chest.

He drew in a long breath and retracted his hand. Cal snuck out of the room with Peter's vest still draped across his forearm.

After walking the winding avenues of the scenic clockwork city, Peter returned to the rented quarters he shared with Apello and Cal. He found the room empty, with no sign that either man had visited the accommodations since their arrival. Prae left Peter to take a private stroll of the city before the evening grew too late.

Peter did not wait long for one of his roommates. Apello barged in, still lost in thought.

"We missed you earlier," Peter commented. From anyone else, the statement might have come across as petty or barbed. From Peter, though, it was earnest.

"I was tending to business."

"Oh, really?"

"Yes. I have accounts with one of the local banks. I needed to make a withdrawal before we departed for Greater Decedistadt."

"Oh. Some spending money for the trip? Going on a shopping spree?"

"Something of that sort."

Peter turned to the window and wedged a pair of fingers between the blinds. Evening had set in and their second-story quarters looked down on the intersection at the front of the building. Long shadows from distant buildings crawled along the cobblestone street. A pair of recently-lit streetlamps cast a sallow halo which highlighted the walking forms as they headed to other locations.

Before he pulled away, Peter saw a lone figure standing in the darkness. Draped in a hooded cloak, the immobile shape looked eerily similar to the mechanical man from Ala'ydin.

When Cal pushed his way into the room in his usual noisy fashion, Peter nodded politely and turned back to the window.

The hooded person was now gone; the sidewalk was empty except for a shopkeeper who whisked a broom diligently in front of his doorstep.

"Here," Cal stated as he handed Peter his vest.

"Thank you," Peter accepted it graciously. He retreated from the view that no longer held any intrigue for him.

19

Though they left only the barest evidence of their stay behind in Ala'ydin, it proved more than enough to leave a lasting mark. The impact of their brief visit would be recorded in the Repository for posterity. Had Prae exhibited more than a rudimentary understanding of command inputs for the mainframe, she might have arranged to end all activity upon their departure.

After connecting the damaged golem, Masina, the string of instructions Prae entered into the ancient database was not as stringent as she thought. With more extensive experience of contextual code-input statements, she might have known that certain routines began running the moment she asked the two devices to interface. With the dismembered machine still attached, the Repository continued background processes that passed data between the two.

While the topographical map on the viewscreen remained long after their departure, it was only once a trio of underlying programs completed their tasks that this information minimized to the far right corner. In its place now appeared long strings of vertical icons that scrolled across the display at a pace far too fast for human eyes to read.

Where the glowing icons along the pyramid had once shimmered in an array of hues, now they pulsed gold and yellow. The pattern of lights fluttered in a downward flow, directed into the android, as if a waterfall poured into the semanifesture bridge.

After a length of time, activity within the Repository came to a stop. When the scrolling wall of text halted, the silver halos between Masina and the machinery vanished.

The faint buzzing that served as a soundtrack to the machinery's activity faded. Before the silence took root, gears whirred to life from beneath Masina's chestplate. The limbs began to jerk erratically until the android eventually acquired viable motor function.

Though its mannerisms were shaky, Masina managed to lurch forward. Without the use of its dismembered limb, it struggled to sit upright. While part of its face was a shattered wreck, the light behind one eye-slit now glowed yellow.

After a few attempts that ended in clumsy failure, Masina finally rose. With its senses hampered from the earlier damages, some time was required before the golem gained its bearings. Eventually, it marched from the room. Once in motion, it moved swiftly with only a few issues as it changed direction.

Masina turned down one of the intersecting bridges in the main chamber and pushed on until it reached a connecting antechamber. Beyond that was a series of rooms, brimming with equipment, which had once served as a machinist's workspace.

As it arrived at the first workshop on the left, a musty space lined with shelves, Masina located the tools it required. After a scan with the red beams of light from its outstretched palm, it began to gather an array of instruments. Each was deposited with care on the central workbench, next to a handheld acetylene torch at the edge of the desktop. This sequence required a couple of trips, during which fluids from its mangled limb left a faint trail along the floor.

A subsequent search for replacement parts proved unnecessary; the unfinished remains of an older-model mechanical golem like those at the entrance was spread across an adjacent workspace. Masina examined the orderly arrangement of unassembled parts before it focused on the detached forearm.

Following a brief pause, in which Masina mapped out the steps in its repair program, it began to remove the tattered remnants of its arm. Tools were picked up, used in as efficient a manner as possible and then returned to their place. Once the wreckage was picked clean, it spun laterally for a moment, grasped the welding torch and refocused on the replacement components to the side.

With an inhuman precision, it began to weld the new arm in place, attaching the rods and gears to the closest analog from its own ragged limb. Once complete, Masina raised the oversized appendage to test its response. Though the fingers were clumsy, it appeared to exercise control over the articulation.

Almost immediately, Masina shifted its posture to compensate for the weight of the new attachment and returned its attention to the worktables.

It progressed onto the next step in its field triage. Masina reached up and began to pull broken shards of the faceplate free from where they loosely hung, barely attached to the framework beneath. From behind the cracked metal, the occasional spark still flickered and the components that were once its right eye were smashed beyond repair.

To the side was a half-finished head piece that featured an unpolished brass beak and a crown of iridescent plates arranged to look like feathers. The eyeholes were placed in a more human fashion, facing forward beneath a curvilinear brow line. The empty shell was just a faceplate that would have been mounted to the front of the cranial casing.

With its good hand, Masina clasped the curved metal shell. It placed the sloping cover atop the ragged remains of its own. A few spot-welds later and the falcon-shaped features were in place.

After delivering a series of knocks along the surface, Masina departed from the workshop and headed for the entrance.

20

As the sun sank on the western horizon, Prae and her companions arrived in Ilgyngate, exhausted and hungry. The long and winding course through the Itiri Uplands took its toll on the passengers. A sense of relief and trepidation came over the travelers when they spied the jagged skyline over the final rise only miles to the north. In light of the fact that Prae had never visited the city before, Cal and Peter informed her of what to expect.

Though Ilgyngate served as a border city between Greater Decedistadt and the rest of the continent, it was steeped in industrial and manufacturing commerce. Lower-class residents toiled at one of the many assembly lines or loaded outbound transports destined for other locales. Few were what one might consider well-to-do; the population at large appeared locked in a daily struggle just to make ends meet. The air itself was a polluted haze that not even a steady breeze from the southern coast could dilute.

The plan was to remain for the evening and take the first train to Greater Decedistadt in the morning. Just as they reached the city limits, the last scheduled transport for the day departed along the Langspur. A plume of smoke from the engine rose above the horizon as it pulled from the depot. They settled on rooms at a small brick building in a back corner of the market a few miles from the station. Though it wasn't flush with amenities, it served their purposes.

It was decided that after checking in, the group would reconvene in the adjacent courtyard and head on for supper before calling it a night. Cal took this opportunity to slip away from Peter and Apello, informing them that he would meet up with them before too long.

Cal hurried through the inn's narrow halls to where Prae and Oebe roomed. Once he reached the dark wooden door, marked with a brass number six, he came to a stop and began to fidget.

Cal waited out in the hall as he mulled over the same topic that had preoccupied him since before their departure from Viisibourg. With their impending arrival in Greater Decedistadt there was two matters of business he could no longer put off.

To return to the metropolis empty-handed was a certain death sentence. Their visits to Natx Hollow and Ala'ydin failed to yield something immediately valuable to someone like Jaefor. While he'd been on the lookout for an alternative of any kind, Cal came up empty.

As he was now only a day's travel away, he was left with only one option: the only objects that might appease Jaefor's fancy rested within the adjacent room.

On top of that was the matter of Oebe. Realistically, he needed to return her to the Athenaeum. It was the responsible thing to do. Sure, the others could tend to her and even see her home, but he had to admit he'd grown to like the An-Sebban.

After a long sigh thick with resignation, Cal banged against the door with the meat of his hand. There wasn't a lot of force to his knocking; he hoped that no one would respond. When the doorknob began to turn, he let out his breath. The door opened to a crack and revealed Oebe's curious face.

"I won't be too much longer," she announced, to which Cal cocked a single brow.

"Sorry..."

"You've not spoken with Prae?"

He shook his head slowly. Without another word, she retreated and offered him entrance to the room. Once within, Cal noticed that Oebe's hair, which now hung well past her shoulders, was still damp. She was half-dressed; the shawl was deposited on the end of the nearby bed.

"She went on ahead to meet with you and the others. I advised her I wanted to stay in the bath a little longer and that I would join in a few minutes." Oebe left Cal by the entrance as she retrieved a towel and began to slowly pat at her moist locks.

Thinking quickly, Cal shifted gears. "Well, I needed to talk about—"

"There is the distinct possibility that you might not be able to complete your task as assigned. It is not possible for me to return," Oebe interrupted. Her usually soft words came across as unusually cold. With her back still turned to him, Cal was unable to see her expression.

"How's that?"

Rather than repeat herself, she continued. "It is in the best interest of our current efforts that I fail to follow the process which would have me return to add my recently-acquired knowledge to the Central Archives. There are things I know now that would be dangerous for the Athenaeum to acquire. You know this to be true, as does Peter. It's why Prae spoke of being able to decide what information could be shared and what would have to be kept secret."

"She likely didn't understand your situation," Cal pointed out. "That as an An-Sebban you have no control over what data is available during the——"

"Irrelevant," she cut him off as she dropped the towel on the mattress. "What she knows and what decisions I must make are not the same. She placed the responsibility of such revelations on *our* shoulders."

Cal was taken aback by the tone of Oebe's voice. He had to admit that she was likely more capable of responsible decisions than he had ever been. Over the time that they were away, she had slowly begun reasserting her personality. There were more and more moments that she was "herself" and not the detached An-Sebban he first met. It had occurred so gradually over the length of their travels that Cal failed to fully appreciate what was happening until he stood alone with her in the midst of such a critical discussion.

"They will send someone to collect you at some point,"

Cal stated matter-of-factly. "If I don't escort you home, someone in the League will eventually be hired to track you down. Whether you like the idea or not, you are a possession. You have value to them."

Oebe nodded. "That is, if you don't report back with a manufactured story that I perished. Or something to that effect." Oebe was not one for subtext, but she implied something that he had hoped would never surface. "You're good at telling stories. I think you could arrive at a believable narrative."

"I'm beginning to think that isn't exactly true."

Oebe picked up her shawl and draped it across her shoulders. There was a coyness in the smile that she offered Cal. "Shall we head on, then?"

"Certainly," he responded with a wave that ushered her towards the exit. As she reached it, he opened the door and waited for her to pass through. Once she was in the hall, he paused.

"Hey, why don't you go on without me," Cal suggested. Oebe gave him a curious scowl, but before she could comment, he followed up with "I left the cash for the tickets tucked away in the bottom of your bag. I... I'm not good with money. Tend to be a spender rather than a saver, so I figured if I kept the money, you know, not on me, it wouldn't get spent."

"I can see the logic in that."

"Well, why don't you meet up with the others? Once I'm done getting the boarding passes, I'll join."

She paused as she looked into his eyes. When he refused

to flinch or look away, she nodded before she headed on. Cal watched her walk away before he returned to the empty room.

He moved quickly. Oebe's leather satchel was on the floor, her An-Sebban vestments its only contents. He lifted it, removed her clothing and set them on the nearby bed. Instead of digging further, he faced the opposite bunk and Prae's duffle.

Cal quickly untied the top and opened the pack, which revealed the jumbled pile of her armor. Set on one side, draped in Prae's black bodysuit, was the ornate helmet. He reached in, dug out the metal headgear and quickly shoved it into Oebe's empty sack. More than once, the sharp edges caught on the fabric.

He retied the drawstrings and nudged Prae's bag to make it appear unchanged. His travel-mates might think that he went out on the town for the night. Any lead he managed would have to do.

Cal closed the door as he tucked the purloined headpiece into the crook of his arm. He grimaced slightly as one of the horn tips jabbed him in the side. *Suffer through it. Hopefully, this will cover my debts with Jaefor. If not, well… I'm certain I'll be feeling a lot worse than having a few pieces of metal sticking me in the side.*

After their earlier visits to Attis Grove and Viisibourg, Ilgyngate struck Prae as a community rife with churlish day-laborers. Whereas the northern townships seemed idyllic with their relaxed atmosphere, there was a surliness to the border city's populace. This was made worse by the feeling that everything was coated in a fine layer of soot which billowed from the chimney stacks that rose from the skyline.

Across from the inn was a small square, lit by a pair of street lamps, with a sole bronze statue of a long-deceased founder. Metal and concrete benches were arranged at cardinal positions; none were in use currently. With the sun long gone, most of the locals were in a rush to be elsewhere. What little chatter could be overheard was spoken on the move.

It was in this plaza that Prae, Peter and Apello waited for the remainder of their company. When he earlier scouted their dining arrangements, Apello located a smorgasbord of excellent reputation a few blocks to the west.

Peter cleared his throat as he shifted impatiently. During their transit, Peter had remained introspective, as if consumed with sorting out a plethora of ponderings that filled his head.

"Tell me about Erudatta," Peter requested as he locked eyes with Prae. "You made mention of him earlier. I assume you know him in some capacity and I'm still trying to understand his role in all of this."

Prae snorted sarcastically. "He was Hierarch of the Scientia, headmaster over all practiced disciplines in the fields of science. Anything that ended in −ology or −tics was under his purview. No one began an authorized project or experiment without the appropriate documentation passing through his office. To his name were credited legions of discoveries and breakthroughs. He was the creator of the first mechanized golem. Spent many years perfecting the technology, as we were all witness."

"So it would be safe to assume that it was his work that greeted us? In Ala'ydin?"

"Different models separated by eons, but yes. That was his handiwork. Masina had all the telltale signs of refinement upon his previous designs. There were design elements in the craftwork that were distinctly his. He might as well have signed his name to it. I would gather that he's had plenty of time to improve upon his original creations."

"Are we to expect others?" Apello spoke up from where he leaned against the statue. With their sights set on Greater Decedistadt, a renewed drive seemed to overtake him.

"If I'm to give an answer in absolutes? Unknown. It should not be unexpected that he would keep one or two about as protection. We'll need to prepare for such a probability."

"Wait, really?" Peter's voice raised an octave. "We had our share of trouble with only one."

Prae was about to comment when she noticed as Oebe exited the inn.

"A discussion for another time," Prae noted as she hailed the smaller woman with a wave of her arm.

Since the lion's share of his inquiry went unanswered, Peter opened his mouth to press the matter, only for words to fail him. Before long, another question came to mind.

"Where is Cal? I thought he was going to pick you up?" Peter inquired. "I mean, it *is* his job. I have half a mind to file a complaint with the League about the cavalier manner in which he handles his duties."

"He said: 'Why don't you meet up with the others? Once I'm done getting the boarding passes, I'll join.' I left him as he was recovering his money. By his own admission, he concealed it at the bottom of my luggage for safe keeping." Her imitation of his cadence was surprisingly spot-on.

From behind Peter came the sound of Apello's stifled groan.

Peter began to mull over her words. *Wait, I thought he didn't have any money. Or, barely enough to get him and Oebe back. It makes so much sense now that he bailed on us earlier, telling a fib that he was going to fetch Oebe. That lying bastard, skipping out on the check like that. Cal and I are going to settle up before we're done. I'm out a good bit of my savings for this jaunt and I may not even have a job once we're done.*

"Let us head on, then," Apello announced. "If he is to meet up with us, he will. If he plans to find his night's entertainment elsewhere, then it's best to not waste time waiting for him."

"You don't think—" Oebe began before Apello cut her off.

"That he's made himself scarce to tend to his indulgences? Yes, I do. I would rather partake of a certain meal than gamble with the chance that he isn't plotting a night of debauchery."

Oebe scowled briefly. After a resigned shrug of her shoulders, she fell in behind Apello.

"Who knows? Maybe he went to go get a drink. Or meet up with a lady friend. There's no telling with him." Peter spoke in an upbeat tone. "He could have connections in town that we don't know about."

While the others strode off, Prae looked to the second story of the nearby hostel. For a moment, she bit at her lower lip. Before losing sight of her companions, Prae took off at a light jog.

If she had waited only a few moments, she might have caught sight of Cal as he came out of the servant's entrance into the alley.

Cal travelled unmarked back streets to avoid the foot traffic as best he could. He was of the opinion that the fewer people who might have reason to recall his face, the better.

In his rush to escape, Cal hadn't exactly hammered out all of the finer details of his plan. So, when he was halfway between the inn and the Langspur Rail Station, it occurred to him that there would be no outgoing train that evening. He swore aloud and kicked at a piece of debris, which bounded noisily into the nearby avenue.

He paused in the darkness of the alley and considered his choices. There were options available, though organizing or even paying for them might prove challenging.

Chartering a boat from the southern docks was a possibility, however he doubted he could afford it. He could try to hike along the Langspur, though the prospect of such a walk was unappealing.

Lost in his thoughts, Cal failed to hear the footfalls until someone spoke to him from the darkness. Through the thin slivers of yellow light that stretched along the passage, Cal eventually picked out a hooded man who slowly crept towards him.

"Reeger." The raspy voice came across as muffled. Once the light from the distant lantern reflected off of the bronze chin that jutted from under the hood's shadow, Cal swore to himself.

"Raxus," Cal sneered as he went into a defensive posture. A cold sweat broke out across his brow. With the trophy still tucked in one arm, he dropped his free hand to his holster.

"Don't even think about it," Raxus growled. He made a quick motion with one hand. A pair of associates dressed in gray Kevlar body armor with riot batons entered the lane and approached Cal from behind. When it became clear to Cal that he'd not seen either man in Jaefor's employ, his muscles tensed.

"I've got what Jaefor wants," Cal stated as his eyes danced from target to target.

"I doubt you have any idea of the things that Jaefor desires," Raxus spat. "You've took me on a merry chase, fool. Should've ran for it when you had the chance. I caught up with you in Viisibourg, walking around like some kinda tourist." He made another wave of his hand and the two men closed in.

"How many did you leave dead in your wake?" Cal taunted Raxus. He just couldn't help himself. The man had a reputation for violence that bordered on sociopathic. If he was hired to locate Cal, odds are that Jaefor's prize would keep him alive.

"Take him."

At Raxus' order, the pair converged on Cal. One struck him over the head with a baton before Cal could even consider moving for his revolver. His knees buckled. As his vision blurred, Oebe's sack dropped from his grasp and struck the paved walkway with a clatter.

With the dazed Cal held upright in his men's hands, Raxus crossed to the pack and picked it up. He peered inside. In the poor light, Raxus was forced to open the bag wide before he could see its contents.

"Well, well," he muttered before closing it again. "You get to live, at least for another day. That is until I can figure out whether this is worth anything or not."

At that, a black sack was pulled over Cal's head. He was struck in the stomach and over the head a second time before he blacked out completely.

21

Cal's head pounded something fierce. It felt as if someone was angrily beating a tympanum from behind his eyes. Between the constant jostling and the dull throb from his scalp, he awoke confused. He had no idea where he was or how much time had passed.

His eyes flickered open to darkness. He wasn't dead, yet, that much he knew. Only when he felt the sackcloth brush against his cheeks did he realize that a bag had been placed over his head.

As his senses began to return, he grunted and twisted his shoulders. There was something fleshy tucked under each armpit that restrained his movement. He could feel the rope that kept his hands bound. The coarse fibers dug into the meat of his wrists. A second attempt to move his arms was met by a sudden nudge to his ribcage.

"Stop yer fidgeting," a voice barked angrily into his ear.

It was then that everything began to fall in place. A pair of men was carrying him by his shoulders. As his feet scraped along the ground, he grew certain the walkway was paved. The surface did not have the rough texture associated with stones, bricks or pavers, so they were presumably within civilized city limits. Even through the bag over his head, he could pick out the familiar stink of the city: a mélange of burnt oil and human sweat mixed with an undercurrent of brine. Gone was the scorched aroma of soot that was indicative of Ilgyngate.

"Here. Bring him here," a voice from somewhere in front ordered. Raxus and his men were taking him somewhere until the value of Prae's helmet could be determined.

"Where exactly are we going?" one of his captors inquired.

"Got a meeting place with… our benefactor set up not too far off."

The screech of a steel door as it scraped against its frame helped Cal gain some sense of direction. He was being led into a building a few meters up on his left. Without the feeling of warm sun against his skin, he had to consider this location was somewhere off of the beaten path. From the lack of crowd noise, he considered they were now in an abandoned stretch of the back alleys far away from the more populated areas. If he was in Greater Decedistadt as he thought, Cal figured he was being escorted through one of the industrial sectors.

Once through the entrance, Cal's kidnappers came to a stop. He could still hear the scuff of boot heels on concrete just up ahead. There was a sound of movement, accompanied by the banging of metal against metal.

"Ugh. What the hell is that stink?" the man on Cal's right grunted as he halted for a moment. From the shift,

Cal guessed that he moved a hand to cover his face.

Cal knew immediately what he meant. He could smell a pervasive aroma of rotting flesh that persisted in the air. Something had died here recently.

He once again felt himself dragged forward when a scuffle of boots on distant steps rang out from in front of them. At this, the two men who held him came to a sudden stop. Behind them, the door slammed shut.

"What in the hell?" Raxus barked.

"What's going on here, Raxus?" the man on Cal's left inquired. Cal could make out the fear in his cracking voice. "Were you expecting—"

The world around Cal was thrown into chaos. As he was released, Cal was pushed aside. Still bound, he immediately toppled over. When he landed on the cold floor, the side of his skull bounced off the surface.

Cal's senses were a mess. Even if his vision hadn't been hampered, the blow to his head caused his brain to spin. The fragments of sound he did catch were jumbled. He heard the clatter of combat. Male voices grunted as heels scuffed across the flooring. A piercing scream cut short by a bone-cracking blow. A string of swears that Cal was certain came from Raxus was quickly followed by the crash of broken glass.

Just as soon as it began, everything fell silent. Footsteps approached where Cal still lay.

When the dark cloth was yanked off of Cal's head, he flinched. After blinking for a few seconds, he saw a form towering over him. Leaning in close, no more than a foot or two from his face, was the imposing obsidian helm of a Magistrate, the tips of its metal horns inches from his scalp. Cal could see his stunned look reflected in the red-glass panel at the center of the faceplate.

"Oh shit," he groaned with a roll of his eyes.

"Name, citizen," the Magistrate commanded, his voice disguised and amplified by a speaker hidden just beneath the helmet's jawline. The tone was deeper in timbre and held a hint of static that became noticeable in the sharper consonant sounds.

"Does it *really* matter?"

Cal's head craned to one side as a blow caught him across the mouth. Pain radiated along his jawline where the metal glove struck him. Within seconds, he could taste the blood on his tongue and his lips began to throb.

"Your name, citizen. I won't request it again."

"Reeger. Cal Reeger."

At this, the officer lifted him up by the collar of his shirt. Cal spotted a second Magistrate a few paces away who towered over the broken and bloodied bodies of Raxus' henchmen. In one hand he held Oebe's pack. Cal turned back and forth as he looked for any sign of Raxus.

After a quick assessment of his surroundings, he realized that the location was a vacant workhouse. Row upon row of abandoned machinery stood in an adjacent room. The thick layer of dust and debris left Cal to wonder how long it had been since the building was in use.

When he caught sight of the shattered window at the

other end of the hall, he realized where Raxus might be found.

"My escort?" he asked as he was set on his feet. He wobbled as he attempted to keep upright. Seeing this, the armored man grabbed him by the rope which bound his hands and jerked upwards. A sharp pain shot up both arms.

"Not your worry." At this, his captor turned. "Where do we deposit this one?"

"Upstairs." He hooked a thumb to the stairwell at the end of the corridor. "There's a room that'll do just fine to detain him until we're done here. I'll go ahead and call this in."

"Be sure that we get paid *up front*, this time," the first officer commented as he forced Cal forward with an elbow to the back.

"Yeah, yeah. Not so gullible as to let that happen again."

Cal was swiftly escorted to the second floor, where dilapidated offices had been left for months, if not years. The Magistrate shoved him into a side room that only contained folding tables and a trio of rusted filing cabinets. At the center was a steel chair that was bolted to the floor. Around this a spattering of dried blood stained the linoleum flooring. A ceiling lamp hung from the center of the room; the bulb, which glowed a glaring yellow, surprisingly still received power. Cal was forced into the chair as his restrained limbs were hung over the back.

The Magistrate produced a strip of plastic that quickly molded into handcuffs. He used this to lash Cal's hands to the chair. He left the room and closed the door with a slam.

Some time later, one of the Magistrates returned and dropped Oebe's pack on the nearby table. He also delivered a pair of holsters and revolvers that Cal immediately recognized as his own. These were placed beside the stolen helmet.

Cal waited for what felt like an eternity. The prospect of his dwindling future weighed heavily on his mind. He could hear the occasional footstep from somewhere in the building, but no one came to visit. More than once, he tested the strength of his bonds. Since the chair was bolted to the floor, he focused on whether the plastic tie could be broken. After a series of tugs, each more violent than the last, he slumped into the chair, defeated. His arms began to hurt; the bindings themselves were wearing at the skin around his wrists.

Things don't exactly piece together just right. I get hiring Raxus to make sure I came back. Dude's always hanging around D'rian Obix, even if only as paid muscle. Makes sense for Jaefor to send him out after I didn't come back right away.

But, where things get odd is our friends, the Magistrates, showing up like they did. Was this an unrelated—Naw, it couldn't be. They were looking for me. Asked me for my name, even. Someone paid them to grab me. Oh, shit, someone paid Magistrates… Jaefor. Has to be. No one else has that kind of money. Unless… what about Prae's 'friend' Erudatta. Would he be the kind of person to bribe law enforcement to do grunt work? Naw, that can't be it. That doesn't seem like the kind of thing her people would do. He'd send another golem, and even then, why would he want me, in particular?

It's gotta be Jaefor, but if that's so, then who hired Raxus? He ain't the kinda guy to do things on his own without a payday. And, we don't know each other enough for him to hold a grudge—

At the sound of steps on the metal staircase, his concentration was broken. The footfalls were softer, those of someone lacking heavy armor. He sat upright and waited. The door opened to Jaefor standing in the entryway, silhouetted by the sunlight that filtered through the dirt-caked windows.

"Mr. Reeger," Jaefor called out as he entered the room. One of the Magistrates stepped in beside him, only to be brushed aside with a flick of his hand. The constable returned to his post and closed the door behind himself. "It has been some time since last we conversed. While you were late in your return, I knew I could count on you to eventually turn up like the bad penny that you are."

"Nice…" Cal's mouth ached.

"Having said that, I would now like to peruse what potential addition to my collection warranted such a sequence of events," Jaefor continued as he strode forward. He was dressed in a garish ensemble of silk and velvet. A violet three-piece suit practically glowed in the drab surroundings. "Between the delay in your arrival and the ill-advised machinations of my former employees, I am of the opinion that this *must* be an invaluable object, worth more than you've seen in your entire life."

"Oh, come on," Cal grunted. The swelling of his lip

and the bruising along his jawline caused him to slur. "You can't exactly blame me for what Raxus did, can you?"

"Not just Raxus," Jaefor corrected as he raised a finger. "But, Illgosses as well. I am now out one accountant and one mercenary. The only reason I'm not more cross with you is that Illgosses' maneuver outed him as a liability. His role will be filled with someone far less ambitious as to think for themselves."

"Well, ain't that convenient for you."

Jaefor offered a cockeyed smile. He kept any mirth he may have felt to himself and continued. "The last time I spoke with you, you were struggling not to shit your pants in my presence. I stood naked before you—you were armed even—and yet, you shook in your boots. How is it that you have so much bravado, now? Men of far greater quality would tearfully beg for their lives. Bargain with all that they have."

Cal coughed up a laugh that came with a dollop of blood. "At this point, I really got nothing left to lose."

"Your life."

"Worthless. I stole from one of the few people who, even for a little while, didn't think I was complete gutter trash."

Jaefor paused as he examined Cal's countenance. Jaefor's inspection ceased when Cal looked away.

Before Jaefor could press the matter, Cal spoke up. "I take it you have friends in high places."

"The Magistrates? Not so difficult to employ if

one knows the right people, or has the correct amount of money by which to bribe. In my time, I've hosted a few gatherings for people of power. Men with specific *depravities*. I tend to their needs and from time to time, they tend to mine."

Jaefor went to the folding table, opened the bag and reached inside. Carefully, he removed Prae's helmet and held it up to his face. As he spun it from side to side, Jaefor examined the craftsmanship. He rotated it and inspected the circular ports at the base of the skull. Jaefor ran a finger along the seams for a second. Though he made the occasional pleased sound, he did not speak a single word. In the end, he nodded with a hum and placed it upright on the table.

"Impressive. I would usually have this examined for its tangible market value, maybe even its cultural and historical worth, but the man I would usually turn to—Illgosses—is otherwise disposed. This leaves me in a bit of bind, as it were."

"How did you know?" Cal inquired. "About Illgosses and Raxus, I mean."

"Is this the part where I spill my grand scheme to you purely out of hubris? Where you get me to blather on incessantly while you attempt to extricate yourself from your bindings? Just so you know, there is no escape for you. I'll have you understand, once I'm done here, the two Magistrates waiting just outside will be tending to your situation." He pointed over his shoulder and winked. A perverse grin grew on his face.

"Well, I won't lie and say I wasn't hoping for at

least a little delay before you decided to kill me," Cal admitted with a shrug of his shoulders. The movement was humorously stunted by his restrained arms. "At this point, I'll take any extra second I can get."

"Hoping to give your rescuers a chance to arrive in the proverbial nick of time?"

Cal scoffed. "Ain't no one coming to save my hide today. You know it as well as I do. Just… just wanting to be a little older before you put me down. Every man tries to delay the inevitable. I ain't no different."

"Fair enough. I will concede to your request." Jaefor cleared his throat before he continued. "I was alerted to Raxus' departure along the Langspur Line by one of my contacts in the Central Judicia. As you are well aware, he is not a man that one might call inconspicuous, even dressed in a hooded robe as he was. A few inquiries later, it was abundantly clear that some of his known associates had likewise shipped out to Ilgyngate. Those camped out in and around the station in Greater Decedistadt were quickly picked up."

Jaefor paused as he brushed a few flecks of dust from his lapel. "Have you ever heard of the interrogation techniques employed by Magistrates when they *really* desire information a person might have?"

"Can't say as I have. The beat-downs they hand out for petty theft are bad enough. I don't know that I want to guess."

"It's for the best. Unpleasant work, it is. Especially for those of weak constitutions. Effective, though. Nothing like making a man's fingers bend the wrong way to loosen up his tongue. I mean, I could have just as easily paid for the information, but I was already in for nearly six figures with the rental of law enforcement. Didn't make sense to double-dip, as they say." He snorted to himself. "As you might expect, it did not take long for Illgosses' name to come up. A quick audit of my accounts unearthed a few *irregularities*."

"Is that accountant talk for 'he was stealing from me'?"

"Worse. Yours was not the first time he sought to intervene by hijacking the payment of outstanding accounts." Jaefor fell quiet as he returned his gaze to the objects on the nearby tabletop. "How much do you think these are worth?" Jaefor motioned to the pair of revolvers.

"Does it matter? Take them. Sell them for pocket change. I'm sure it won't cover what I owe." With the tailored cut of Jaefor's suit, Cal assumed he was not carrying a gun of his own. If death was to come by way of a bullet, it would probably be from his own armaments. *The only thing I actually ever owned and it'll be the death of me. Pretty sure Jaefor would like the irony of that. Does seem a little easy, though. I figured him for the kind of guy to make a person suffer. Maybe he's got a blade. Cut me up pretty bad first. Nah, wouldn't want to soil such a nice suit. Probably'll let the Magistrates do the dirty work for him.*

"Of course it won't." Jaefor looked back to Cal.

Just as he opened his mouth to add something else, Jaefor stopped. From outside the closed door rang the sounds of shuffling feet and raised voices. A clash of steel was quickly followed by a single shot from a rifle. His eyes widened as Jaefor looked over his shoulder but remained in place.

After Jaefor stepped into the storeroom, the Magistrates were left to loiter in the second-story hallway. The payment they were promised for the diversion from their daily rounds was enough to keep both men waiting happily. Jaefor had arrived alone and his only instructions were to remain until he finished his business with the prisoner. Once the door to the room closed, they lingered nearby.

They chatted about the unpleasant task of cleaning up. It wasn't until the first step clanked on the metal staircase that they ceased their conversation and faced the end of the hall.

"Were we expecting someone else?"

"No. Jaefor was supposed to come by himself. Wanted to keep this hush-hush."

"Maybe we should check…" The Magistrate trailed off.

Prae stood alone at the end of the corridor. Except for the missing helm, now replaced by a stern look, she was fully dressed in her armor. The two Magistrates withdrew their batons and began to slowly approach her. Electricity crackled along the surface of their cudgels.

"Halt!" one called as he raised a hand to her. "This is private property. Your presence has been deemed an illegal action. Retreat or we shall be forced to administer justice."

At this, Prae unsheathed her weapon. With a flick of

her wrist, the blade telescoped. The armored pair went into defensive postures. Before either could move, she created a halo of red light above the flat surface. She folded her thumb inward and swept four diagonal lines across the circle of light. She then swung her hand in a downwards arc, which caused the semanifesture to become absorbed by the steel. A string of icons glowed vibrantly in sanguine hues.

"Let us see you try," Prae taunted as she raised the weapon.

One of the Magistrates strode forward, his baton above his head. As he drew within a few paces, he barked at her. "You've no idea what you're asking for!"

Prae attacked with lightning quickness. She turned the sword horizontally and brought it across his chest. The impact was so sudden and unexpected that he had no time to recoil. The strike caused him to drop the baton as the steel plates on his chest bent beneath the violent force. As the Magistrate stumbled, red energy hung midair where the blade had struck his armor.

Before he could recover, Prae brought the sword around in an arc over her head. The blade came down at an angle and caught him in a glancing blow across the helmet. The momentum spun him like a top before he collapsed to the floor. When he failed to move, Prae stepped back and turned her attention to the Magistrate in the distance.

The second combatant discarded his baton and went for the rifle slung over his shoulder. As she faced her opponent, Prae observed this maneuver. With her blade still held across her waist, she raised her free hand and extended a pair of fingers. A few quick movements produced an amber disc marked with angular icons. The circle pulsed once before it expanded to a six-foot tall barrier that hovered before Prae.

The Magistrate leveled the rifle and fired off the first round. A sharp crack rang in the air. As Prae expected, the bullet slammed into the semanifesture and dropped impotently to the floor. She stood silent and watched as the armed man loaded the next round and aimed at her head.

The second shot's outcome was the same; the projectile was briefly caught mid-air before gravity dragged it to the floor.

Rather than delay any further, she made a quick downward sweep of her hand. While the amber light scattered, she launched forward. Flecks bounced off of the sharp angles of her armor as she pierced the dissipating barrier. The speed of her approach forced the Magistrate to stumble in retreat.

As she reached him, her weapon rose in an upwards arc. The flat tip caught him along the abdomen. A flash of sanguine energy burst on impact and he was tossed into the air. With an unholy clatter, he spilled to the floor and skidded to a halt a few meters down the hall.

Prae charged to where the dazed combatant was splayed. She drove the heel of her boot into his head and it bounced off of the concrete floor. A faint grunt was joined by a gut-wrenching crunch which indicated painful injury. The crimson glass at the center of the helmet's faceplate was cracked from the severity of the blow.

She glanced about cautiously. When neither opponent rose, she turned to the entryway they guarded. With her blade still in hand, she kicked at the doorknob. The impact snapped the brass handle and splintered the wood; this forced the entry wide open.

Once inside the room, she found Cal lashed to a chair, his face bruised and bloodied. Despite his position, he cracked a smile as he snorted sardonically. To his left was an older gentleman in a velvet three-piece suit. In his possession were Cal's revolvers, both held aloft with unsteady hands. He leveled one at Prae as the other was shakily aimed at Cal. Prae caught sight of her helmet on the tabletop behind the would-be gunman.

"So good of you to join us." Cal chose to break the tension in his usual manner. At this point in time, he had nothing left to lose. If Jaefor didn't shoot him outright, Prae would probably exact her own brand of revenge. "Jaefor, this is Prae Ganvelt, the original owner of what *was* to be your prize. I've got the distinct feeling you won't be walking away from here with it like you were hoping."

"You bastard! What is this, Reeger? Is this some kind of set up?" Jaefor's voice screeched as his hands shook. Cal had never seen the man in such a state. Face-to-face with a far more intimidating opponent, any bravado he once displayed quickly disappeared.

Cal chuckled at the implication of his so-called treachery. "That's rich."

After a few seconds, Jaefor attempted regain his deportment. Cal could still see the trembling in his hands. "Look, Miss..." Jaefor began.

"Ganvelt," Cal spoke up. "Trust me, you don't want to get it wrong."

"Look, there must be some kind of arrangement we can come to," Jaefor spoke in a casual tone that seemed intended for cautious negotiation. He addressed her in an even baritone an octave lower than his usual register.

Focused on Jaefor, Prae's stern gaze failed to falter. "You will find my capitulation cannot so easily be purchased."

"It's true, she can't."

"Cease your prattle!" Jaefor snapped at Cal as he nudged the barrel ever closer to his forehead. Cal only smiled as his shoulders relaxed. Though there was still discomfort from the way he was bound, Cal felt relief.

"Just so you know," Cal continued to prod Jaefor. "Before you decide to go all gun-happy, there aren't any bullets left in the revolvers."

"What?" Jaefor turned to him, brow furrowed. His face became flushed.

"Well, it's not like I've been able to afford ammo for some time now. You know how my finances are, right? I mean, that's why we're here, isn't it?"

Jaefor angled one of the revolvers so that he could look inside the cylinder. It was the exact distraction Cal wanted.

In that brief moment, Prae crossed the short distance. Held in both hands, her blade flicked upwards and caught Jaefor along the right arm. The cutting edge slid through flesh and bone like hot butter. Still grasping the firearm, the dismembered limb fell to the floor. As the pain came to surface, Jaefor staggered backwards and dropped the second gun as he clutched at the stump that proceeded to gush a torrent of blood. All color in his face quickly faded as he slumped against the back corner of the wall.

Cal twisted as far as he could to look at Jaefor. The rope dug into his flesh.

"Oh, that looks permanent," he muttered under his breath before turning back.

Ignoring Cal's presence, Prae went to Jaefor. Though he struggled to apply pressure to the wound, he maintained enough awareness to pull back from her approach. Blood covered his hand and soaked the violet fabric of his suit, staining it a muddy brown.

"Please, no more," he croaked as tears rolled down his cheeks. "I beg you, spare my life!"

She stood over him silently, her weapon aloft.

"Cal, speak to her for me," he pleaded. "Tell her what I can offer her in return."

Cal's only response was to chuckle.

After a few tense seconds, Prae spoke. "Cease your blathering. I have killed over a thousand men, whether directly by my own hand or through anonymous orders that led to their eventual demise. Each time, it was deemed that their deaths were for a greater purpose. Now, that I stand before you as executioner, I have the distinct impression that your own passing will make this world a better place."

Before Jaefor could continue his supplication, she

brought up the sword and drove the edge into his head.

Cal heard the sickening crunch but chose not to look. The splatter of fluids that struck the floor was all he needed to hear.

After a long hushed pause that grew more unnerving by the second, he cleared his throat. He might be next in line.

"Look, I don't expect that you came to get me, but if you'd at least cut me loose, I'd really, really appreciate it. I mean, if you didn't kill the Magistrates out in the hall, they'll do what Jaefor wanted to before you showed up. Leaving me behind is only gonna delay the inevitable."

Cal felt a hard tug at his bindings. A second later, his hands were free. He brought them forward and tossed the slit rope to the floor. The skin around his wrists was rubbed raw.

Before he could rise, Prae came around and leaned in. Her sword had already been returned to its scabbard and she held one of his revolvers. She placed her right hand on his chin and lifted his face to meet hers. Cal was immediately surprised to see relief in her usually-stern face.

"Are you well?" she asked as she looked over the bruised jaw and swollen lip.

His eyes flickered briefly. Her shift towards concern left him stunned. "I'm okay, considering. Still confused as to why you bothered to help me, though."

"I owe you a debt. Your actions saved my life in Ala'ydin. I do not forget those who helped me."

"But I—"

"By the evidence available, it is clear that, in some capacity, you were coerced into a scenario that you would not have found yourself in otherwise." She stood upright and offered him a hand. "Unless, this is how your compatriots usually complete such business arrangements. If so, it is for the best you find other friends."

"You're being pretty magnanimous about this." Cal eventually took the offered help. She pulled him up and placed a supportive hand behind his back. He had been sitting in the chair for so long that his legs had grown weak. He had to lean against her shoulder for support.

"I have no time to waste on the cycle of anger, acceptance and eventual forgiveness that would usually accompany this kind of event," she announced.

"Don't you even want to know *why*?"

"If it will make you happier to unburden yourself, then feel free to do so."

"I, uh, well…" he stammered at her bluntness.

"There is good in you. It may be hidden beneath layers of questionable decisions, but it is there." She looked him directly in the eyes. "I've seen it. Whether you wish to play such a thing off with a show of sarcastic bluster or not is up to you."

He frowned for a moment, puzzled. Then, he remembered the semanifesture at Ala'ydin. The colored haze that had displayed the aspects his character. He never inquired what she had divined from the vapors.

After a few minutes, Cal was able to stand under his own power. He proceeded to stretch his arms and legs, to work out the worst of the stiffness.

Prae reached down and retrieved the revolver from the dismembered hand. Now back with its mate, she offered both to Cal. "I won't pretend to understand the day-to-day issues you and your kind must suffer through. I have never gone without, never had to worry about surviving the mundane existence that besets you."

Instead of expressing his usual sardonic nature, Cal nodded quietly as he took his weapons. Eventually, a thought occurred to him.

"How did you find me? I can't imagine Raxus was so sloppy as to leave that much of a trail."

"By this." She extended her index and pinky fingers and quickly produced a blue circle of light. With a few additional movements, this was filled with three smaller concentric rings. The last contained a trio of diagonal lines in a Z-formation. Prae tapped at the center with a finger, which caused it to extend into a beveled cone shape. After a second, the semanifesture spun about and pointed directly at her helmet.

"Of course."

With a toss of her hand, the energy form dissolved. Prae collected her property and deposited it in Oebe's bag. She tied the end to a belt loop and looked at Cal, who had already strapped his holsters to his waist. As he slid the guns back in place, he avoided glancing at Jaefor's remains.

"Shall we, then?" Prae motioned to the open doorway.

"The others?" Cal inquired as he slowly strode forward. There was still a stiffness to his gait, but not enough to keep him in the room any longer.

"Peter is looking for the entrance to Erudatta's containment cell. Apello is with him. As is Oebe. I came to retrieve you on my own. This was non-negotiable."

Upon seeing the bodies of the Magistrates, Cal understood her reasoning. Apello may have been a fierce combatant, but he would have only gotten in her way. With no such impediment, Prae had dispatched her foes with an alarming haste. Cal thought that neither law-keeper proved a match for the centurion.

"And how are they about all this?"

"None of my concern. Any personal complaints they have to take up with you can be settled on our return."

The admission did little to assuage his anxiety. Oebe would likely treat him no different. Peter might be cross and pepper him with bitter language. Apello, on the other hand, might administer justice for Cal's thievery with his bare hands if Prae did not intervene.

"Okay... So, where are we supposed to meet up with them?"

"A location within Nipir'x Sector. Peter determined Erudatta's point of origin was somewhere in the area. Oebe announced that you would know the way."

"Of course she did." Cal groaned. An image of the campus, bound on all sides by its ivory-colored walls, flashed into his mind. *It would be just my luck...*

As they reached the first floor, Cal paused. The fallen bodies were left were they fell. Small puddles of blood were slowly drying in the cracks between the dust-coated tiles.

"They're beginning to rot something fierce," Prae commented as she placed a hand over her nose.

"That stench was here when we arrived. Before things went to shit," Cal mentioned as he looked back and forth.

"If so, then—"

"Something else has been dead around here for some time. Wouldn't surprise me if this is Raxus' dumping grounds." With that said, he slowly moved down the hall, giving the recently-dead a wide berth. As he passed a doorway, he nudged it aside with one hand.

When Cal recoiled from the scene, Prae moved up beside him. Beyond the opening was a cleaning closet. Long-unused supplies were still arranged along a pair of metal racks. In between was a body, left prone in the middle of the small room. Cal immediately recognized the thinning hair and diagonal scar along his scalp. A pair of broken green-tinted glasses rested just out of reach of the dead man.

"You know of him?"

"Yeah. I guess I really don't have to pay that debt anymore. Probably not in my best interest to stay around the city after we're done with our business."

22

As they took their overdue leave through the front door, Prae stopped long enough to retrieve her robe, which hung from a doorknob just inside. She quickly draped it over her armor. While it was not intended to cover the bulkier gear, it was enough to obscure the attire. If anything, the average person was likely to be drawn to the metallic copper of her hair before they took notice of her apparel.

Once they departed, Cal was able to confirm his earlier estimation: they were already in Greater Decedistadt. By the position of the sun above the crooked roofline, he could tell it was already midday.

Before they were too far away, Cal came to a halt and looked back to the entrance in the distance. Noticing Cal's hesitation, Prae likewise stopped.

"No one's gonna know this even happened, are they?" Cal's voice was heavy with melancholy.

"By the lack of foot-traffic and the secretive nature of such dealings? I would gather that they will not. Your man, Jaefor, may be missed, in the technical sense of the term, but I doubt they will discover him in the near future. Whoever rises to take his place may not desire a resolution on the matter of his disappearance. Such matters cause confusion in the midst of transition." After a few seconds, she reached out and placed a hand on Cal's shoulder. "Will you be okay?"

He gulped with a nod. "Yeah, eventually. I… by all rights, I should be dead."

"Well, you aren't." Her fingertips squeezed tightly. Cal was surprised to find comfort in her grip.

"Thank you."

"Consider us even," she said with a smile before motioning that they should be moving along.

Cal made a quick perusal of the surrounding abandoned warehouses. They were somewhere in the northern part of the city, probably no more than a mile from the harbor.

Back onto the more inhabited avenues, Cal shook off the dark mood and chose to lead. It took him a few seconds to pick out the nearby landmarks and street signs. When he determined their approximate location, he quickly ushered Prae to the west. As fortune would have it, they were not too far from Nipir'x Sector. It would only be a half hour's walk to reach it via a series of side streets.

It wasn't long before they arrived at the main avenue. On one end, it fed into the circle which surrounded the An-Sebban campus. Through the undulating throng, Cal spied the ivory walls in the distance. A sour feeling grew in the pit of his stomach as they drew near.

Eventually, they located the rest of their party waiting at a nearby delicatessen a dozen yards from the blackened iron gates of the Athenaeum's estate. They were seated at a table in the establishment's veranda, among a group of other customers who were enjoying an early supper. As Cal and Prae emerged from the crowd, a look of stunned disbelief showed on Peter's and Apello's faces. Though Oebe's brow piqued, she seemed more relieved than anything.

Once surprise gave way to anger, Apello's countenance changed. Just as the pair stepped into the shade of the canvas awnings, Apello shot up from his chair, knocking it back with a clatter. He lunged forward to meet Cal and grasped him by the collar. Consumed with rage, he lifted him off the floor.

"Apello!" Peter cried out. With a quick glance to their surroundings, he noticed as a pensive curiosity infected the other patrons. None made an attempt to flee; rather they watched to see how the distraction would play out.

Apello spoke through clenched teeth. "You wretch of a man. I do not know how you tricked Prae into—"

"Do whatever you want to me, man," Cal cut him off. "I've been pulled from the reaper's grasp. I'm not all that scared of what you can do to me anymore."

This caused Apello to hesitate. Cal saw conflicting emotions play across the man's coarse features.

"Set him down," Prae ordered as she moved in beside Cal. Apello turned to her. After a few seconds of tense silence, Apello let out a long breath. He dropped Cal to his feet.

Prae continued. "I have spoken with Cal and taken a measure of the situation. Facts presented to me when

I located him gave me a better understanding of his circumstances. I arrived at the conclusion that his decision, while questionable, came because of exterior forces exerting pressure on him. This was not a choice he made out of greed, but out of self-preservation. It is my opinion that, ultimately, such a choice, though regrettable, is understandable, given the nature of those with whom he was dealing. I hold no grudge with Cal and I would suggest you set aside your own for the time being."

The harsh grimace slowly softened as he released his grasp. There was a lengthy pause while he processed the situation but, eventually, he eyed Cal and nodded once. "I... I will relent. I am not unfamiliar with taking actions in light of events beyond one's control. It is not something so easy to understand unless one has been there before. If you choose to forgive him this transgression—this theft of your property—I see no reason not to stay my hand."

"Uh, thanks," Cal sputtered as he backed away. Apello's comment would certainly stay with him. Now was not the time for such conversations, but his curiosity had been piqued.

"And you?" Prae shifted to face Peter, who had not yet risen from his seat. "Have you any grievances to air on this matter?"

The combination of their surprising appearance and the subsequent flurry of activity was enough to briefly discombobulate Peter. He wordlessly acknowledged the inquiry with a nod. Eventually, he shook his head and spoke up. "Uh, timing's inconvenient, but with all that's happened so far, I really got nothing to add. Questions, sure, but now isn't really the time or place."

Oebe rose from her seat and went to Cal. He leaned in as she extended an arm to him.

"Your face," Oebe stated as she reached over and ran her fingers softly along his jaw. Cal flinched once as she brushed at the worst of the bruising.

"It's okay. I was born with it like this." He let her gingerly touch his face for a few seconds. Once she retracted her hand, Cal faced the others, who had gathered around the pair.

"In light of our recent, uh, dust up, might I suggest we move along?" Peter motioned his head sideways, reminding them of the curious glances they were still receiving.

"I recall there being an empty storefront a ways down the street," Apello noted as he scanned the vicinity. "It looks like we did not arouse the interest of the local constabulary, so perhaps we should reconvene there."

They departed from the delicatessen. The group made their way through the afternoon traffic and located the boarded-up establishment. The abandoned building was at a nearby street corner. The exterior windows and front entrance had been shuttered some time ago. Reddish corrosion discolored much of the steel door.

They slipped into the adjacent alley and quickly discovered an employee entry, which was only barred by a tarnished padlock. Prae delivered a quick blow to the rusted metal, which popped the lock, and the party entered the building.

From the remaining furnishings, it was clear that it had

once been a greengrocer. A thick cloud of dust, an odor of water-logged cardboard, and the smell of spoiled produce hung in the air. Apello headed to the front of the shop to peek through the space between the blinds. His eyes scanned for any sign that their unlawful entry had been noticed.

Cal cleared his throat and spoke up. "So, I know I'm gonna regret asking this, as I've got a pretty good idea of what you're gonna say, but have you figured out where we need to go? Prae made mention it was somewhere in the sector."

Peter pointed to the north, where Cal was certain the An-Sebban estate rose in the distance. "Somewhere beyond those walls." There was an edge to his voice and a crease in his brow.

Cal groaned. "Of course. Figured as much."

"What seems to be the issue?" Prae inquired.

"*That* would be the campus for the Athenaeum of the An-Sebban. It's where I was supposed to bring Oebe back once she was done at Natx Hollow." The sharp pain from his earlier wounds caused him to wince. "In light of the situation, do we even want Oebe to come along with us?"

"You can't exactly leave her behind," Peter implored. He looked horrified at the possibility.

"And we can't just walk *her* in there." He turned to Oebe hoping for corroboration.

"Cal isn't entirely mistaken," she admitted. "I conversed with him earlier about my decision not to return to the Athenaeum. There is a wealth of information of which I am now in possession that would be dangerous to have added to the Central Archives. The location of Ala'ydin. Knowledge of the Progenitors and Prae's Blue Room. With any of this, others might begin to hunt for Prae and her kind. Worse, they would certainly attempt to enter Ala'ydin only to find themselves attacked by its guardians.

"With that said, though, my experience on the premises would prove invaluable. Recently—ever since our visit at Ala'ydin—I have unearthed specific recollections about familiar locations within the main administrative building that may lead us to where we need to go. Memories from a time prior to my last session within the Archives."

"Wait, what? You can remember something that far back?" Cal sputtered. "I thought, well… I don't know what I thought."

"As I explained earlier, there are memories, devoid of factual data, that exist, submerged in the deeper layers. Because I have been out amongst the world in general, the recently-acquired information has provided a stimulus that allows me access to such recollections. When we were in Ala'ydin, I witnessed a series of structures that triggered a familiarity which took time for me to understand."

"I, uh… yeah, whatever," Cal tossed his hands up in the air. "I'm just not smart enough to get this shit anymore. I'll take your word for it."

With a frazzled look, Peter raised a hand in the air. "So, and you'll forgive me if I haven't been following too closely, but what exactly *is* the plan?" Peter asked. "We just waltz in and peek about, however you please? Can't imagine that'll go over too well."

Cal lifted his shoulders before replying. "I don't see us successfully using stealth, so we may as well just walk in the front door. Barge in and act like we own the place. Keep on the move and never let them know we don't belong there."

"Not the worst plan I've ever heard," Apello announced with a dry chuckle from his sentry post. "Considering our situation, it's as good as we can expect."

"I get the distinct impression you've done something like this previously," Prae stated as she shot Cal a sideways glance.

"Maybe. When we get inside, just follow my lead. We'll need to waltz past a bunch of people who may or may not even care we're there. Someone may recognize Oebe, so that'll be a thing that we're gonna have to deal with when it happens."

"Do we know where we'll be heading once we're on the property?" Peter asked of Oebe. "I rather think wandering around, looking for a needle in a haystack, is only going to increase our chances of being found out."

"Not exactly," Oebe replied. "I will know it when I see it. I have a faint recall—slivers of memories that are not exactly in what one might call order—that it's in the older part of the main building. Once we're within, I should be able to pick out familiar markings."

"The cathedral? Near the Archives?" Cal asked.

"It *is* the oldest part of the building."

"Okay, then stick close to me," Cal pointed to her. She nodded in response.

"That's it?" Peter inquired as he looked between Cal and Prae. "That's what we're going with? I mean, no offense, but Cal's last plan obviously got him beaten. By who, I have no idea. Discussion for another day, I guess. Are we really going to just 'go with it'?"

"You could always stay behind," Apello commented.

Peter let out a resigned sigh as he watched the others file out of the building. Wasting only a second on fruitless consideration, he called out for them to wait as he scurried after them.

By the time they returned to the main avenue, the traffic was beginning to thin and they could clearly see the ivory walls a few blocks to the north. Cal placed a hand on Oebe's shoulder to ensure she was never out of his reach. Though she wasn't dressed in her formal garb, he doubted she would go unrecognized for long.

As they pushed on through the crowd, Apello came up beside Cal and spoke. "Sorry about earlier. I didn't know—"

Cal held up a hand. "It's appreciated but it's not your job to manage my baggage. Think nothing of it."

It seemed as though Apello wanted to say something else, but he swallowed the words. Cal found Apello's sudden change to be a bit curious; perhaps the Thosan remembered a few questionable decisions of his own.

The gates were unmanned and the group passed

through the courtyard without issue. For a moment, Cal considered the lack of visible security on the property. From memories of his earlier visit, Cal was certain he hadn't seen anything that remotely resembled a security staff. Maybe the upscale northern location was enough buffer to deter the usual vandals and petty thieves that populated the more southern regions.

Cal found the concourse beyond the entrance unchanged: lush with blooming, well-tended foliage and occupied by a mix of An-Sebban and administrative staff. Crossing the brick-laid walking path, he kept a wary eye on those they passed. The few An-Sebban they saw kept to themselves, disinterested in the visitors.

Cal spied a pair of concierges in conversation as they casually patrolled the well-tended greenery. When one headed towards Oebe, Cal hurried his pace. The others followed suit as he rushed towards the central administration building. The towering edifice of gray limestone cast a long shadow across the yard.

Upon entering the foyer, they were relieved to find it empty. Cal was unsurprised. The Athenaeum did not strike him as an organization with a full social calendar.

As they crossed the lobby, a thin, sharply-dressed man emerged from a nearby door. It took Cal a second to recall the name, but the charcoal suit and flaxen hair looked familiar.

The instant she recognized Hru-Gatta's personal assistant, Oebe side-stepped to hide behind Cal. Peter noticed this and sidled up beside her.

"Mr. Reeger," the man hailed him. "So good to see you again. It's been some time since your departure." The insincerity of Golette's greeting made Cal's skin crawl.

"Golette..." Cal trailed off as he recalled the man's name.

"Is Miss Nsu-Ogette with you? We've been waiting for her return for some time. She's late for her scheduled appointment with the Central Archives. Grande Dame Hru-Gatta was concerned for her as such delays can prove problematic."

Cal wanted to be done with Golette after only a few seconds. To his right, Apello looked to Cal, who immediately let out a sigh and nodded. At this sign, Apello strode forward and took Golette by the arm. Shocked, Golette gasped but found himself unable to pull away. Apello clasped a hand over his mouth.

"Mr. Golette," Cal began as he came up beside him. "I have had one hell of a day and just felt like being a dick to someone. You, my friend, rose to the top of my list only because you're right here, right now. Sorry."

Golette looked over Cal's shoulder to where Oebe waited with Peter a few paces back. She offered him a wry smile. He glanced to Prae, who came up behind Cal, and for a moment his eyes grew wide. Cal noticed this reaction. The idea that Golette and Prae were somehow acquainted was hard to swallow, but Cal began to wonder if he made some association from her angular features and iridescent hair.

"Okay, I'm going to ask my friend to remove his hand

so I can ask you a few questions," Cal stated in a low tone heavy with menace. "You're not going to cry out for help and we're not gonna be forced into harming you, isn't that right?" He nodded for a second before Golette did the same. At this, Apello slowly removed his hand.

"Wh-what do you want to know?" Golette sputtered. Once again, he glanced over toward Prae, who eyed him suspiciously.

"My friend, here." Cal hooked a thumb over his shoulder. "You're familiar with her. Somehow. Don't know how. Don't care how. And, don't lie to me about it; you're not that good of a liar. I would know. We can smell our own kind. Spill it."

"I-I don't know her, per se, but I know of someone who shares her likeness."

"Who?" Prae snapped as she leaned in. Cal sidestepped just enough to place himself between Prae and Golette.

"Be quick about it, champ," Cal said with a smirk. "I get the feeling you may know what she's capable of. Or what kind of damage she could do to a twig like yourself."

Golette began to stutter. Sweat dotted his pale face. "I-in the Central Archives. I swear I've not met one in p-person. I was doing some research for the Grande Dame and I ran across an entry of hers from back when she served. I was curious as to what she might have observed during her service, so I began reading through the files. Some time ago, she came across an older gentleman, went by the name of Erudatta, who was on the property."

"How long ago?" Prae asked.

"I can't quite recall. Hundreds of years, maybe."

Cal's eyes widened. It took a few seconds for his brain to register the implication. He looked to Oebe. To the question on his face, she offered a smile before responding.

"While the process stunts our physical growth, it also lengthens the average lifespan of an An-Sebban. At some point in the upcoming month, it will be 82 years since my date of birth."

This caught all but Prae by surprise. Cal shook his head and refocused on Golette.

"Okay, back to this Erudatta fellow."

"There was a holographic record of his face in the files. He had very unique facial features. Something I had never seen before in all the collected anthropometric data. Until I saw her, I thought I'd not see its like ever again. He was a statistical anomaly, genetically speaking." Golette took a breath and before he could continue, Cal placed a finger to his lips.

"That's all good and well. Let's change topics for a second." Cal tried his best to form the question in his head before he spoke. "We are looking for a, uh, *unique* section of the property that's potentially fairly old in age. One that Oebe may have accidentally wandered into earlier. Any of that ring a bell? I get the feeling that a part of this building may have been built over it."

"N-n-no. N-nothing of the sort. Maybe b-back in what used to be the cathedral. That's the oldest part of the main building. You've been through it before, have you not?"

Cal affirmed with a bob of his head.

"The only room back there I've never had access to is the Grande Dame's personal quarters. At the back of the right hall just off the entrance to the Central Archives." At this point, Golette was speaking a mile a minute. The manic responses let Cal know he might not provide much else.

"That works for me. Thanks so much for the info." He patted him on the forehead before turning back to Peter and Oebe. "Works for you?"

"Makes reasonable sense," Oebe replied. "I do recall slivers of memory in which I visited the Grande Dame, though the topics of such events elude me."

Peter pointed to Golette, who looked on the verge of hyperventilation. "So, uh, what do we do with—"

Before he could finish, Apello balled his fist and struck Golette across the side of his temple. The impact snapped his head violently. As his eyes rolled back, the thin man collapsed to the floor in a heap.

"Apello!" Peter barked as he dropped to one knee beside Golette. After a quick check of the man's pulse, he glared at Apello with a cross look. "There was no reason to do that."

"Yeah, there kinda was," Cal quickly disagreed as he joined Apello. They hastily dragged the unconscious body to a nearby closet, where he was left propped against the back wall. As he closed off the cubicle, Cal continued. "We ain't got time to waste with tying him up or some such shit. I don't even have ropes or anything. Golette knows both Oebe and me. You heard him. If we had left him alone, he would have eventually gone to Hru-Gatta. Then we'll be in it deep. Or deeper than we already are."

"Well, uh, can we go the next ten minutes without resorting to violence? Is that asking too much?" Peter implored.

"No promises," Cal stated. When he marched for the oaken double doors, the others quickly followed.

Peter muttered to himself. Things were progressing fast and he was growing increasingly nervous.

Cal seemed to have a fair recollection where they were heading. Though the dormitory was almost labyrinthian in its complexity, Oebe only once had to advise him of the correct turn. They ran across a few ambling tenants along their way, though none seemed to give the group a glance in passing.

As they advanced through the residential halls, Peter slipped up to Oebe and spoke in a low voice.

"So, you're 82?" Peter asked.

"Almost," she replied without missing a beat. "I thought that was obvious."

"No. No, it wasn't."

At the end of the hall, they came across a set of stairs that curled downwards.

"This is it," Cal announced as he pressed through the entryway at the bottom and into the converted cathedral.

Unprepared, Peter came to a sudden stop as his breath caught in his throat. His eyes scanned the aged structure. As he pondered the historical significance of the location, the others were already heading on without him. He groaned and picked up his pace.

Halfway down the vaulted nave, Cal began to feel growing anxiety. There were a pair of assistants posted at the circular desk on the other end.

"We're not going to the Central Archives, are we?" Cal inquired nervously as he nudged Oebe's shoulder with his elbow. This caused her to look up to him.

"If Golette's word is to be believed, not exactly. I don't remember there being any access to the Central Archives outside of the main door. Though there is a door to the right at the top of the steps."

As they approached the service desk set in the apse, Cal cleared his throat and stepped forward. Much like before, the concierges that manned the circular desktop were too entranced in their own readings to acknowledge his presence.

"I'm from the Merced League. Just returning Ms. Nsu-Ogette to Grande Dame Hru-Gatta," Cal announced to the pair, neither of whom made an effort to respond. "So, uh, we'll be on our way, then."

"Smooth," Apello said under his breath.

Cal bit his tongue as they pressed on to the lone staircase at the back of the chamber. The continued disinterest of the workforce towards their visitors worked in their favor.

On reaching the top of the steps, Cal came to a stop just before the entrance to the Central Archives. He glanced back to the desk and was quickly relieved that neither employee had deigned to turn. Their unflinching diligence was unnerving.

He hung a right and found the doorway that plainly sported a "No Entry: Administration Only" sign. He slowed on approach and looked back as Oebe cleared the last set of steps.

"This it?"

"Yes."

With that simple confirmation, he reached out for the polished brass knob and was surprised when it turned easily. For some reason, he anticipated that the door would be sealed firmly and that they would be forced to either pick the lock or just kick it open.

Cal wasn't exactly sure what to expect when he strode through the doorway. In his mind, he assumed that there would be an area even older than the last; something much like Ala'ydin. Instead, he stumbled into an L-shaped corridor with doors to three unmarked chambers. It was carpeted, with cream-and-brown striped wallpaper, and lit by frosted-glass sconces mounted at regular intervals. A quartet of landscape paintings which were hung in the open spaces seemed to be from a more personal collection than the artwork on display in the dormitory.

"Whoa," Peter said as he came up beside Cal. "Not exactly what I was expecting. Though, at this point, I really should stop assuming anything."

"Yeah, there's a severe lack of... uh, consistency—yeah that's the word—in how this place is put together."

The group split up and began to explore the hallway.

The first two rooms held little of interest. One was an office space spartanly decorated with a mahogany desk and matching chair set. The other had the appearance of a personal library, with bookcases that lined the walls. In the center was a steel desk covered in machinery with a lone display, all of which was leashed to the nearby floor via wires and tubing. Oebe announced it was likely how Hru-Gatta accessed the data from the Central Archives.

For a moment, Peter wondered if he might procure similar access. Such a wealth of data beckoned like a siren's call, but when Apello called out from the far end of the hall, his focus shifted. When they caught up with him, Apello had already opened the final room by force. From the state of the broken jamb, Peter assumed that it had been locked.

Beyond lay the Grande Dame's personal quarters. Having never met the woman before, Peter entered with no idea of what to expect. Much like the adjacent library, the walls were covered in stacks of books, tightly packed within the limited space. A chaise lounge was arranged atop a woven rug at the center of the room. On the far side was a green velvet curtain hung from a ceiling-mounted rod in front of what he could only assume was her sleeping space.

"Well, I guess it's good that she wasn't here," Cal cracked dryly as his eyes scanned the surroundings. "*That* would have been awkward."

"Do we know where she might be?" Peter asked Oebe, who shrugged.

"Not here," Cal responded. "Which is fortunate. For us. Maybe she's looking for Golette. Wouldn't that be a laugh? As it is, I say we don't dawdle any longer than necessary.

Someone might get it in their head to call for Magistrate intervention once we get found out."

When Prae derisively snorted, Cal shot her a look.

With a quick glance over his shoulder, Cal found Apello stationed at the room's entrance. The Thosan kept watchful eye on the connecting corridor. Oebe stood alone only a pace away, seemingly in a daze. Cal wondered if she recognized the room from some prior visit. He opened his mouth only to have the question die on his lips as Peter went to check on her.

"Let me guess," Cal said as he began to peer over the wall of bookcases. "She's hidden the entrance behind one of these. Isn't that how it always is? Pull a book with some witty title and the bookcase swings open. Something like *The Passage* or *Secrets From Another Room*."

He chuckled to himself.

"Not exactly," Prae commented from the back of the room. Cal looked to her as she motioned at something hidden by the curtain.

Both Cal and Peter quickly joined Prae. Where both thought a bed would be placed was an open archway along the back wall. Left askew, propped against a wall just beyond the entry, was what they assumed had once been the passageway's door. The bronze-paneled slab had been ripped from its hinges and discarded haphazardly.

As Apello and Oebe joined them beside the drapes, Peter took a cautious step forward. Beyond was a short hall of gray limestone which extended a few yards to an octagonal atrium floored in brass-plated tiles. On the other side was a staircase that spiraled downwards into the darkness.

"Well," Cal said with a sigh, "That's that. Easier to find than I would have originally thought."

23

With their course set before them, the party left Hru-Gatta's chambers behind. There was no quibbling among them. The discovery of the open doorway failed to generate an extended back-and-forth about how the Grande Dame accessed such a location or the nature by which they found it. The violently-discarded door was a curious item that created more questions than it answered.

While Peter and, to a lesser degree, Cal took in the scene about them, Oebe strode forward with no sign of surprise. Apello, who remained vigilant with a hand behind his back, came up behind her as he scanned their surroundings. Once it was clear the entryway was unguarded, his shoulders slumped ever so slightly.

"This is familiar to me," Oebe eventually announced as she came to a stop at the top of the steps.

"I can imagine it would be," Prae noted as she cautiously progressed into the atrium. There was wariness as she inspected the concourse's features. "The architectural concepts are comparable to those at Ala'ydin. Similar to most of the work being done in the later years. A significant portion of their development was invested on longevity rather than visual aesthetics."

"That's not exactly what I mean. I have a specific set of memories of visiting this exact location."

"How so?" Peter inquired.

"When we were in Ala'ydin, I came upon an intersection that was analogous in both material and design. At that time, I was reminded of a similar passage of which I had faint recollection. The architecture elicited a sense of familiarity in me, which, at the time, caused me some concern. For the longest, I struggled to understand how such recognition was possible, but now I know."

"You've been here before?" Peter ran his hand along the bannister. The steel was cold to the touch.

"It is safe to make such an assumption. I cannot say how deep I traversed, not without viewing what lies at the bottom of these steps, but I can attest to making it this far." She turned to Peter just as he opened his mouth to speak. "And before you wish to inquire about the events that led to such a proceeding, I would remind you that I have no detailed memory of whom I was with or why I was here. Such information has surely been removed during the transfer process to the Central Archives between now and then. All that remains are threads trapped in the deepest layers of my memory, so deep that not even the Athenaeum's machines can excise them."

Peter blew out a disappointed snort.

"That's nice an all—" Cal spoke up as he headed for the steps. "—but I think we should be on our way. Sticking around here running our mouths isn't exactly in our best interest."

No one chose to argue with Cal. One by one, the group descended the limestone staircase. By the time they reached the third flight of steps, Cal stopped long enough to cast a glance over the side. Visibility was poor and he could only make out a few yards before darkness masked the details. When he noticed that they were nowhere near the bottom, he let out a moan.

Their descent grew more arduous the further they traveled. By the twentieth flight, there was a dull pressure in the atmosphere that made the seemingly never-ending march more exhausting. Even though the air itself retained its coolness, Peter's forehead was drenched and he had to regularly dab at it with his handkerchief. Another dozen floors down, they began to notice a thin, iridescent fog, lit by a faint blue luminance from below.

With this hint that their downward trek may soon be at an end, there was a renewed vigor in their pace. In a few minutes, the group spilled out to an enclosed foyer. On the other side was a vaulted archway. Wasting no time, they pressed on.

They found themselves within a massive cavern much like the one in Ala'ydin, thick with a vapor that glittered in blue and green, lit by thin beams that radiated along the flatter surfaces. An elevated walkway led away from the entrance to a series of interconnected platforms. While it was difficult to see clearly though the muddled haze, they could make out rows of stone columns that ran parallel to the walking path. These pillars were dozens of yards in diameter and lined with shallow alcoves, the majority of which were filled with stone tablets marked with alphanumeric symbols.

Cal thought the surroundings reminded him of when he first met Oebe in the Central Archives. When a whirring of gears caught his attention, Cal noticed mechanical armatures extending from the columns along steel tracks along the circumference. These artificial limbs moved about slowly as they arranged the slabs in some as-yet-undetermined order. From time to time, one would extract a block only to place it in the open slot of an adjacent column.

Cal thought to himself that, with time, a smarter man might be able to discern the scheme of organization.

"What is it?" Peter inquired as he came up beside him.

"Uh... oh," Cal sputtered. "Just a memory. This is kinda like the Central Archives. Not exactly the same, but—"

"It shares similar technological concepts," Oebe joined in. "If I was inclined towards contemplative research, I would posit that some of these—" She pointed to the nearby tablets. "—may have come from above. Perhaps moved into a long-term storage of sorts when the data they contain is deemed outdated or unnecessary."

As they moved along the walkway, the group came to an intersection where the path split into three. Apello knelt down and began to examine footprints in the thin layer of dust. He reached out a hand but made certain not to disturb the markings.

"There are two distinct sets of footsteps here," Apello stated as he pointed. "One is walking towards the stairs in a straight line. Large feet with wide flat surfaces. Long strides."

"What are the odds that they would come from Masina? The golem from Ala'ydin?" Prae inquired as she watched Apello. "His geolocation history led us here. I would think that he had to pass through, at some point."

He remained quiet for a moment. Eventually he said, "Would make sense. I did not take the time to examine its feet, so I cannot be entirely certain. If he, in fact, came from here, then it would be fair guess."

"And the second set?"

"Smaller steps arranged in an erratic pattern. Like someone more interested in the scenery than where they are heading. Moving back and forth, as if they've arrived and departed at least once. Looks like they're wearing some kind of soft leather loafer."

"Like these?" Oebe asked as she came up beside him and turned up the heel of one of her own shoes.

It took Apello only a second.

"Yes."

"The Grande Dame," Peter stated as he searched their surroundings for evidence of additional visitors.

"How long ago would you say they were made?" Prae followed up. Apello stood upright as his eyes remained on the tracks.

"Hard to tell. As with Ala'ydin, I imagine things do not deteriorate with the same speed as they do elsewhere. It is as if this vapor about us retards such processes. As if they were created to help preserve the aging locations. Could be earlier today, could be weeks ago. For all I know, it may have been as long as years for some of these. There is overlap with Masina's own steps, which leads me to believe she was down here after his departure."

Apello's theory about the mist's unusual effects went without challenge. The concept itself might have been ridiculous had they not bore witness to an eons-old subterranean dwelling that looked no older than a few hundred years old. Something had to be the cause and the rich fog, which smelled of phosphorous and ozone, was as good an explanation as any. Either way, this made the age of the layered footprints difficult to determine.

As Apello continued his examination, Cal slipped up beside Prae. With a whisper, he began.

"So, how do we handle this?"

"How do you mean?" she inquired without looking.

"Erudatta. When, or if, we find him. Is he an enemy? Are you expecting a fight?"

Prae took a second before she answered. She seemed to be tempering her anger. "It's… it's for the best if we attempt to treat with him. There is no telling what defenses he may employ. Despite my misgivings about his role, I would be remiss not to allow him to defend himself."

"Okay," he said with a nod.

"Uh, so which way do we go?" Peter hailed from the center of the nearby intersection. His query put an end to their conversation.

"This way," Apello pointed. "The golem's tracks come from that direction."

While this was enough to prod the group along, Cal lingered for a moment as he groaned to himself. They might be in for a walk before they reached anywhere of note.

He took a second to look over the bannister at the iridescent vapors. Cal began to pat at his pockets to find a cent. By measuring the length of time it took to hit the bottom, he could estimate how far above the cavern's floor they were.

He once again found himself without a coin to his name. Even the last bit of his stipend was gone, probably stolen by one of Raxus' men.

Cal let out a disappointed grunt and headed on, picking up his pace when he realized he was being left behind.

After about ten minutes of a continuous march down a central aisle through the heart of the chamber, they arrived at a juncture. A quartet of bridges stretched almost a hundred yards to matching limestone towers. Each was fifty yards in diameter and presented a surface that was almost entirely featureless. Lost in the darkness and mists, neither the top nor bottom was visible.

Apello strode forward, following Masina's footprints back to their source. Noticing that the set of tracks abruptly terminated at the stone column in the distance, Prae overtook Apello as she charged toward the nearby structure.

As she stood at where the bridge met with the face of the tower, Prae looked intently over the exterior. At her feet was half of a footprint, as if someone had walked through the unmarked exterior. She reached out and ran an open hand over the surface. There was an expectation in her movements. When no red beams of light flickered, indicating an opening, she scowled and clenched her jaw.

After a second fruitless wave, Prae drew in a deep breath.

"Erudatta!" Prae bellowed as she drove her fist into the curved surface. The echoes floated into the empty hollow around them.

Shocked, both Peter and Oebe jumped.

Prae continued. "Unfasten this barrier! I am here to have words with you. Do not think I will be ignored! I am of a mind to tear your domicile down around you if needs must."

Prae stood still for a few seconds, focused on the column before her. Gingerly, Cal slipped up and whispered.

"Not sure if he heard you."

"*Not* in the mood for your acerbic tongue."

"O-kay..." Cal rolled his eyes as he spun away.

A rumbling began to build from deep within. As gears ground from behind the wall, a seam formed along the surface. After a few seconds, the oval-shaped pane receded into the structure. Once it sank a few feet in depth, the door slid to the side and disappeared into a recess.

"It has been some time," a voice cracked from underuse called out. A male silhouette came through the pale gray light framed by the doorway.

Prae dropped her hand to the hilt of her weapon.

"There is no need for violence. Please, stay your blade, Centurion." His soothing tone put her off guard.

Erudatta stepped forward, his arms spread out welcomingly.

24

As he shuffled forward, Erudatta became visible to all. Draped in a drab ochre robe, he was a thin man who stood nearly as tall as Prae. While he moved with some stiffness, he did not exhibit any kyphosis as a result of advanced age. While his face was lined with vertical creases in his cheeks and horizontal furrows across his forehead, his crystal blue eyes still retained their spark. Though it was thinning, a mop of silver hair shimmered like polished metal in the light.

The longer Cal examined their host, the more it became evident that he and Prae shared similar genetic heritage. The bridge of his nose and brow were formed from sharp angles and his cheeks were flat and wide.

When the folds of Erudatta's robe shifted, Cal could make out parts of an exoskeleton that was bound to the man's frame. A thin strip along the base of his skull became visible as his head turned and the loose strands shifted. His right hand had been replaced with a tool that caused Cal to rub his own extremity in sympathetic pain.

After a cough to clear his throat, Erudatta turned directly to Prae. "So good of you to visit. It has been some time since we've had the opportunity to speak." Cal immediately noticed the low resonance beneath every syllable. On first meeting her, he had observed that same vibration in Prae's own speech.

Prae took a menacing step forward. "Do not labor under the pretense that this is a social call. I have very specific questions that you are going to answer before I am done here. First and foremost has to do with this location—"

"Please," he cut her off. "It is something we will discuss in due time."

This did not sit well with Prae, whose eyes bulged.

Erudatta raised his left hand, as if to ask for patience, before he beckoned her to the open doorway. "Please join me in my humble abode. I would be a poor host to not invite you and your friends in. I pray your forgiveness as I don't have much in the way of amenities. I don't regularly have company."

In response, Prae eyed him warily. She did not move, but a clenching of her jaw revealed a lack of trust in her fellow Progenitor. Erudatta noticed her temperament, shrugged and receded into the darkened arch.

When Oebe strode to join him, Peter and Apello were quick to flank her on either side.

As he watched the others move past, Cal looked toward Prae. Despite the cold expression, he could pick out the faintest hint of concern. After a sigh, he placed a pair of fingers on his revolver and passed through the ingress. Prae eventually relented and joined them. Once she was through, a curved slab of steel moved back into place and sealed the chamber from the outside world.

Within Erudatta's quarters, they moved through a small hall to a set of stairs that wrapped tightly around the circular interior. By the time Cal reached these, Erudatta was almost at the top. Even with a palm pressed against the wall for stability, he moved with an unexpected speed.

Cal noticed no sentries. Whether Erudatta hid his handicraft elsewhere remained to be seen, but as of that moment, Cal felt a sliver of relief.

"You must pardon the condition of my domicile. As you may imagine, I was not expecting guests." Erudatta cast a wave to the adjoining workroom. He gave Prae a wry smirk, which only seemed to enflame her simmering temper.

"I am not one for your placating banter!" Prae barked as she charged up the steps. Upon her approach, he retreated without turning his attention from her.

"I see your humor has not improved over the millennia."

"Oh, you have *no* idea," Cal said under his breath. As his line of sight fixed on Erudatta's laboratory, he joined Peter in contemplative silence.

As Erudatta moved to his worktable, Cal glanced at the console and display behind him. On one side of the flat screen was a rectangular view of the exterior walkway. To the right was a list of entries transcribed in what Cal believed was the Progenitor's written language.

The elderly man took a measure of those around him.

Only when he spotted Oebe, who stood quietly beside Peter, did he pause for any length of time. Once done with his assessment, he addressed Prae with a crack in his voice.

"Now, if I could get you to calm down for a moment—" Erudatta implored to Prae, who lingered in the doorway. "—we might discuss this like civil adults. I take it by your presence here that you were not brought into the Waking State through the normal means. Perhaps by your retinue?"

"You know that I was not," she said through clenched teeth. "There was an arrangement amongst us. Every man and woman was to have their time in the Waking State. As you well know, I should have woken far sooner. How long have you being doing this? How long have you been hiding here, keeping the rest of us in stasis? I would have not known about your culpability had I not run across your golem. Oh, you and yours went on and on about the detrimental impacts of remaining in the Dormant State for too long. Pompous assholes blathering on about the importance of responsibility in the face of our prolonged existence. And yet, you're the one who threw off the cycle!"

Erudatta snapped. "Cycle? Damn your cycle. You always were too preoccupied with thinking small." His left hand fluttered erratically as he spoke. "You never were able to see the big picture. There are machinations set in motion long ago which are no longer within our control to circumvent. I am doing what I feel I must to stave off yet another potential extinction event."

"What? What exactly are you yammering on about?"

"Did you never consider why the third and fourth eras

fell so quickly? Dead before they even reached the second tier of sociological, much less scientific, development. And why the fifth is just *now* flourishing? Did you not have any vague inkling of by what manner it transpired? Or, were you too busy hiding yourself away in whatever hole you chose to occupy? Well, Centurion, I do."

"You speak with the tongue of an experienced orator," Prae stated. Her words were rich with derision. "Educate me on such matters. I would enjoy the opportunity to hear the reasoning behind your actions."

"It is fair that the accused be permitted to defend the logic in his choices," Erudatta began. "I know that in your mind, you wish to place the yoke of blame solely upon my shoulders. You're a soldier, incapable of seeing the subtleties inherent in such decision-making. That my decision was made in a vacuum, without cause."

"Cease the condescending prattle and get to the crux of your argument."

"I assume you retain some recollection of Magromous, do you not? One of our fellows and a seasoned virologist by trade." He paused as if waiting for verbal confirmation. After a few seconds of silence, he continued. "Did you know by what title Magromous goes? What horrific moniker the ancient texts have bequeathed to him? That those who eventually fell victim to his efforts branded him in writings salvaged at the end of their eras? The Poison that Kills. Every time Magromous comes out of hibernation in his turn in the cycle, his sole drive is to deliver a pathogen of one breed or another to the world in hopes of wiping out the current populace."

"But... I… How is such a thing possible?" Prae stammered, noticeably shaken.

"He failed to kill the populace of the second era the first time around. The 'Great Mortality' as it was branded, was a strain of virulence called Yersina pestis that did its work well, but not to the completeness of his liking. But, his time in hibernation gave him eons to dream over how best to improve and deliver his breed of death. It is because of Magromous that I have been forced to break your precious cycle. If I were to return to the Dormant State, it would set processes forward that would eventually turn him loose upon mankind again. None would survive, not even your precious entourage." He flicked a pair of fingers at the others.

Prae eyed him suspiciously. She shifted her weight from one foot to the other. "And how did you arrive at such knowledge?" she eventually asked. "These are heavy allegations to be leveling."

"Belamis, the Last. He scribed a lengthy testimony describing what he witnessed upon his awakening at the end of the second era. He wrote about the dying throes of humanity as they limped towards the grave. He transcribed their tales of the monster that had brought death to them. A reaper who walked among them, giddy at his success. Belamis stood witness to the funeral march of these people and then left his notes with Naucilous, to bring awareness of what had transpired. He knew that Scroturea would eventually start the seeding process again, but the problem of Magromous' madness was left to Naucilous who then passed it on to me to discern a method to halt him.

"There were those of us, Scroturea and Na-Exetase in particular, who tried in vain to alter the human genome. To make them resilient to his plagues. Even then, it was never enough. It was penned by their wise men that death came to them with a smile every time."

"What caused Magromous to turn genocidal?"

"While he ceased recording his thoughts in the Repository not long after the end of the second era, we do have some inkling as to the spiral he took. Magromous was already prone to an obsession with disease. Rather than see the lands blasted clean of life by nuclear fire, he looked to create a way in which mankind alone could be removed. It seems he cared more for the wildlife than the descendants of our efforts. Perhaps, ultimately, he was merely not strong enough to weather the effects of the Dormant State and it affected his decision-making ability. We went into this knowing the myriad of potential side-effects of such a process. Did you, yourself, not report bouts of depression during the early stages of the third era?"

Prae looked sharply away.

Seeing her discomfort, Peter joined the conversation. "You speak of how Magromous has killed previous civilizations again and again. How then are we to be saved?"

Erudatta offered a grim smile. "Your world needs not salvation but inoculation."

Peter gasped at his bluntness.

"Spare me your verbal sleight of hand," Prae stated harshly.

"You fail to grasp the enormity of events that have

transpired. You hid yourself away, buried your head in the sand as you wallowed in grief and paid little attention to the larger maneuverings at hand. The second era... let us not paint too pretty a picture. They laid waste to themselves. True, it was by our hand that the seeds of such knowledge were gained. And Magromous did his best to smother the last of them while they struggled on their deathbed. But, they could not help themselves. In their rage, they burned the land clean, spoiled the earth, made it unlivable. We had no choice. Kayvurim did what he felt he had to so that we would have a clean slate to begin again. Tilled the soil, so to speak."

"And yet, here we are."

"You were not the only one who felt distraught at the loss. Kayvurim hated to find his greatest achievement ruined. Scroturea wrote volumes on the topic of waking to a lonely world. Though he diligently did resume his work, starting from what he felt was the beginning all over again, it wore on him to see the land so empty."

This caused Prae to fall silent, her earlier anger long ago dissipated.

Erudatta crossed to Oebe where she stood by Peter. Both Apello and Cal grew apprehensive as he approached. "Ah, this one. How strange that you would find yourself in Prae's company. You must be one of my children," Erudatta said like a doting grandparent as he leaned in. "Not in the literal sense, mind you. More a progeny of my arrangements."

"Oebe? Or the An-Sebban in general?" Peter inquired as he placed a supportive hand on her back.

"The entire line, though in actuality none are related by blood. Sad result of the process, that is. Forces the administration to enlist new recruits instead of allowing their altered nature to be inherited. Though, I am unsure of the hereditary nature of such severe alterations. I imagine the restructuring of the brain and how they retain memory cannot be passed along so easily. That is, if they weren't already rendered sterile by their transition. But I digress... I was there when the Athenaeum was founded. A silent benefactor. One might say I watched from the shadows. I provided the seeds of their fruition. The basis for all of their efforts to come. The Central Archives are fashioned by my own designs."

"And the An-Sebban themselves? Did you create them?"

Erudatta cast a sideways glance at Peter. "Not in the manner in which you might think. I have no interest in abiogenesis. There are no homunculi here. T'was an abandoned project of Na-Exetase's that I co-opted for a greater cause. The first of their kind were molded from those without families all their own. Nowadays, I have no idea from where their source materials are culled. I expect that the process of conversion remains the same. Orphans treated with chemical cocktails and a touch of body modification which paved the way for such a perfect device to record information."

His hand hovered only inches from her face. Oebe made no effort to pull away. After a second, he turned back to Prae.

"It has been some time since I've been abroad and just

as long since this body was capable of lengthy transit. I've not been capable of the journey to Ala'ydin for hundreds, if not thousands, of years. For that reason I needed to establish a database that I could readily access from these confines. It took many decades for the cumulative data acquired to begin to approach what we had in the Repository. Even then, there are millions of years of knowledge outside of my grasp."

Erudatta cleared his throat as he began to shuffle back to the center table. "The only access to the remnants of our world I was able to procure was a data feed via semanifesture to a point on the mainland. During the fourth era, I uncovered a hub buried in one of the mines. From this, I was able to secure a connection, limited as it was, that advised me of the status of the other containment cells."

"Could you use it to track back to the others?" Prae questioned.

"I had no desire to invest in the task. We had made an oath to—"

She let out an incredulous laugh. "You dare talk of promises? Now? If you truly thought Magromous was so dangerous, why did you not take the opportunity to hunt him down?"

"And what?" Erudatta raised a single brow. "Strike him down where he sleeps?"

Prae and Erudatta locked eyes in conflict. Peter chose this moment in time to break the tension.

"I, uh, you'll forgive my professional curiosity, but I

am intrigued by this location. Mind you, I'm no expert on said subject. I work for the Bureau and have extensive proficiency with pre-historical sites, especially those in the Quartewuste, but your own structures are a new experience for me. In speaking with Prae, I was led to understand that Ala'ydin was some form of final bastion. But, as we stand here, I feel that is proven wrong."

"Truthfully? T'was a lie," Erudatta stated without an ounce of guilt. "Or rather a lie of omission. Topheth has been in existence in one form or another for as long as Ala'ydin, if not longer."

"There is no record of its founding," Prae interjected. "This is the first I am hearing of it. Through what subterfuge were you able to hide such a place for so long?"

"My dear," Erudatta began in a tone that reeked of condescension. "Such a matter is possible when one controls the flow of information. Topheth was established in the later years of the first era by those in certain sects within the science division. There was a schism that led to a splinter faction of the Scientia founding this very location. They had the site erected in secret and had not things turned how they did, it might have eventually overtaken Ala'ydin's role. My choice of residence here was no whim. That such a metropolis as Greater Decedistadt would be founded above Topheth was purely providence."

Peter looked at Oebe before inquiring. "And the connection to the Athenaeum's Central Archives?"

"As you probably are aware, it's an extension of the technology already present. You've seen the legion of storage capsules housed along the central aisle. When the Athenaeum was founded, I saw to it that they were outfitted with the technology they currently employ. In a manner that ultimately benefited me, for certain. The founding fathers—or rather *mothers*—we're so very enthused to have such a well-connected patron that they never delved too deeply, both metaphorically and literally. Or, never chose to peek, lest the answer became part of public record. The first Grande Dame was a willing partner who founded her campus in a place most convenient for our partnership. It served two purposes, though any boon to those of your kind was purely coincidental." He addressed the final statement to the others in the room.

Prae once again roared. "You took it upon yourself to intervene? To offer them unearned gains in technological advancement for your own advantage?"

"Look, Centurion Ganvelt," Erudatta now raised his voice. By this time, Cal began to notice that Erudatta's use of her title was something other than a measure of respect. It had the ring of someone reminding a soldier of their place. "You'll exhaust yourself before too long if you choose to be enraged at every sliver of information I provide you. I know it is not in a Centurion's wheelhouse to think of grander schemes—"

"Never was more an apropos term as 'scheme' spoken."

"There are much bigger concerns to the world at large." Winded by the lengthy conversation, Erudatta leaned over and began to breathe deeply. Perspiration dotted his forehead and cheeks.

After catching his breath, Erudatta reclined beside the console at the back of the room.

Peter took advantage of this momentary diversion. "Sir, would you be opposed to Oebe and me taking a brief tour of the premises? Purely as an academic exercise. I assume you'll understand an An-Sebban's curious nature." Oebe looked up to Peter with a smile.

Erudatta gazed at Oebe and then back to Peter. He relented with a nod. With Apello in tow, the pair headed down the curving staircase. Before he was through the doorway, Apello glanced pointedly at Cal.

Cal knew to remain on guard. Despite his advanced age, Erudatta was to be regarded as a potential danger. He had created Masina; there was no telling what other volatile creations he had stashed on the premises.

Prae moved in beside Erudatta and spoke, her voice soft. Cal strained to listen while pretending not.

"You know you cannot live forever, right? There was a reason we resolved to use the containment cells."

With a scoff, he waved her away. "It was never my intent to remain abroad forever. I had hoped to discover some means to counteract Magromous' work, be it through a vaccination to be dispersed amongst the populace or a cure of the man's own madness. It appears... that neither is within my immediate grasp. Only Na-Exetase could have provided such answers, but I fear that it would be far too late by the time his turn came to pass."

"Really? You believe mankind incapable of surviving Magromous' return?" She cast a brief glance to Cal, who stood sentry on the other side of the room.

"The initial strain of Yersina pestis proved devastating

even before its later evolutions. It cleverly hid within the vermin and their parasites. The demise of its victims was not enough to remove its presence. To rid the earth of it, all forms of life had to be eradicated. Mankind did its best attempt to burn the disease out, whether they knew it or not, but it was too little, too late. Magromous' most-recent version was fatal and virulent on a scale that made the original strain look like hay fever."

Prae bit at her lower lip. "And to locate Magromous? To take matters into your own hands, so to speak? You talk of decisions made to circumvent his genocidal inclinations, nevertheless there is a solution yet untaken."

"To kill one of our own?" He scowled in distaste. "Even if I were so capable or inclined, the matter is impossible. You've been to Ala'ydin. You know, by intent, there are safeguards in place to prevent discovery of where the others slumber. Your discovery of Topheth was a convenient miracle as it was, though if you met with Masina, not wholly unexpected."

"Yes, we ran into your creation. Or rather, ran afoul." At this, Erudatta frowned. When he made no comment, Prae continued. "Due to a misunderstanding, we were forced to strike it down, rather than allow it to harm us. In the end, I used a semanifesture to connect him to the Repository and trace his path back here."

"I see," he mumbled as his eyes dropped.

"My apologies for the damage of your property," Prae offered her regrets. "We were unsure of its intent and before the situation could be sorted out, it had devolved into violence."

With a brush of his hand across his wet eyes, Erudatta replied. "It is understandable. Masina was not yet fully formed. In my haste to have him investigate your arrival to the Waking State, I dispatched him before his completion. He lacked… certain processes that would have prevented such an issue. It is my own fault to dispatch him with a mind comparable to that of a simpleton."

The pair fell into silence, which made Cal uncomfortable. He excused himself from the room. Erudatta took this opportunity to speak privately with her.

"Prae, in light of the current situation—as it is—I must make you aware of something. I cannot compel you to return to the Dormant State. It would be the height of hypocrisy. If and when you make such a decision, let it be known that the cycle will be restarted. You will return to slumber and the processes of moving on to the next of our kind will begin as if nothing had changed."

"And there is danger in this?"

"No. I am aware of the order. My containment cell will fall between yours and Magromous. Because of this, I myself can never return. My own cell must remain online even if it is never put to use again. The cycle will stall again once it reaches my turn. My death is preferable for the greater good of all."

Prae scowled. Before she could respond, he held out a hand in a patting motion that asked for patience. As footsteps sounded from the staircase, Erudatta brought the talk to an abrupt end. With Prae's aid, he rose to his feet.

Preceding the others, Cal re-entered the workroom. He

crossed to meet Prae and Erudatta at the workbench. As he was about to comment on the dreary décor, Cal's attention was drawn to the viewscreen. He squinted at the female form that came into view.

"Looks like you have a visitor," Cal commented. This caused both Prae and Erudatta to look back. "Or, well, another, *newer* visitor. I guess you're kinda popular today." Cal hadn't yet recognized the person as they stepped over to the main console.

By now, Peter had returned and was immediately curious by the development. He quickly joined Cal and peered at the form. "Who is it?"

"It's unmistakable who it is by the attire," Oebe announced from where she and Apello hung in the doorway.

Both Peter and Cal turned back to her for a moment before returning to the display.

"You should know this already," she added.

It took Cal only a moment to place the charcoal suit and ivory ascot. Oebe was correct.

He spoke up. "The Grande Dame."

25

A coldness filled the air.

Erudatta squinted as he peered into the display. A thin groan slipped from his lips before he leaned back and stood upright.

"So it is. Disregard her," Erudatta ordered. "She will tire from the exertion and go away before too long. This is not the first time she has fruitlessly clamored for my attention. That one, I should not have made the error in judgment of speaking with her when I did. Once, I thought direct intervention, however inconsequential, was vital to my work with the Athenaeum. Minor nudges to move things in ways I thought beneficial. Now, I know better. Such stimuli are not only unnecessary, but often harmful to the larger scope."

"Uh, I don't think you're gonna get rid of her so easily, this time," Cal said sardonically. "We may have busted up one of her assistants on the way in. She *might* be a bit miffed. If she found him already."

"Might?" Apello added with a snort.

Erudatta fluttered a hand dismissively. "Whether you

caused a problem with the staff is of little concern to me. She can voice her concerns with you upon your departure." Erudatta turned from the viewscreen with a roll of his eyes. "Consider yourself fortunate that, if you did assault her employees, she doesn't have some form of law enforcement waiting for you on your return."

This caused Peter to stand bolt upright. "Would she? I'd always heard the Athenaeum liked to avoid outside assistance. Except for the occasional contract with the Merced League. I think now I understand why."

"What she would or would not do is irrelevant to me. If you wish her gone, deal with her yourself."

"Erudatta," Prae began. There was an imploring tone that struck Cal as strange. "If Hru-Gatta finds Oebe here, she'll be compelled to return to her life as an An-Sebban. Do not punish *her* because of your own indifference." She pointed to Oebe, who only stood quietly in place.

"Return?" Erudatta coughed a dusty laugh. "There is no variability of status to her existence. It *is* what she is. Don't delude yourself with her congenial nature fostered by time spent abroad. Turning her over to the Athenaeum would be a kindness."

"No, you can't," Peter retorted as he placed himself between Oebe and Erudatta. The elder gave a condescending roll of his eyes.

Before another word could be spoken, Apello withdrew his khukuri. "Enough of this petty bickering," he growled. "I will tend to this, even if it requires her to be driven away by fear for her life."

"Hold," Erudatta beckoned before he disappeared. "Rash creatures that you are. There is no need to resort to violence. I will see that she is dispatched." He paused to level an admonishing finger at the group. "The lot of you has brought drama to my life in such a short span of time. I expect you to depart once I have sent this woman away."

Prae opened her mouth but eventually chose to remain silent.

As Erudatta strode through the room, the others moved out of his path. Apello waited until Erudatta began to descend the stairs before he followed in his footsteps. The elder made no effort to brush him aside or to tell him to wait with the others.

Prae crossed to the doorway and watched. With his blades still in hand, Apello lingered at the entryway as Erudatta lumbered into the connecting hall.

Cal turned back to the display. Framed in the glowing rectangle was the An-Sebban headmistress, who scowled impatiently before opening her mouth to speak. Since no audio emanated from the machinery, Cal had no means of making out what she was saying. "Well, doesn't she look a bit, uh..."

"Heated?" Peter finished the thought.

"I mean don't get me wrong. I guess I can understand. If I actually had something like property to call my own, I'd probably be pretty pissed about people walking about it like they owned the place. Doing a number on the help and all." Cal then glanced to Oebe, who quietly observed the viewscreen with no sign of emotion on her face. "So, you think she's ticked off? I mean, in your experience did she ever seem like she's got that kind of fire in her?"

Oebe frowned. "I don't recall any consistent patterns of emotional outbursts. Hru-Gatta was always an even-tempered person."

"Well, ain't that nice. I guess we found her tipping point," Cal said as he stepped away with his hands tucked into his pockets.

Though he looked over Erudatta's workshop, he occasionally glanced to the display on his right. Hru-Gatta remained central, her diminutive frame filling almost the entire view. It was only when something caused a distraction behind her that she turned away.

Oebe raised her voice in concern.

"Look," she said as she pointed. This caused both men to spin around.

Lurching into the frame was a creation of segmented steel plates, molded in an imitation of the human form.

Its limbs were mismatched; one of its arms was much larger and moved clumsily as it swung like a pendulum. The added weight of the appendage seemed to pull its torso to one side. This caused its steps to be uneven and jerky. Atop its head was a bronze faceplate fashioned into the visage of a falcon's head. The metal exterior was weathered and sun-bleached in places.

"What in the hell is *that*?"

"Masina," Oebe announced matter-of-factly.

"Wait…" Peter squinted. After a few seconds, he stood

upright, nodded softly and let out a breath that whistled between his parted lips. "I'll be damned. It is."

Before anything else could be said, Cal dug into his belt and removed his revolvers, one at a time.

"What are you doing?" Peter shot him a look. He saw that Prae was missing from the room's entryway.

"You stay here with Oebe." Cal's tone grew dark. "Someone's gotta make sure our friend doesn't get past Apello and Prae."

Peter stood with his mouth half-open as Cal marched off.

Apello waited in the shadows at the other end of the connecting corridor. He watched as Erudatta raised his good hand in the air. Though he struggled to hide it behind a balled fist, a small yawn still spilled out. Apello was tired. With all the travel and the never-ending chain of events that led them to this place, he was worn out. Not even a decent night's sleep would be enough. Whether things were settled or not, he knew that he would not be departing the city in the company of his travel companions. Their trip to the Athenaeum property had already delayed him too long.

When a small square, composed of green and blue light, flashed to life and lit the passage, he shook his head and refocused. Erudatta pressed his palm into the construct for a few seconds and a series of hidden gears slowly began their task.

"Dearest Hru-Gatta," Erudatta began in tones rich with condescension as he waited for the door to open. "I advised you in fairly certain terms the last time we spoke that I—"

Before he could finish the comment, Erudatta was viciously yanked up from his feet. This sudden disruption caught Apello off-guard and left him stunned and alone in the hallway. Apello swore to himself and dashed out into the cavern.

He arrived at a scene so unanticipated that he immediately skidded to a halt.

It took him a few seconds to process. A deformed metal monstrosity stood in the walkway, only a few yards from the entrance. Apello came to realize that somehow this thing had once been Masina. The sloppily-welded additions caused Apello to pause, but once he recognized the iridescent brass feathers, it all made sense.

Erudatta was held aloft by the smaller of Masina's hands, which gripped at his throat. His feet dangled back and forth above the tiled pathway. Without the rigid exoskeleton, Erudatta's body might have fluttered like a limp rag in the clutches of his creation.

Behind the pair, discarded like a broken toy, was Hru-Gatta's body. While her torso lay prone, her head had been twisted a full 180 degrees. Dead eyes stared up into the murky haze that concealed the ceiling above. A trail of blood leaked from both sides of her open mouth.

As he hung in the air, Erudatta struggled to command his handiwork. Even with the addition of unfamiliar prosthetics, the design was easy for him to recognize.

"Masina, s-stand down, P-protocol C-c-caesum. Re-response s-string."

The mechanical golem no longer communicated in a pattern of chirps. Instead, a warbling static seemed to pulse at random intervals from beneath the new head covering.

Though he did not fight against his captor, Erudatta attempted once again to order the android into submission. "Masina! Protocol Caesum. Response str—ugh."

Before he could finish, Masina rattled him with a shake of his arm. A sharp sound that grated on the nerves cut through the air.

At this, Apello sprinted to where the android stood with its back turned as it remained focused on Erudatta. As before in Ala'ydin, Apello lashed out at the mechanical man. Once again, he found that his weapons deflected impotently off of its exterior with only a few marks on the finish as evidence.

Undeterred, he struck again with a pair of upward swings. Likewise, these failed to draw Masina's attention. Apello could hear Erudatta's ragged breathing as the older man flailed against the rigid limb holding him airborne. When a faint sound of gears from beneath the metal carapace sounded, Apello shifted his weight to his back foot.

Little did he expect the sudden upswing of Masina's mismatched limb, which had, up to that point, hung listlessly from its socket. The launch of the bulbous end struck him in the midsection and drove the air from his lungs. As pain flooded his nervous system, he released his weapons and stumbled backwards clutching at his abdomen.

There was a moment when he thought he might vomit.

Stunned by the fierceness of the first blow, Apello struggled to stand. Even with the sturdiness of his leather breastplate, he was certain that at least one rib was broken. Out of the corner of his eye, he saw Erudatta discarded, thrown like a rag doll, to the ground. The old man crumpled immediately on impact as his body rolled twice before falling still.

Masina swung around and marched to where Apello waited, hunched over as he drew in a series of rapid breaths. He made no effort to move out of the golem's range. When Masina brought its oversized hand around like a club, Apello wilted under the impact. Blood spilled from his mouth as he was driven into the railing.

In that moment, he fought to regain his senses. His vision was blurred and he had difficulty focusing. Apello reached out in an effort to drag himself upright by way of the railing. Once on his feet, Apello propped himself against the steel bannister.

A blurry trio of images shifted back and forth, overlapping long enough to make Masina's approach visible. This was enough to allow Apello to recoil from the incoming blow; at full strength, it might have knocked him unconscious. Even still, the impact lifted Apello and sent him over the balustrade.

Through divine providence, Apello kept a tenuous hold on the railing with his right hand. The precarious upheaval caused a jarring in his shoulder that sent pain screaming into his chest. Though a sharp agony that lanced his wrist left him fearful of damaged tendons, he resisted the overwhelming urge to release his life-saving hold. The edges of the manufactured surface dug into his skin. He could feel warm liquid running from his palm and down to his wrist.

Once he shook off the dazed fog that filled his head, Apello flung his free arm up and clasped the bannister. He was able to bring his legs up and place his boots against the bottom edge of the walkway.

As he struggled to keep a grip on the cold steel, Apello watched Masina lumber closer. It began to raise the oversized limb. Though he flailed as he ineffectively tried to pull himself back up, Apello braced himself for the impending impact. With each twist of his torso, pain from his damaged ribs flared.

When a terrifying wail screeched, Apello expected to be knocked free. Instead, he was relieved to see Prae lunge into view. Surprised by the war cry, Masina halted midstride and attempted to change its course. Before it could redirect, the flat of Prae's sword struck it across the shoulder. Flecks of red energy crackled at the point of collision.

As metal clanging against metal rang like a tolling bell, the golem was quickly driven backwards. Prae pressed her advantage and struck additional blunt blows to force it to retreat further from Apello.

With a thin sigh of relief that was stifled by the ache in his chest, Apello attempted to slowly drag himself up. Pain radiated from his palms and the muscles in his arms were rubbery with fatigue. Fear settled into his chest. Apello began to falter; it occurred to him that he might not be capable of lifting himself to safety.

"Here," Cal called out as he came into view. "I gotcha!" He reached out and grabbed Apello by the edges of his armor, along the seams under his armpits. As he dug in with his feet for leverage, Cal hoisted Apello to the solid surface.

After a few swears about his weight, Cal released his grip and began to rub at a catch in his back. Apello slumped to the floor as an exhalation that was half-laugh and half-sob escaped. The persistent throbbing in his ribs was made all the more uncomfortable by his slouched posture.

He held out his hands and examined the abrasions. Most of his flesh was rubbed raw; both palms were distorted and discolored from the hardened steel. From cracks in the skin, two streams of blood trickled. A sharp pain accompanied any attempt to turn his right wrist.

Apello took in a few deep breaths and uttered a voiceless prayer of thanks before he scanned the bridge for activity. While his peripheral vision remained blurry, he found Prae and Masina. Cal had already left his side and was on the move. Though the muscles in his arms were weak, Apello feebly dragged himself up as he watched Cal withdraw his revolvers.

At this point, Prae had forced the golem back to the platform that connected the quartet of towers. It was there that she chose to square up her stance and face it directly in combat.

From the glowing iconography etched across the length of her weapon, Apello could tell that Prae had deployed a semanifesture before diving into the fray. Any advantage that Masina had once enjoyed was countered by the empowered ferocity of her strikes, each delivered with an electrical flare.

Every lunge forward by the golem was met in kind; she deflected its blows with angled flicks of the blade. To counter these strikes, she lashed out with a flurry of attacks, many of which ricocheted off of the bulky metal hide. With each slash, red embers sparked. Though the prosthetic made its movements slower and clumsier, Masina used the thicker armor plating to its advantage.

Apello stumbled to Erudatta, who was splayed across the tiled floor. With Erudatta's robe undone, Apello was able to get a clearer idea of the man's injuries. His breathing was inconsistent and shallow; at times it stopped only to be followed by rapid respiration. There was bruising along his chest and his pale skin was dotted with abrasions. The exoskeleton itself was bent and cracked in places as a number of the supports had broken or twisted on impact.

When Apello shook him, he uttered a pained groan. The man's mouth was filled with blood and he made no response to the snapping of fingers by his ears.

Apello turned to Cal, who lingered on the walkway, somewhere between himself and Prae's ongoing fight. The man stood frozen like a statue, one arm held out straight as a rail. Though he seemed paralyzed by indecision, the revolver in his hand did not waver.

"What are you waiting for? If you have the shot, take it," Apello barked at Cal.

"Can't chance it," Cal said as he watched the fight's to-and-fro.

"The old man doesn't have much time left."

"Not helping," Cal mumbled as he wiped the sweat from his brow with the back of his sleeve. His right-hand revolver bobbed before he leveled it at Masina's new cranium. *I ain't that good of a shot,* he thought to himself. *Don't need the added pressure.*

Once it became evident he could not gain a clean shot, Cal sidestepped to his right, hugging the platform's curved rail. Though almost entirely absorbed on the melee with her assailant, Prae recognized his flanking maneuver. Her eyes flickered to where he stood. She took a pair of steps that drew Masina away from Cal's position.

When he found a decent-enough angle from behind the golem, Cal focused on the spaces between sections of armor that opened up ever-so-briefly as Masina moved back and forth. The man-shaped machine's awkward movements as it fought failed to provide the predictable pattern Cal had hoped for.

After a few seconds of pondering, Cal swore to himself. There was never going to be a perfect shot. He squinted as he fixed on the sights of his revolvers.

He squeezed off a trio of rounds, the first which deflected off the recently-added cranium. The second struck the back of the neck only to rebound on impact with part of the spinal column. The third bullet punched through a cluster of exposed wires. A flash of sparks lit between the plates of armor.

Masina quickly abandoned Prae and spun to face Cal. Another string of warbled buzzes sounded from a muffled speaker beneath its head. Though arcs of electricity continued to fire, Masina's lumbering movement seemed unimpeded by the damage.

"Probably not my best plan," Cal mumbled as he squeezed off another pair of shots. Both ricocheted off of the oversized feather-shaped metal plates.

As Masina trudged towards him, Cal took a step in retreat. When his back immediately pressed against the bannister, his eyes shot open.

The monstrosity drew in close. Masina raised its club-like appendage and began to charge forward. When Cal fire blindly, the bullets failed to do more than scratch the bronze-plated steel. Dented slugs plopped harmlessly to the ground.

The revolvers clicked impotently; the hammers no longer struck live firing pins but Cal continued to squeeze the triggers.

Prae sprinted up behind the mechanized creation with her sword trailing behind her. Just as it was about to close in on Cal, Masina dropped its arm in a downward arc like an executioner's axe.

With an ear-piercing scream, Prae slung her sword in an upwards arc. Propelled by unfettered speed and strength, the blade disappeared from sight for an instant. Only once it impacted Masina squarely between the legs did the weapon become visible again. The crunch of metal warping filled the air as flakes of shattered bronze peppered the floor.

The force lifted the golem from its feet and flung it off to the side. Masina was tossed head over heels into the air.

This sudden reprieve caused Cal's fear to dissipate. With a flinch to avoid the spinning android, he dropped and turned. With one bent arm, he tried to protect his head. He heard the raucous clatter as Masina slammed into the railing. Top-heavy as it was, this was enough to send it tumbling over the side.

After a few seconds in which he heard nothing, Cal let out a sigh and uncovered his head. Prae stood a few paces in the distance, her gaze on where Masina had fallen beyond the bannister. Her eyes were wide as the taut muscles of her hands clutched the sword out in front of her.

Patting himself down for any sign of injury, he eventually exhaled with a half-hearted laugh and took a curious peek at the roiling mist beneath. He hoped to see a Masina-shaped hole punched in the fog that would slowly dissolve as the seconds passed.

"Oh, you have *got* to be shitting me," he groaned as he quickly brought up his revolvers. Masina still hung from the bottom edge by one arm.

Prae hustled to his side and discovered Masina still clinging to the masonry. A string of static-filled notes warbled as the metallic man attempted to pull itself up. The ponderous weight of its recently-added limb hampered its efforts.

Prae was about to comment when she heard Apello beckon to her.

"Prae!" he called out with a frantic wave of his hand. She looked to him with confusion in her eyes. When she saw the sprawled body at his side, they immediately widened. Without looking back, she placed her sword in its scabbard and spoke to Cal.

"Take care of it."

"Yeah, uh, sure," Cal eyed her for a second as she rushed to Erudatta. "I'll get right on that."

He holstered one of his guns and proceeded to reload the other. With a quick upturn of his wrist, the empty cartridges were dumped with a soft, almost musical, tinkle. Kicking them with the side of his boot, Cal brushed the empty brass off of the platform. He refilled the chambers one by one, with a half-dozen rounds from of his belt. After spinning the cylinder with a flick of his thumb, Cal closed the revolver and aimed it at the hanging Masina.

"Sorry that this has to be done," he said under his breath. "I'm not much for killing, though I don't know that you're exactly alive. I don't figure you understand what's going on here. I barely do. Perhaps you weren't all there to begin with and the smashing you got before turned you into this. But, deed's gotta be done."

The mechanical man held on to the strip of metal that jutted from the side of the platform. It might never let go on its own, but Masina could no longer lift itself up. The makeshift repair job had turned part of its body into an anchor.

Cal picked out a gap along the wrist joint where the plates opened to a width of two inches.

He cocked the hammer, closed one eye, and lined up the sights. He took a few breaths through his nose. Cal squeezed the trigger and the first round punched through the joint. A viscous gray liquid oozed from the opening. Cal was reminded of the gunk that had soiled Oebe's robes.

Cal fired twice more. By the time the last round struck home, Masina's weight began to tear at the weakened components. Under the strain, wires severed and hoses tore. The screech of metal against metal caused Cal to grimace as support rods within the forearm slipped loose from their joint housing.

While the hand still retained its hold, Masina's arm tore free. The golem made no sound as it was quickly lost in the ocean of mist.

Cal counted the seconds. He gave up after he reached thirty.

26

The flickering light of the display illuminated Peter and Oebe as they observed the proceedings. Silently locked in place, unable to offer assistance, it felt as if they were forced to view a teleplay featuring their friends. The pair watched on in horror as Apello was knocked off his feet and Masina closed in on him. Both sighed with relief when Prae and Cal came to his rescue. When Prae drove the golem back to the nearby platform, the fight moved out of view.

After Cal came to Apello's assistance, he quickly moved off-camera to join Prae. Apello struggled to rise and hunched over. Once able to keep upright, Apello staggered to where Erudatta's body was discarded. With the hazy details on the grainy display, it was difficult to tell if the elder was still alive.

Every time one of Cal's revolvers fired, Peter flinched. From where they waited within the tower, the echoing clap sounded like distant thunder from an approaching storm.

In the top corner of picture remained the body of Hru-Gatta, who had not moved since being violently dispatched by Masina. They'd helplessly stood witness as the golem lifted her and effortlessly spun her head about. Oebe remained mute with her eyes were locked on the display.

When Apello and Prae carried the limp and bleeding body of Erudatta back into the tower, Peter knew that the battle had come to an end. He let out a long breath that felt like it had been held for far too long. He looked to Oebe, only to realize she was no longer at his side.

"Oebe?" Peter backed away as he looked about. When it was obvious she was gone from the workroom, he rushed to the doorway.

"Oebe!" he exclaimed. Having lost sight of her, his heart rate accelerated. His face flushed almost immediately. Taking the steps two at a time, he descended, only to see her as she turned and disappeared into the connecting vestibule's darkness.

Focused on catching up with her, Peter lost his footing as he reached the doorway and stumbled into the steel frame. From the throbbing along his shoulder, he was certain there would be bruising before too long.

After a shake of his head, he spied Oebe's tiny frame by Hru-Gatta's body on the walkway, almost a dozen yards from the entrance. As he departed from the tower, he ran into Cal, who watched Oebe as she dropped to her knees beside the Grande Dame.

Peter made no effort to speak to Cal as he slipped past him.

"Hey," Cal called out and he took Peter by the shoulder. Peter's brow furrowed until he met Cal's eyes. "Give her a moment, okay? She's still a little gir… uh, well, she's still a woman. Even with all they did to her, she still has to have human emotions in there. She knew Hru-Gatta personally."

After an extended pause, Peter nodded in response. Cal released his sleeve and disappeared.

Peter waited and observed her from afar. She was seated on the ground with a hand on the chest of her headmistress. Tears rolled down her cheeks and there was a hitch in her breathing.

After a few minutes, Peter chose to join her. There had to be something he could say to comfort her.

After stooping to one knee and clearing his throat, he spoke up. "H-how are you doing?" He inwardly groaned at how awkward the question sounded. "Sorry, I have a pretty fair idea, but—"

"It's customary to pose an inquiry that you already know the answer to in hopes of broaching a topic with someone in a perceived state of emotional disarray." Though the words were spoken with her usual cadence, there was a sogginess caused by her sorrow.

Even with her reassurance, Peter stammered. "Well, uh, how are you… What's on your mind? What are you feeling?"

"The Grande Dame is the only person I've known for any extended period of time," Oebe responded as she retracted her hands and placed them in her lap. "Or, rather, the only person of which, through regular interaction between data transfers to the Central Archives, I've retained memories. She was… stern. Not what one would call a caring individual. I would not claim her to be a surrogate family or even a friend. And, yet, I still cry for her passing. I… don't exactly understand why."

"It's because you're human," he said as he placed a hand on her shoulder. "It's what we do. We cry when someone we know passes away. Even if we weren't what would colloquially be referred to as 'on good terms.' Hru-Gatta was a non-insignificant part of your life. Her passing ushers in a change for you that can't exactly be dismissed."

"That makes sense."

Peter produced a handkerchief and used it to wipe the tears from her cheeks. Though her eyes were still red, she turned and offered him a smile. As he rose, Peter reached out to her with a hand, which she willingly accepted.

"What is to be done with her?" she inquired.

"I… I don't know," Peter mulled over the matter. "Perhaps we should return the body to her quarters so she can eventually be interred. Proper burial, ceremony and all."

"Is that such a good plan? When she is discovered, it will be known to all that she was killed. Considering the criminal nature of our appearance, this would place us as prime suspects in her murder. Golette will surely run to the Central Judicia and lay the blame squarely on us."

"Well, then, as Cal might say, it'd be in our best interest to be gone before they find out."

This elicited a thin smile from Oebe as they began to walk away.

"Still, it will make things harder for each of us."

"Which would make *you* feel better?" Peter cut to the

heart of the matter. This caused Oebe to frown.

After a few seconds, she looked up. "I would like it if she was properly buried. Even if I cannot be there. It's the right thing to do."

Peter smirked as a thought occurred to him. "Sometimes doing the right thing is all that matters."

Cal arrived just as Erudatta was placed on the flat slab that acted as his bed. Even laid out as gingerly as possible, his body was a crumpled mess wracked with pain. One of his legs was bent in an odd angle and his arms were curled tightly across his chest. From the ragged raspy breathing, he was struggling just to stay alive.

"How is he?" Cal blurted as he came up beside Prae. She stood hunched over beside the extended bunk upon which her kinsman was spread.

"Not good," Apello announced. He waited on the other side of the room, near the rust-colored slab of metal that stood out from the drab walls of the living space.

"As Apello said," Prae spoke grimly. "His extended time in the Waking State has taken an adverse toll."

"So, uh, what should we do with him? I mean, I'm no doctor. I don't even know that we could get him to one before... well..." Cal trailed off.

"His wounds are too severe," Prae brushed off the idea with a shake of her head. "As it is, the exoskeleton allowed him to be more active than he should have been. There are advanced signs of atrophy in his limbs."

Cal shot a glance back to the etched metal door. "Well, is there something here we could use? Like, put him in his containment cell until we can get someone to help him? Ya know, put him on ice until we can get him some medical treatment? I mean, I know it probably doesn't work that way but I don't have any better ideas."

"Now is not the best time for your usual sardonic wit."

"Sorry. Defense mechanism," he said with a grimace as he backed away.

Prae thought to say something else but was stopped by a tug at her arm. She turned and met Erudatta's gaze. Crystal-blue irises, now glazed over and incapable of retaining their focus, swam in the blood-filled sclera of his eyes.

"Prae," he spoke. His voice struggled through the fluids that filled his lungs.

"Clear the room," Prae commanded. Both men nodded. As they departed, Cal offered a hand to his ally; Apello's injuries caused his movements to be sluggish.

Once they were out of the room, Prae leaned in.

His speech was breathless, interrupted by short bouts of coughing. "L-leave me. You… you can't return me to the Dormant S-s-state. You know that. Leave… leave me here t-to die."

Prae kneeled beside the bunk and placed a hand on his cheek. Erudatta did not react to the warmth of her touch on his skin.

"Are you certain?" she eventually inquired.

He responded with a small twist of his head, almost a nod. "My quarters will seal... behind... tend to the entrance to Topheth. With Hru... Gatta's death, no one should know what's here."

"And yourself? How much longer do you have?"

A faint groan bubbled up.

Her brow creased, Prae rose and closed her eyes. After a few seconds of contemplation, she reached out with her left hand and quickly fashioned a semanifesture that hovered inches above his face. After a few clumsy flicks of her fingers, the manifestation coalesced into cream and pink hues that throbbed with a faint pulse.

"My apologies that this isn't stronger," she stated as, with a tap at the light formation, it lowered onto Erudatta's strained face. Within seconds, the energy disappeared as it scattered and sank into his skin. "Analgesics—medicine in general—was never my strong suit. This will have to do."

As his features slackened, Erudatta's eyes closed. With each shallow breath, more blood seeped from his wounds and stained the soiled robe beneath him.

Prae lingered for a moment. Once the tension in his extremities slowly gave out, each slumped limply. Broken bones in his limbs caused them to lie at unnatural angles. When she felt she had seen enough, she turned away and strode from the room.

Once through the doorway, she stopped and bit at her lower lip. After a few seconds, she continued up the steps, only to find Apello and Cal waiting patiently for her near the exit.

To her relief, neither man said anything.

There was no delay in their departure. Prae marched onward, as if unconcerned for the abode she was to vacate. Much like the rest of Topheth, it was an abandoned tomb, a place she hoped no one would ever encounter. Moments after they stepped from the entrance to Erudatta's tower, the lone access closed and sealed tight.

Cal paused to examine the exterior one last time. Once he could no longer locate the door's seams along the curved surface, he shrugged his shoulders and hurried to join the others.

As they strolled away, Prae cast a glance at Cal, who had acquired one of Erudatta's hand-held welding torches. He carried it in his arms like a newborn baby. She shook her head and focused her attention on where Peter and Oebe waited.

There was a short discussion about what would be done with Hru-Gatta's body. Despite the problems such a choice created, they collected the Grande Dame's remains and took it with them.

After a lengthy and tiring climb, they reached Hru-Gatta's residence. To their relief, there was no sign that anyone else was aware of their presence. The private quarters were still empty and appeared unchanged.

Peter and Oebe laid the deceased on the chaise lounge

with as much care as they could. Though tears clung to her cheeks, Oebe nodded with an appreciative smile.

Apello and Cal used the welding torch to seal the damaged door that had been discarded on the atrium's floor. Through some muttered cursing, between Apello's physical discomfort and Cal's clumsiness with the tool, they eventually closed the doorway. With Prae's assistance, a pair of bookcases was moved to hide the barrier as well as possible.

As they left, Oebe lingered for a moment. When she turned back, she found Peter waiting for her. He placed a comforting hand on her back.

Within the hour, they were gone. Night had fallen long ago and the nearby streets were largely empty. They hurried from the ward and located meager lodgings to the west.

For most, slumber did not take long to come. While Oebe slept silently in the same room, however, Prae remained awake well into the early hours.

By daybreak, Apello was gone without a word of goodbye.

27

After a night of broken sleep due to the aches of his untreated injuries, Apello slipped out of the inn and disappeared into the pre-dawn metropolis.

The air itself was cool and thick with a fog that would not burn off until well after sunrise. He wrapped his kaftan tightly about him to ward off the chill as he vanished into a side-alley.

Hours later, he turned up at the southernmost docks of Okanus Sector, where he found Gelhda in residence at a local inn. She had been in hiding there for weeks now and was elated when Apello finally walked through the door. Standing almost a foot shorter, she embraced him tightly for what felt like forever. When she pulled away, she noticed the discomfort on his face.

Once they retired to her quarters, Apello explained, in vague terms, the reasons for the delay and his recent injuries. Gelhda tended to his wounds. She bound his wrist and torso with elastic bandages.

Apello took this time to observe his sister. Except for the evening in which he had put her on a southbound train away from Viisibourg, it had been years since they shared company. He did not recall her looking so thin and weary. All the evidence of a hard life was there: her skin was ashen, her hair brittle, and her brown eyes dull. Apello suffered the pangs of shame. He felt failure at his inability to rescue her from Sert earlier. His efforts to earn their way back to Thosa Prathvi had not transpired quickly enough.

Sensing his contemplation, she took his face in her hands and thanked him. To his relief, their discussion never turned to Sert.

Two days later, they were on a chartered vessel heading across the Byrathium Sea. It would be the first time in almost ten years that either had walked the beaches of Thosa Prathvi.

Gelhda wept openly upon seeing the golden shores of her homeland.

Despite misgivings, Peter eventually returned to the central offices of the Archeology Bureau in Rian Sands. His nerves were almost his undoing as he climbed the stairs. Twice he considered turning around and fleeing the desert city altogether.

Once through the vaulted doors and into the central hall, he was greeted by the staff with open arms and relieved smiles. He discovered that the expedition in Natx Hollow was ended after the discovery of Quillin's body. The revelation provided both relief and sadness to Peter, who was mostly thankful for the distraction.

After later meeting with Master Contrell in his office, Peter learned the details of what transpired. Found by his colleagues with his throat slashed, Quillin's death was blamed on the Harenas. When Peter and Apello failed to return, it was feared that they might have fallen prey to a similar fate.

When the topic turned to the subject of Apello, Peter stumbled over his words. He wove a tale that he and Apello became separated during an attack by the Harenas weeks prior. He admitted to having not seen Apello since, which left his whereabouts up in the air.

Contrell ordered Peter on a forced leave of absence. Weeks later, he returned to work, though his workload was initially reduced.

Peter eventually unearthed his documentation, stowed within crates in the basement storage. His papers had been collected by the Bureau before they quit the site. After scouring his notes, he penned a thesis on the markings found within Natx Hollow's Blue Room. Instead of revealing even a sliver of what he had witnessed in his time away, Peter theorized that the etchings were some form of ancient language. While his essay was met with a tepid response from his colleagues, it was enough to sustain his career as Junior Associate.

Sometime later, rumors began that Peter shared his apartment with a female roommate. Gossip was infectious within the insular community of Rian Sands; one that was comprised mostly of Bureau staff. Descriptions of the unnamed companion were of a small woman, easily five years his junior, with long brown hair that hung down past her shoulders. She favored wearing tent dresses draped with knit shawls.

When confronted, Peter remained evasive. Though he took great efforts to keep his public and private lives separate, his roommate joined him as an assistant when he left for the expedition to the Gul Lyceum in Zehngrad the following year.

Despite months on location, they never located any evidence of the familiar vertical markings on site.

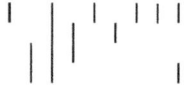

Following the unexplained disappearances of Jaefor and Illgosses, certain interests in Urigo Sector came under new ownership. Local competitors moved into the ward at the first sign of a power vacuum. The changing landscape of proprietorship caused some contentious growing pains that resulted in escalated violence in the streets. For a few months, there was an increased presence of Magistrates in the area.

Their bodies would not be discovered for almost a full year, and even then they were deemed unidentifiable. A conflagration that broke out in the dilapidated warehouse sector drew the attention of fire and recovery teams that swept the area for survivors. Upon finding a pair of deceased Magistrates, the Central Judicia took control of the scene. The story behind the strange assortment of dead bodies in the building was never made public.

The Fifth Era of Man

Even as the surrounding plains displayed the autumnal shift in seasons, the Quartewuste remained a bleached ocean of sun-blistered sand. Heat rose from the dunes in waves that distorted Cal's vision. Constant course-corrections in the ever-shifting desert caused the westward trek to take longer than planned.

As he disembarked from the transport in the shade of a nearby ridge, Cal was surprised to find Natx Hollow uninhabited. The remnants of the Archaeology Bureau's camp told a story of hasty exodus. While the staff was long gone, most of their tents remained where they stood, seemingly abandoned in a rush. Harsh winds of a particularly unkind fall season had already scattered a number of them.

In a half-broken shelter at the northern end of the camp was an assortment of equipment in crates that were almost entirely buried by sand drifts. Cal was surprised to unearth a half-dozen demolition charges and a handheld detonator packaged in a foam-lined aluminum case.

"Well, ain't that irresponsible," he mumbled as he closed the container, hefting it with one hand and taking it with him.

Natx Hollow itself appeared largely unchanged. Cal could see no obvious visible reason for the Bureau's flight.

Upon entering the main temple, he made a beeline for the the courtyard and descended to the substructure. From the footprints on the sand-coated tiles to his left, he immediately knew which path Prae had taken. Despite his efforts to convince her otherwise, she had minced no words. Her mind was made up and all he could do was honor her wishes.

After making a stop in the bottom-most corridor, Cal discarded the aluminum case and pocketed the detonator.

Eventually, he tracked Prae to the Blue Room, where she stood beside the open containment cell. She was dressed in her armor, her helmet deposited on the nearby table. The fearful visage watched her as she made preparations for her long slumber.

As he entered the room, Cal cleared his throat. "Now, help me to understand this, but why again do you need to do this?"

"You know why." This was not the first time the matter had been raised since their departure from Greater Decedistadt.

"No, in fact, I don't."

She looked up from the container as it began to fill with an iridescent vapor. "Look at what my kind has done. What the Progenitors, as we're referred to, would continue to do. We can't help ourselves anymore. The only way your kind has a chance to survive is without our interference. Without our presence."

"What about—"

"Magromous? Erudatta made it clear that he would remain in the Dormant State."

"That doesn't mean—"

"Cal." From the stern tone of her voice, Cal knew she could never be persuaded. As the inevitability of the situation sunk in, Cal finally came to terms with what he had not accepted before now. He sullenly realized it was best if he dropped the subject and at least departed on good terms.

"Will you dream?"

Prae paused at the question. After a few seconds, she offered Cal a smile and the simplest answer possible. "Yes. Yes, I will."

"Good," he said with a soft nod. "I hope they're good ones at least."

Prae reclaimed her helmet and strode to where he lingered by the doorway.

"So do I."

Without warning, Prae leaned in and kissed Cal on the cheek. Her lips were soft and wet against his dry skin. Cal only stood silently.

"Of all the people I have encountered, you are the one I will miss the most," she whispered into his ear.

He watched quietly as she donned her helmet and slipped into the sleeping chamber. After hoses and gears came to life, it closed back up into place. The seams disappeared into the etched surface as the reddish discoloration of the walls slowly faded away.

A few minutes later, everything fell quiet.

With a disappointed sigh, Cal departed. His march back to the surface was slow, as if loitering would improve his memories of Prae.

Once he cleared the front steps of the temple, Cal paused and removed the detonator. He looked back over his shoulder and depressed the red button. Seconds later, a staccato of explosions rumbled from below. Moments passed before a plume of dust ejected from the open entrance.

Cal tossed the detonator aside and headed north through the ancient village and basecamp.

With the deed done, Cal slipped into the sand-blasted transport. The green paint was worn down to the metal along the front of the vehicle. In the seat beside him rested his jacket. He lifted it up and shook the white grit from the fabric. Beneath was a small canvas satchel that contained the last remnants of money he could claim to his name.

Even though it pained him, he pawned his revolvers in Nibin Ray to pay for the transport rental. With what was left, he figured he could make Einnlande to the northwest in a few days.

He folded the leather coat and replaced it on the seat.

Before starting the vehicle's engine and driving away, he paused as something caught his eye. In the floorboard behind the passenger-side seat was a duffle bag. Cal reached back and opened it with a tug on the tie-string. Within, folded and left in an orderly stack, were the clothes Prae had purchased in Viisibourg.

For some reason, the red of the tunic struck him as especially vivid. Beneath that was a linen robe.

"Sleep well, Centurion," he said to himself before driving away from the camp.

About the Author

Author of *Not Gods But Monsters*, Joshua Banker was born in Greece in 1973. He grew up in the San Francisco area before moving to Chattanooga where he attended the University of Tennessee at Chattanooga and received a BFA in Graphic Design. After moving to Charlotte, NC, he ran an independent entertainment review website from 1999–2006. Now living in Greenville, NC, his day job is graphic designer and analyst for a Fortune 100 company. Josh is a writer, painter and illustrator, loves all things H.P. Lovecraft, is married and has two cats and a dog.

Visit **joshuabankerbooks.com** for updates.